THE LUCKIEST
WOMAN EVER

(Molly Sutton Mysteries 2)

NELL GODDIN

Beignet Books

To my extraordinary teacher, Helen Tanner

CONTENTS

Chapter One

2005

In the grand old mansion on rue Simenon, in the center of Castillac, sitting in a deep armchair covered in a fabric so expensive it could have paid for a small car, Josephine Desrosiers was watching a game show. She was wearing a nightgown her husband, long dead, had bought for her in Paris thirty years earlier. She blinked as the host talked rapidly in his forced jolly tone, lights on the set flashing as a contestant managed to mumble out the correct answer.

Madame Desrosiers was seventy-one, and her hearing was as sharp as ever. She heard the door to the kitchen close three floors down even though Sabrina, the housekeeper who came each morning, was a quiet girl and not remotely a door-slammer. Josephine got to her feet and snapped off the television set, then smoothed the cushion of the armchair so it looked fresh and unsat-in. And then she nimbly climbed into her vast bed with its ornate posts and carved headboard, and squeezed her eyes closed.

Sabrina could not clean the entire four-story house in one day, even as young and hardworking as she was. That day she did all of the first floor and most of the second, but never came up to Madame Desrosiers's bedroom. Madame Desrosiers had told her that she was very ill and did not have the wherewithal to see visitors, including Sabrina, so she was left alone. She had a box of crackers under her bed and a bit of Brie that was past its prime—quite enough sustenance thank you—so she never rang the servant's bell.

When Madame Desrosiers heard the door softly shut at the end of the day, she slid out of bed and turned the television back on. Then she did her exercises in front of an enormous gilt-framed mirror, counting her movements, bending to the right and then the left, breathing heavily from the work of reaching for her toes. She was preparing for the best part of the day, when she sat at her desk and wrote letters. Each one was a harassing and maligning and instructing sort of letter, every single one of which, when opened, was greeted with the same feeling of deflation and even shame in its recipient, just as Josephine intended.

Josephine Desrosiers had been a lucky woman, in material respects. Her family had not been wealthy, but her husband had invented something that made him millions. (She couldn't say what exactly—something electrical, she believed?) And now she was able to play the significant role of Rich Widow, complete with younger members of the family gathered at her feet, hoping for the odd crumb to fall their way.

Well, there was one family member who did that, anyway: Michel, her nephew. He would likely come around tonight as he usually did late in the week, trying to butter her up. Very occasionally she wrote him a small check. She liked sometimes to think of herself as bountiful, and with impressive self-control, she denied any connection in her mind between Michel's attentiveness and the money she gave him. As she thought of Michel, the doorbell sounded and she heard him let himself in. She was not quite dressed and she enjoyed making him wait. Josephine liked the idea of the young man sitting in her salon, twiddling his thumbs, with nothing to do but look forward to the moment when she appeared at the top of the wide, curving staircase.

A vanity table stood in a corner of the expansive bathroom off her bedroom, covered with crystal bottles of perfume and old tins of eyeliner and foundation. She sat gazing at herself in the mirror, brushing her wisps of white hair straight up. She dabbed her fingertips into a pot of rouge and reddened up her wrinkled cheeks. She applied lipstick and blotted it with special blotting papers. It occurred to her, not for the first time, that some music might be pleasant to listen to while she made her preparations, but the record player had broken decades ago and she had no wish for anything ugly and modern in the house.

Finally, with a spritz of perfume, Josephine Desrosiers was ready to greet her nephew. She was spry for her age and she had no trouble with the stairs. She nearly hummed to herself as she descended, but stopped herself because she thought humming was a low-class pursuit. Her nephew, chewing on a fingernail, was sitting on the very edge of the sofa cushion, his brown hair falling down over one eye.

"Ah, Michel, *comment vas-tu?*"

Michel jumped up from the sofa and kissed his aunt on both cheeks, murmuring the most polite murmurs he could come up with.

He loathed his aunt.

He thought her mean and narcissistic, which did not take an abundance of perception.

"What would you like to do this evening, my dear?" he asked her, so solicitous he almost believed himself. "How about a bit of television? I hear there's a new—"

"Television is vulgar," said Madame Desrosiers.

"Ah. Well, shall I take you out to dinner then? Are you hungry?"

She considered. She did like to enter a restaurant and see the people she knew jump up to come say hello. But on the other

NELL GODDIN

hand, the tiresome service! The expense! She had lost her appetite for food years ago, and she didn't see the point in spending that much time and money on something she wasn't especially interested in. "If you would make me my usual," she said.

Michel sighed inwardly and went to a sideboard. He took a dangerously fragile cordial glass from inside the cabinet and placed it on a silver tray. Then he poured some Dubonnet from a crystal decanter and took the glass to his aunt. The stuff smelled musty like the rest of the house and he did not breathe until she took it from him.

He would have welcomed a drink himself, but had learned that helping himself, or even asking politely if he might join her, was a mistake. And with Aunt Josephine Desrosiers, you did not want to make mistakes. Not if you wanted to escape without a cruel dressing-down.

And definitely not if you wanted to inherit her money.

MOLLY SUTTON RUBBED her sleeve on the window trying to wipe away the condensation blocking her view of the meadow, but it was not fog on the window, it was ice. On the inside. Her first winter in France, and oh it was a cold one. Lowest temperatures in decades, and *La Baraque*—her beautiful, odd, old house—was not insulated.

She had moved to the village of Castillac at the end of the summer. A fresh start in a beautiful place: a life of gardening, eating fabulous food, running a *gîte* business, and talking to goat farmers—that was what she had imagined. Instead, she had discovered a corpse in the woods and gotten involved in a murder investigation, not exactly the peace and serenity she was going for.

But on the whole, Castillac was even better than she had

dreamed: she had made friends, even good friends; the beauty of the village and the surrounding area never failed to take her breath away; and the pastry was *sublime*.

Molly was willing to pronounce any day that began with an almond croissant from *Pâtisserie Bujold* at least a partial success. Now of course, they were at their peak when utterly fresh, so that meant walking the kilometer and a half into the village to buy one first thing in the morning, still warm from the oven. And *Café de la Place* was only two steps away from the pâtisserie, after all—why not stop in for a *café crème* and say *bonjour* to that blindingly handsome server, Pascal?

She wasn't flirting with him, not really. She was too old for him anyway. Nevertheless, they showed their appreciation for each other as he took her order with a twinkle in his eye, as if to say: in a parallel universe I'd have a romp with you, oh yes.

Molly allowed herself a twinkle back.

But that was a summer sort of exchange, all that twinkling, when sitting outside with the sun on your back felt so good, and the days were so long it was sometimes hard to fill them up. Winter was a whole other matter. Restaurants closed their terraces, and everyone wrapped themselves up in heavy coats and sweaters. It didn't feel very sexy. Instead of warm, loose, and easy-going, life felt stiff and closed in.

Molly's best friend in Castillac was Lawrence Weebly, but he had taken off for a month in Morocco, and December had begun to drag a little. She was lonely.

Instead of going into the village she booted up her computer and checked her email. No inquiries about booking the cottage. Make that lonely *and* anxious about money. But at least the first problem was easy enough to solve. She emailed Frances, her best pal from the U.S., and invited her to come for a long visit. The cottage was empty anyway and Molly would love the company.

Frances must have been sitting at her computer at the same time, because in three seconds she emailed back: PACKING.

Molly grinned but had a pang of regret at her impulsiveness. Yes, Frances was an old friend and gobs of fun, and Molly loved her. But Frances was also, well, the sort of person trouble seemed to follow. Houses burned down, cars were stolen, epic misunderstandings—this was Frances's daily life. Molly could only hope that her black cloud would stay on the other side of the Atlantic, or that perhaps by now Frances had outgrown it. They weren't far from forty, after all.

Someone banged on the front door.

"Coming!" yelled Molly, wishing again for a dog. She always felt a spark of worry, opening the door when she had no idea who was on the other side. Was she too suspicious? Overly anxious? She made a mental note to ask Frances if she felt the same.

Constance, the young woman who occasionally came to clean, stood on the front step with a toothy grin. She had her hair scraped back into a high ponytail that Molly knew was her ready-to-work hairstyle. They exchanged greetings and Constance came in and stood in front of the woodstove.

"It's really cold in here, Molls," she said. "Are you sure you don't want Thomas to put in some electric heaters so you don't freeze to death? I'd hate to come over and find you all stiff and iced over!"

"Nah, it's not that bad. Spring's right around the corner anyway."

"It's December."

Molly shrugged. "I'm sorry I don't have anything for you to do today. I knew bookings would fall off once the weather turned, but it's worse than I expected. I guess anticipating something isn't the same thing as going through it. No one's set foot in the cottage since you cleaned it last."

Constance looked crushed. "Well, but—how about I clean your house instead of the cottage?" She looked around the living room and raised her eyebrows at the line of bark and twigs that had trailed over the floor when Molly brought in armloads of wood.

"Sorry, Constance. Without bookings, I don't have the money to pay you. Want a cup of coffee? How about you sit down and tell me all the news. I *know* you have news." Molly smiled and gestured toward the living room.

Constance smoothed a stray lock of hair behind one ear. "Well," she said, "have you heard about Madame Luthier? You know her, she lives in that decrepit house over on rue Saterne?"

Molly shook her head while getting another coffee cup. Constance was a terrible cleaner, no getting around that, but she did always have news, and she wasn't stingy with it either—qualities Molly esteemed quite highly. At least as high as being adept with a vacuum cleaner, luckily for Constance.

"I think I met her at the market one day. Dresses all in black, with really thick hose?"

"Yeah," laughed Constance. "And black shoes that, I don't know, look like she'd like to kick someone?"

"Did she do something scandalous?" Molly handed Constance the coffee and sat on the sofa, leaning forward and hoping for a juicy tidbit.

"Depends on if you think cutting her daughter out of her will is scandalous."

"Ooo, maybe not. But mean. Did the daughter do something horrible? Or is Madame Luthier just a controlling battle-axe?"

Constance tittered. "Well, maybe I shouldn't say cut her daughter out, because in France you can't do that. But she's leaving only the portion required by law, which I think anyone would agree that if the daughter had to put up with Madame Luthier all these years she deserves more than that!"

"You mean there are laws about what you do in your will?"

"Oh, yes," said Constance. "Your children automatically get half or something? Oh, I'm not good with the details," said Constance. "Math was so not my thing, and it's not like my parents are going to leave me anything but debts. But so anyway, I heard the daughter—her name is Prudence and everyone used to call us Pru and Con, although I don't personally see what's so funny about that—so Prudence is supposedly furious. But she better not kill her mother unless she changes her will!" And Constance slammed back against the sofa laughing hysterically at her former schoolmate's predicament.

Chapter Two

⚜

The next day was even colder. *I knew Castillac wasn't exactly the south of France,* Molly was thinking, *but I did think it was south-ish.* She put on a heavy jacket and went out to the woodpile, grateful that at least the wood was dry. Constance had generously vacuumed the living room yesterday, and here Molly was dropping bark and sawdust all over the floor again.

That's life, huh? An endless cycle of tidying up the mess you've made.

She stoked the fire, put on some blues, and settled on the sofa with a blanket and some gardening catalogs she'd brought with her from America. It was less than practical to pack catalogs she wouldn't be able to order from in France, but Molly loved looking at the photographs and imagining the plants in various combinations in borders on her property. She wasn't shopping; she was looking for inspiration.

Certain plants she loved deeply: all the artemisias, definitely baptisias, most of the roses. And for some reason, other plants made her feel slightly ill to look at them—kniphofia, amaranth, and especially astilbe. She didn't understand why this was so, because the revulsion she felt couldn't simply be a matter of aesthetics, could it? Yet the aversion was pretty powerful. Half of them she'd only seen in catalogs anyway. Maybe if she saw them in a garden she would feel differently.

A slow hour passed. She put more wood in the stove, fiddled with the air intakes, swept up the mess. Had another cup of coffee. Thought about inviting her neighbor, Madame Sabourin, over for a cup of tea. Except Molly didn't like tea. She considered calling Lawrence in Morocco but remembered he had said something about turning off his phone, taking a break from the electronic world. There had been a moment—and a night—when she thought maybe something had sparked between her and Ben Dufort, the chief gendarme, but the moment seemed to have passed and she didn't know what to make of that.

Not that she was looking for romance anyway.

She had come to France in part to recover from a divorce. She hadn't been especially happy in the marriage, but still, its ending had knocked her for a loop. And this French winter, with everyone hunkered down in their own houses and the village quiet as a tomb, it let some of those crummy post-divorce feelings come back, like a high tide leaving a line of detritus on the beach.

Thank God Frances is coming. I desperately need some distraction.

Eventually she shoved the catalogs under the sofa and went out for a walk around her property. She had two hectares, just shy of five acres, with a small patch of woods and a sloping meadow in addition to the lawn and gardens around the house. It was difficult to imagine lush gardens in that chilly weather, so she thought about buildings instead. At the moment she had only the one cottage to rent out, but to get anything close to financial security, she needed more buildings with beds in them. An old *pigeonnier*—where some former owner had raised pigeons for dinner—was starting to crumble but would make a charming *gîte* to rent out, if she could find a good mason.

When she returned to the house and peeled off her coat and scarf, she realized she'd forgotten to put more wood in the stove before going out, and now the living room felt like a freezer.

This is ridiculous, I might as well have stayed in Massachusetts!

But she had not moved to France for a change in climate. She had wanted calm and peace and pastry, and she couldn't find them in her Boston suburb, where the crime-to-bakeries ratio was all wrong.

But the truth was, now that she had calm, she didn't want it. She wanted stimulation and excitement. Maybe not as exciting as finding a corpse in the woods.

But *something*.

JOSEPHINE COULD NOT SLEEP. It was one of the insults of getting older, and she did not take it well. She got out of bed, took off the nightgown her husband had brought her from Paris, let it drop to the floor, and wandered around the house naked. The heat was turned way up so she was not cold, and the shutters were closed so she had privacy, with only the faintest moonlight coming through the slats to see by.

She was looking for something, but she had no idea what it was.

No one ever calls. All those cousins who live in Paris, do they ever come visit? No. My sister barely even calls anymore. All I've got is that mewling excuse for a nephew who has never amounted to anything at all.

She came into a sitting room on the second floor, a room where her husband Albert used to work on his inventions. Back then it had been a big mess of tools and parts and boxes of strange things he had ordered from somewhere, and books and papers in towering stacks, threatening to suffocate the man.

What a bore Albert had been, she thought. Always working. Always had his head in some manual or something. Never paying me, his *wife*, the attention I deserved.

After he died—out of nowhere, a heart attack and he was dead on the spot, she had no warning or time to prepare at all—

Josephine had ordered all of his junk taken out of the room. Every last wire, every nut, every bolt. And she had bought a pair of sumptuous love seats and a stuffed ostrich, put candelabra on the mantel and tables, and hung thick brocade curtains at the windows. Following the transformation she found it an agreeable place where she liked to sit and feel tragic about being widowed when she was still so young.

She had been fifty-two when her husband had dropped dead—not exactly a dewy ingenue, but it was true that fifty-two felt like a very long time ago now.

Josephine went to a small antique desk, bought long after Albert died. She opened the bottom drawer and took out three letters tied with a pink satin ribbon. They were tucked in yellowing envelopes without name or address. She slid the top letter out and began to read:

Ma belle,

I am not a poet and words are not easy for me but I want so much to tell you how much our time together means to me. You are so lovely and I find myself thinking of you when I should be studying.

All my love,

A.

The old woman's eyes burned with tears. She put the letter back in its yellowed envelope, retied the satin ribbon, and put the packet back in the bottom drawer of the desk. Though tears were spilling down her wrinkled cheeks, her eyes glared and her mouth turned down. On her way out of the room she caressed the stuffed ostrich's neck, which was showing some signs of wear. She wished the candles were lit but did not want to search for matches.

She could not sleep.

Suddenly she clapped her hands and went down to the kitchen. It was four in the morning. She had not been in the kitchen in several years, so at first she had to turn on a light and rummage about, deep in the pantry, until she found what she was looking for.

Ah! I knew they must still be here!

And then she stood in the kitchen, fingers stroking her chin, pondering just where to set the rat trap so that Sabrina would catch her fingers in it.

Chapter Three

"It's so totally beyond awesome that you really, really did it!" shrieked Frances, dancing around Molly's living room and looking everywhere at once. "You moved to *France!*" She grabbed Molly's hands and spun her around. "Hey, wanna put some music on? We can dance together just like in our wanton youth!"

Molly laughed but made no move for music. "Want me to show you around? House first?"

"Yes ma'am! I want to see it all! It's so quaint I may die. Look at these itty-bitty little windows, they're like something out of a fairy tale." Frances reached out to a small leaded window in the foyer and put her hand right through the glass.

"Oh my God, Molly!"

"Jeez, wait, Frances—don't yank your hand back through there, you'll slice yourself to ribbons!" Blood was already pouring down the glass. "Stay right there, don't move, I'm getting a bandage..."

A first-aid kit was on a list Molly had made of things she needed for the house. Somewhere. She got a clean rag from under the kitchen sink and trotted back to her friend.

"It's nothing, really," said Frances. "I've cut my hand a trillion times, you know that. I'm just—I'm so sorry about your window."

"Don't worry about it," said Molly. She got Frances's hand back through the window without further cutting, led her to the bathroom sink and rinsed out the cut. Then she wrapped the rag around it and told Frances to push down on it.

"Oh, believe me, I know how to stop blood loss," Frances said, laughing. "I'd be even paler than I already am if I hadn't learned that pretty quick."

Then, because of the bitter cold, she cut a piece of cardboard and fit it over the window, taping the edge tightly to keep drafts out, choosing warmth over aesthetics at least until she could get the pane replaced.

Molly and Frances had met in grade school. They had both been known for their white complexions—Molly a freckled redhead and Frances dark-haired and long-legged with unusually white skin. They had done everything together and been nick-named The Pales.

Frances was undeterred in her wish to see every nook and cranny of La Baraque, so Molly took her up the front staircase and into every room, down the back staircase and into the pantry, the laundry room, and an odd little room in which the former owner had left some remnants of fabric and a pincushion shaped like a mouse.

"I love how ramshackle it all is—don't take that the wrong way," said Frances. "I mean...how it's so asymmetrical, like one day the owner woke up and said Hey, I really need another room, let's get busy! and that just kept on happening over decades, you know?"

"I like that about it too," said Molly. "I wish I knew its history, but the couple I bought it from didn't seem to know anything. I don't think they owned it for very long."

"You could probably find out a lot in the courthouse, or wher-ever they keep the real estate sales records, and deeds, that stuff."

"Probably so. Though, uh, chances are pretty good I'll never get around to it."

"Yup!" said Frances. "Now let's put on our boots and go tramp around your *Property*."

"It's not exactly *Property*," said Molly, laughing. "It's just a little over five acres."

"Oh, that counts! That totally counts. You're a *châtelaine*, Molls! Have I mentioned I love that you moved here! I bet your family is all pissed off, aren't they?"

"They...weren't in favor."

"Just icing on the cake," said Frances, grinning, and she opened up the kitchen door as she pulled on her coat.

§.

IT HAD BEEN a satisfactory day thus far, thought Josephine Desrosiers with more than a touch of complacency. Silly Sabrina had stuck her hand in the wrong place and had a rat trap go off. Definitely fractured one finger, maybe two. Josephine had waited at the top of the staircase, listening. She was prepared to wait a long time, but Sabrina had found the trap quickly, propped inside a bucket she used for mopping the kitchen floor.

The old lady had closed her eyes and listened to the howling with a serene smile on her face. Stupid girl, not to look where her hands were going.

The afternoon passed with one television program after another, mostly game shows. She felt more energetic than usual and went wandering into a room where several large chests of her old things were kept. Fancy dress after fancy dress, the lace, the taffeta! And what was the point, she thought morosely, running her fingers over the finery. It's nothing now, useless.

She slipped one dress out of the pile and held it up. It was black lace, with a silk sheath underneath. Stunning workmanship. She vividly remembered how she had enjoyed spending her husband's money, with no thought of bank accounts or overdrafts or anything else. And how when she would come out of her dressing room wearing a frock like this one, all would be forgiven.

Josephine decided it would be the perfect dress to be buried in, not that she had plans to go anytime soon. But it felt wrong to try it on. Wear a fancy dress all alone in the house? That's ridiculous. Yet she took the dress back to her room, and stood in front of the mirror, looking at it. It fell just above the knee, not an outrageous length for a woman her age if she had the legs to carry it off.

And I *do*, she thought, nodding at her reflection. Michel is coming tonight anyway, perhaps I will go ahead and put it on. Show the little weasel how a woman of sophistication dresses.

The dress still fit, although it was tight in different places than it had been when she was thirty. She selected some diamond earrings to wear with it, because black and diamonds are so natural together.

Her hair and makeup were finished before Michel arrived, so she was forced to flip through an old issue of Paris Match while he waited downstairs, but finally got tired of that and made her entrance on the grand staircase.

"Well, Aunt..." Michel was speechless. He desperately wanted to laugh at this ridiculous specter coming down the stairs like she was the star at a Hollywood premiere, her hair standing on end with Lord knows how much hairspray, eyeliner gone terribly awry, and stuffed into a dress that ought to be in a museum somewhere. "...you look magnificent."

"Thank you, Michel. Sometimes I get tired of just throwing on any old thing."

"You must have quite a closet full of treasures. Did Uncle Albert let you buy all the couture you wanted?"

Josephine smiled a girlish smile and laughed, "Nearly! Sometimes he could be fussy about money. But most of the time...most of the time he was shut up in his room fiddling with little bits of things, or on the phone talking to one of his colleagues. Such a bore," she added.

"But that fiddling as you call it—that's how you could afford a dress like that," said Michel, who barely remembered his uncle, but felt someone should stick up for him.

Josephine glared at her nephew. "What do you know about anything," she sneered. "Have you ever made more than fifty francs altogether, in your entire excuse for a life?"

Michel sighed inwardly. Her barb did not hit home because he had long ago realized her poison was about her and not those at whom she directed it, and because she was so ridiculous standing on the stairway in what she imagined was an elegant pose, hurling thunderbolts down on his head.

She was a tiresome, noxious old hag.

"Oh, dear Aunt, you have such admirably high standards. I will redouble my efforts to try and meet them." He bowed his head to hide his ironic grin.

Josephine was momentarily mollified. She made her descent, clutching tightly to the handrail, her heels clopping on the stone stairs and sounding like a small pony. Michel went to the sideboard to pour his aunt her usual Dubonnet, which she drank off in two gulps.

"So this evening, my darling. Would you like me to take you out for dinner? I made reservations at *La Métairie*, if you would like to go."

Madame Desrosiers pursed her lips. On the one hand, she appreciated that he had made an effort, in advance, to please her. On the other hand, she wanted to make whatever decisions were to be made about dinner, not follow along with whatever Michel wanted to do.

"Hm. Well, what sort of food is it? It's nothing modern, is it? Not...not *ethnic*?"

Michel laughed at the way his aunt spat the word as though she had suddenly realized there was *merde* in her mouth. "No,

Josephine, *La Métairie* is French, through and through. They specialize in duck, as a matter of fact. I've not had the pleasure of eating there myself, but all reports are extremely positive."

"You mean you can't afford to go on your own."

Michel inclined his head, and forced himself not to roll his eyes. "Yes, Aunt, true enough."

In the end, Madame Desrosiers agreed, and she allowed Michel to fetch her fur coat and bundle her into the economy car she had bought him, so that they could drive the six blocks to the restaurant. Certainly she would have refused his offer had she had any way of knowing what would occur after she arrived, but that is life.

And death.

Chapter Four

Claudette Mercier always had tea for breakfast, with a bit of stale bread left over from the day before spread with some strawberry jam. This had been her routine for close to twenty years, ever since her husband had passed away, and she no longer had to make the more substantial breakfast he preferred. While she waited for the water to boil, she stood in her nightgown and brushed her long white hair and then braided it. Most mornings she remembered how her husband, Declan (his mother had been Irish) had often told her that the long white braid was the hair-style of an old woman. And she had replied that she *was* an old woman.

It made her smile to think she had only been in her fifties then, hardly old considering she was over seventy now. It had been so many years since Declan had passed away, but she felt his presence still. Even strongly so, from time to time, and she believed that some part of him was still there with her, though she could not explain in what fashion that might be possible.

After her tea and bread with jam she went to work in the kitchen, which took most of the morning. There was jam to make, and chutney, and silver to polish. The work was never-ending and she enjoyed the routine and sense of accomplishment. Her father had owned a prosperous hardware store, and her family had been well off by the Castillac standards of seventy years ago. Her parents had tried to keep her out of the kitchen and let the servants take care of those chores, but Claudette hadn't listened. It seemed as though she had spent most of her life cooking and cleaning up, and except for missing Declan, that life had been mostly happy.

At least until the letters started coming.

By about 11:30 she was folding up the last dishtowel and ready to get the mail, before making her lunch. In earlier years, the mail had been such a source of pleasure! Her friends sent postcards and letters when they traveled, and she had some cousins who lived in Brittany who sent a birthday card every year. But people didn't write letters anymore. She still got a few birthday cards, but the mail was almost entirely advertisements now. Except for these letters, written on expensive stationery, which came every few months. Vicious, hateful letters, with the sole intention of causing hurt.

When the first one arrived, Claudette had been excited to see the lovely stationery; it had been so long since receiving a real letter. She opened it standing by her front gate, not waiting to get back in the house, and began to shake and then to cry when she saw what it said. Later on, when others showed in her mailbox and she recognized the stationery and handwriting, she knew the prudent thing would be to throw them directly in the trash, but she could not make herself do it.

Five letters so far. Every word burned into her brain like a scar.

Everyone has weaknesses, or perhaps we can call them areas of sensitivity, where we struggle if prodded too roughly. For Claudette, her heart's desire was also her weakness. All she had ever wanted was a simple life of making food and being with her family, and that was what the letter-writer attacked, telling her she had been adopted and was not the natural child of her parents, and she was lucky not to be a scullery maid which was all she was equipped for.

Now, Claudette had nothing against adopted children, or even being adopted herself, but the idea that her parents had lied to her, never told her the truth, dying with the secret? They must have thought the circumstances of her birth terribly shameful. It was unthinkably painful to contemplate.

She was not a woman who was particularly gullible or dim, nor was she quick to take offense. It was only that the letter-writer had been able to divine the exact thing to say that Claudette could not defend against, finding the one bit of soft flesh showing under the social armor we all put on every day, and driven in the stiletto precisely at that spot. Now Claudette counted the days since the last letter, wondering if the next one would come on the same schedule as the one before, or just possibly there would be no more and it would all be over. But she sensed that the letter-writer would keep on as long as she was able, and Claudette was not wrong about this.

That morning there was no mail, and she was caught somewhere uncomfortable between relief and wishing a letter had been there, just to get it over with, because the anticipation of the pain had become almost as bad as the pain itself.

She kept the letters, for reasons she could not explain. All five were placed in a tin and nestled in her bureau drawer underneath her winter socks. The letters were unsigned with no return address, and no telltale markings or monogram on the fancy stationery. But Claudette had a pretty good idea about who was sending them, and she was not wrong about this either.

MOLLY AND FRANCES had intended to make an extensive tour of

Castillac before going to dinner, but the weather was not cooperating, and their feet complained before they had gotten very far.

"We lost our taxi driver—long story—so we have to walk," Molly told her friend as they left La Baraque. They were dressed up and wearing heels, and looking forward to a meal at La Métairie. Molly had never been to the almost-one-Michelin-starred restaurant but figured her friend's visit was the perfect opportunity to try it.

"I don't know about a fancy restaurant," said Frances, limping a little from an incipient blister on her right heel. "If you'll remember, my palate leans sorta toward the Cheetos end of the spectrum."

"But don't you want just once to eat in a serious French restaurant, where food is art? And yes, I'm regretting the shoes too. Let's explore Castillac tomorrow, if it warms up a little. You don't have to rush home, do you? I meant what I said about the open invitation. I have no bookings so the cottage is yours. And if a miracle happens and somebody wants it, you can always move into the big house with me. I've got a haunted bedroom upstairs that would be perfect for you."

Frances shook her head quickly, her straight black hair whipping around her face. "Haunted? Nope, not for me, thanks. I'm superstitious, Molls. Nuh-uh."

Molly grinned. "Maybe the restaurant has a bar where we can wait—our reservation's not until 8:30."

"You trying to get me drunk?"

"Yup. Then I'm gonna take advantage of you."

They laughed and hobbled arm in arm the rest of the way to La Métairie.

"Gracious heavens, that bartender could be on the cover of GQ!"

"Ha, yeah, that's Pascal. He's usually at *Café de la Place*, I didn't know he worked here too."

"You *know* him? You're friends with that specimen of manly perfection?"

"Well, sort of. We say hello and kiss, like everyone in the village. But we've never really had a conversation or anything."

"I'd like to conversate with him right this very minute."

Molly laughed. She was so glad she'd thought to invite Frances; she felt like she was twenty again.

The coat-girl took their coats, and Frances and Molly entered the ethereal world of La Métairie. The walls were painted a soothing dove-gray, and there were impressionistic paintings of the sea in the foyer. A small bar with four high chairs was off to the right, manned by Pascal, who really was almost too beautiful for words.

"I bet he's gay," whispered Frances, a little too loudly.

Molly shook her head.

"No, really! When's the last time you met a man that good-looking who was straight?"

Molly thought if she didn't respond maybe her friend would shut up.

"*Never*, that's when!" Frances said, her voice reverberating in the small room.

Molly shot her a look and Frances shrugged. "I'm just sayin'," she mumbled.

"*Salut*, Molly," said Pascal, with a dazzling smile.

"Salut, Pascal," said Molly, leaning across the bar so they could kiss one cheek and then the other. In French, she said, "Allow me to present my friend, Frances. She doesn't speak French, which is a blessing, believe me."

Pascal laughed and winked at Frances. Frances gripped Molly's arm so hard she left marks. They both ordered kirs and turned on their chairs to look out at the dining room and the other diners.

"It looks like the Early Bird Special in Florida out there," Frances said, her voice thankfully lower. It was true that almost all the diners were gray-haired. Molly noticed one old lady in a black lace dress that looked like something you might wear to an opera singer's funeral. Her white hair stood on end and she was holding the hand of a much younger man. Not holding it so much as gripping it like a raptor, digging in with her talons.

"Do you think they're a couple?" Molly said to Frances in a low voice, gesturing with her head at the old lady in lace.

"No freaking way," answered Frances. She had turned back around and was making embarrassing goo-goo eyes at Pascal, who was smiling at her charmingly.

The chic woman who had greeted them at the door appeared at Molly's elbow. "I hope you don't mind," she said, a worried expression on her face, "but part of the dining room is going to be used for a private party. If it becomes too loud and you are unhappy with your service, we will be happy to have you come back to La Métairie, free of charge. I'm sorry but this is an unusual circumstance of crossed communications and I hope you will still enjoy your dinner."

The restaurant was so calm, so serene, that it was difficult to imagine a party getting so wild it would be any kind of problem. Molly rather liked a wild party, anyway. She and Frances assured the woman that they were fine, and the woman looked visibly relieved and went back to the front door.

Not five minutes later a troupe of five people came in singing *bon anniversaire*, some hilariously off-key. They surrounded the old lady in lace, all smiles, though the old lady was not smiling even a little.

"Maybe they *are* together, and it's their anniversary, but he forgot to get her a present," said Frances, talking in her normal voice because no one would be able to hear her over the noise of the partiers.

"*Bon anniversaire* means *happy birthday*," said Molly. "Good theory, though!"

The chic woman came by with compliments of the chef, a small tray of *amuse-bouches:* several kinds of clams and something green neither Molly nor Frances could identify. But they gobbled it all up, Molly trying to eavesdrop on the louder conversations of the party and making more wild guesses about how they were all related. Another old lady sat at the other end of the table from the first one; Molly was desperate to know the connection. Were they friends? Sisters? The second old lady had very white hair put up in a braided bun, a hairstyle Molly loved.

She wondered, would it be rude to lean over and tell her so? She knew that generally the French had stricter boundaries than Americans. But what woman doesn't like to hear a compliment?

Chapter Five

Molly and Frances were seated close enough to the party that they felt almost part of it. Frances said she intended to help herself to some cake, if birthday cakes were a thing in France. The group crowded around the old lady, leaning down to kiss cheeks; they chatted to each other in low voices, and to Molly it was obvious that everyone was not terribly happy. The feeling of duty was heavy, and the old lady looked petulant and as though she had a bad taste in her mouth. The woman with the white bun at the other end of the table looked alert and wary, like a bird perched on a precarious twig.

A blonde woman with a limp came in last; she looked to be in her mid-thirties, around Molly's age. She kissed an older woman wearing no makeup (Molly thought she heard "*Maman*"), and then she went around the table to greet the old lady, who did not look at all happy to see her.

One of Molly's favorite things was eavesdropping, and she wasted no time.

"Dear Aunt, you must admit I surprised you this time!" said the much younger man whose hand the old lady was still clinging to.

"Oh, I was surprised all right," the old lady croaked, looking as though she had just bitten into a caterpillar, or worse.

A dark-haired woman with a bandage on her hand stood looking on with a pained expression. Her husband stood with his arm around her protectively. Is she a granddaughter, Molly wondered, never able to say no to a family obligation even though she is a grown woman? No family resemblance though. Molly decided she was a friend, even though she was anything but friendly.

"Well of course she's happy, everyone's paying attention to her!" whispered the blonde to her mother, who was standing close to Molly and Frances's table. She was well dressed and carrying a nice handbag. The older woman nodded and they both rolled their eyes. So chalk up another pair who did not appear to be fans of the guest of honor.

But fans or not, they had brought presents. They were arranged in front of the birthday girl like offerings, mostly small boxes with extravagant ribbons, and one large box that Molly guessed held some kind of clothing.

"Hello, Molly!" said Frances. "Should I just take my plate to the bar and eat with Pascal for company? Actually I wouldn't mind that one bit."

"Sorry." Molly leaned forward and whispered, "It's just fascinating seeing how this family interacts. So much history bubbling up, you know?"

"You know my opinion on families. Most of 'em suck. But this fish?" she said, pointing with her fork. "I swear to Lord Jesus I have never tasted anything so good. I may have to give up Cheetos and just eat this for the rest of my life."

Molly realized she'd barely touched her starter. The members of the party were settling down to the long table and she couldn't make out much of their conversation anymore, so she turned her attention back to her meal. Her sweetbreads were grilled, with a thin layer of crispy breading and a sauce so complex and wonderful she closed her eyes to savor it.

"So what *are* sweetbreads, anyway?" asked Frances. "I have a feeling the name is kind of a fake-out."

Molly laughed. "Thymus gland, I think."

"So like, guts. You're sitting over there willingly putting guts into your mouth."

"Actually guts are tripe. More or less."

"Same diff."

The waiter came by and put another roll on each bread plate with tongs. Another waiter came by and poured them more wine.

"I could get used to this," said Molly.

"I bet half the people who come here say the same thing. And I agree with all of them."

"And to think—this place doesn't even have one star! What must the restaurants be like that have three?"

Frances just shook her head. "Can't imagine. Looks like it's all been a little much for the old lady," said Frances, glancing over at the party table.

Josephine Desrosiers's face was bright red under her caked-on rouge. She said something to the young man that neither Molly nor Frances could hear, but they saw the man lean away from her, and guessed that whatever she'd said had not been welcome.

"She looks like a bitch on wheels," said Frances, a little too loudly.

"Frances, I have to tell you—French people, generally...they're not loud. They don't shriek in public places. So can you keep your voice down? At least when you're insulting people or making guesses about their sexuality?" Feeling annoyed when she started to speak, she was laughing and shaking her head by the time she finished. It was fun having Frances visit, and interesting seeing Castillac through someone else's eyes. Even if those eyes were half-nuts, probably thanks to all the Cheetos.

The friends moved on to a rich chestnut soup that they could

NELL GODDIN

barely sip without moaning inappropriately. Then to plates of roast duck with several sauces to dip the perfectly cooked slices in, along with a mound of sauteéd mushrooms that were so good Molly was convinced some sort of actual magic was involved. They finished their bottle of Médoc, reminisced about youthful hijinks, and enjoyed their splurge immensely.

"I'm too full for dessert."

"Well, of course. But we won't let that stop us."

"No. Pass me the menu, will you?"

"I'm going to the bathroom," said Molly. "Back in a flash. I'm thinking the lavender *crème brûlée* might be in my future."

"Yum," said Frances.

Molly's feet cried a little when she shoved them back into her heels, but La Métairie was not the sort of restaurant where you could pad to the bathroom without shoes. Molly made her way over the dove-gray carpet to the short corridor where the bathrooms were.

Ah, what a fantastic meal. It was worth it to move to Castillac just for that one perfect dinner.

The door seemed to be a bit stuck. Molly shoved harder. Then an extra-hard shove, and she stumbled into the room to see that it was the old lady, the birthday girl, blocking the door. She was lying on the tile floor of the bathroom, on her side, eyes closed, as though she had decided to choose that spot out of all the possibilities to take a nap.

Chapter Six

The chief gendarme of the village, Benjamin Dufort, arrived at La Métairie in less than ten minutes. He lived on the edge of the village but Castillac was not large, and at ten o'clock at night there was little traffic to slow him down.

He kissed the woman in charge on both cheeks, greeting her warmly. "Very sorry about this, Nathalie. No one has been allowed in the bathroom, I hope? You're quite sure the woman is dead?"

"I'm afraid so," said Nathalie, looking rather pale. "One of the diners found her. She came straight to me saying there's a dead body in the bathroom, and I called you first and then went to see if she could use first aid. Sadly, there was nothing I could do for her."

"Was she here with anyone?"

"Oh yes, a whole party. They were celebrating her birthday—seventy-two, I believe."

"They're still here?"

"I believe all of them are, yes. We're trying to get dessert out of the kitchen if it won't get in your way."

"Not at all. No need to interrupt your service. And thank you, Nathalie. I will go see her now."

"Right down the hall on the left," said Nathalie. "I'm just...it's upsetting, having this happen. Death is part of life, I know this. Yet—who wants to be reminded?"

Dufort nodded and went down the dove-gray corridor to the bathroom. He looked out to the dining room on his way, and saw at least one person he knew. "Molly!" he said with surprise.

She waved weakly. Not a month after she had moved to Castillac, she had found the body of a missing woman. She was embarrassed to have stumbled upon a second corpse barely two months later.

Dufort went on to the bathroom and pushed the door. Since neither Molly nor Nathalie had moved her, Josephine Desrosiers was still blocking the way and he had to give her a shove before he could get through. Dufort was thirty-five and had been on the force for over ten years; he had seen his share of death. But unlike most in his line of work, he never got used to it.

He took a series of slow breaths through his nostrils, expanding his belly, and then pushed the air out forcefully through his mouth. Then he took a small blue glass vial out of his pants pocket and tapped a few drops of an herbal tincture under his tongue. His anxiety more under control, he knelt down beside the old lady. He pushed two fingers against her carotid artery searching for a pulse, though he had no doubt from the first sight of her that she was dead. Dufort did not have the expertise of the coroner, but he did have a fine intuition about life, and he could see that the woman lying on the tile was no more.

It was true she did not have the pallor he normally saw in a dead person; her cheeks were almost ruddy, as though she had been out in a bracing wind. She was not yet cool to the touch. Her black lace dress was hitched up above her knees but that was the only sign of disarray. Dufort guessed that she had collapsed in the bathroom, alone. Perhaps not the most dignified way to go, but at least it had been quick, which is all any of us can hope for.

He stood up and walked around Josephine Desrosiers, looking

with curiosity, noting details of the way she was lying, her jewelry, her shoes. Something about her feet in their dark stockings and low heels seemed poignant. Dufort rubbed his hand back and forth over the back of his head, feeling the prickles of his brush cut. He called the coroner on his cell, and then went to look for Molly Sutton.

❧

"YOU LOOK A LITTLE PALE, even for you," said Frances, cocking her head at Molly. The waiter had come around with tiny glasses of cognac for everyone in the dining room, as a way to acknowledge the difficulty they were all going through. No one makes a reservation at the most expensive restaurant in town expecting to have the place crawling with gendarmes and corpses.

"I just...yeah. What can I say? At least she probably died of a heart attack. Although..."

"I can see the rusty wheels in your brain turning. Although what?"

"Funny. It's just that..." Molly leaned across the table and lowered her voice, "didn't you get the feeling that almost everyone at the party hated that woman? Like, *really* hated her?"

"I was focusing on the food, Molls. This grotesquely expensive, heavenly food. But okay, I saw there were some less-than-happy faces, once you pointed them out."

"I don't think they were joking around," said Molly. "It wouldn't surprise me one bit to find out one of them killed her."

Frances cocked her head. "Come on, Molls, you really think so? I mean, people in families not getting along—that's not exactly headline news."

Molly shrugged. "Just a feeling," she said. And instantly got a flash of her ex-husband yelling at her. "Donnie used to get so mad at me. He'd yell 'Feelings aren't facts!' as though if something wasn't a fact, you didn't have to pay any attention to it at all."

"Donnie was a moron," Frances said, and swishing a mouthful of cognac before swallowing. "I will say this, though: I'm pretty mad at that old lady too, because I think she may have cost me that white chocolate mousse I had my eye on."

Molly turned to look for the waiter, wondering if the arrival of Dufort had put the brakes on the service or whether the restaurant was going to try to muddle through.

"Sudden heart attack—that's like my dream death," the young man who had brought the old lady was saying.

"She was always very lucky," said the dark-haired woman.

Molly stood up. "Back in a sec," she said to Frances.

She tapped the young man on the arm. "Please excuse me for bothering you," she said, in her vastly improved French. "But I just wanted to say that I'm very sorry about what has happened, and give you my condolences."

The man was clearly taken aback but he recovered himself and said, "Thank you, madame. I am Michel Faure, her nephew."

"Molly Sutton, pleased to meet you. And I do agree with you —I overheard what you said about a sudden heart attack being your dream—I mean, not that I dream of dying, thank God, but only, yes, since we have to go sometime, that does seem like one of the better options."

The blonde woman approached, one foot dragging. She nodded at Molly and said to Michel, "Is there any reason I should stay? I can think of a million places I'd rather be right now."

"I suppose it would be tasteless for us to sit down and have dessert, and a couple more glasses of cognac? The dinner's on Josephine's bill, after all."

"Michel," said the blonde woman warningly, nodding at Molly.

"Oh. Right. Sorry!" he said to Molly. "Please forgive me."

"I'm Molly Sutton," said Molly, holding out her hand to the blonde, who grasped her fingers gently and gave them a mild shake. Molly had never quite figured out how to greet someone you did not know well enough to kiss. She had gotten so used to the cheek-kissing that not to touch someone in greeting felt weird.

"Adèle Faure," said the blonde. "This *crétin* is my brother. Apologies for airing our family business out in public where it doesn't belong."

Molly smiled and barely restrained herself from saying, "No, please do air it out! I want all of it! More please!" but instead she blurted out, "No worries, Adèle. I hope you won't think it's the wrong moment to say that I love your bag, and it goes perfectly with your complexion."

Adèle surprised Molly by giving her a grateful smile. "Thank you!" she said, looking surprised and a little unsettled.

"Molly!" hissed Frances from her seat. "There's a *crème brûlée* sitting here with your name on it! And I ordered you coffee."

"*À bientôt!*" said Molly to Adèle as she moved back to her seat. "I'm dying for some coffee, good idea. Although..."

"Oh stop it with the *althoughs*!" Frances spooned some white chocolate mousse into her mouth and then gripped the sides of the table while she swooned.

"I wanted to meet the family, to see if there was, well, any dirt to dig up."

"It's a family. Of course there's dirt to dig up."

"It's probably not a good idea for me to get involved. It's not like I don't have a ton of work to do at La Baraque, getting the new cottage ready."

"Well, strictly speaking, it's not you doing the work but the guys you'll hire. But whatever. Doesn't the cop do a good job? He's pretty foxy," she said, growling.

Molly laughed, her eyes on Adèle and Michel, who had sat back down and were drinking coffee, deep in conversation. The rest of the party had cleared out, and it was only the four of them left in the restaurant.

"Dufort? Yeah, he's okay. Probably better than okay. He's had the bad luck to be chief in a village where things seem to go wrong more than seems fair."

"What's that mean, 'things go wrong'?"

"Amy Bennett, the woman I found...she was the third woman to go missing. The other two have never been found."

"And the guy you nailed? He didn't do those?"

"Apparently there's no evidence pointing in that direction. He says he didn't touch the others. So I don't know. Maybe he did. Maybe he didn't."

"You think the cop is a loser."

"No! No, I really don't. He's a smart guy. And not bad looking..."

"I didn't miss that."

"Figured. And he's really a kind man. I could tell his heart was breaking for Amy's parents. Really, I have nothing at all to say against him."

"Except that he sucks at his job."

"Frances! I'm not saying that."

"I think I'll go over to the brother-and-sister team over there, and just tell them that my friend Lady Sleuthington says that the local guy is crap and if they want to find out what really happened to old granny, they should hire you."

Molly laughed. "Let's go home. I swear I'm retiring my civilian badge and focusing on my house and garden from now on."

"Sure you are," murmured Frances, grinning at Molly's back as they waved their thanks to Natalie and hobbled their way back to La Baraque in the cold dark.

Chapter Seven

Thérèse Perrault was the first to get to the station on Friday morning. She was almost always first. She was young and enthusiastic and trying to make a good impression on Chief Dufort, and very pleased to have a job she was interested in, where she could make a difference in people's lives. Even if, in Castillac, that often meant returning Madame Bonnay's dog or Madame Vargas's husband, both of whom tended to wander.

"Bonjour, Thérèse!" said Dufort, striding in. He ran every morning, farther in winter than in summer because he liked working out in the cold. His skin was still bright from the exertion, and he too was glad to come to work, happy for a job where he didn't have to sit behind a desk but could spend most of the day out on the streets, talking to the people of the village and listening to their concerns, and—he hoped—helping with their difficulties.

The third officer on the Castillac force was Gilles Maron. He had grown up in the north, near Lille, and worked in Paris for several years before being transferred to Castillac. Dufort valued his work though they had not become close. Perrault had not decided what she thought about Maron. He was not like the men she was used to—more closed up, sterner, serious.

The three usually met in Dufort's office first thing, where Dufort handed out any assignments that had come up.

"Well, here we are, on a dreary December day," he said. "The village is quiet and I have absolutely nothing whatsoever on my desk. Apparently the people of Castillac are without problems this morning."

Perrault chuckled and Maron did not change his expression.

"Wait, what about Madame Desrosiers dropping dead at La Métairie last night?" asked Perrault.

"She did indeed," said Dufort. "I got a call from the restaurant at close to ten. I drove over and spoke to Nathalie—you both know Nathalie Marchand?—at any rate, yes, the old lady was dead in the bathroom. I called the coroner and went home."

"Heart attack?"

"Haven't heard from Monsieur Nagrand yet, but I suspect so. She was seventy-two—yesterday was her birthday, in fact. No reason to suspect foul play."

"Except that she was a complete witch," mumbled Perrault.

"In what way?" asked Maron, looking awake for the first time that morning. "Garden-variety bitch, or the kind of bitch that makes people want to kill you?"

"I said 'witch'," said Perrault. "But I'd bet on the latter."

Dufort shook his head. "I know you two prefer our work to be interesting, but I don't believe there's anything there. Seventy-two year olds sometimes die. That's life."

Perrault nodded and did not let on that she intended to give Desrosiers's niece Adèle a call. Perrault's older sister had been schoolmates with Adèle, and Perrault could remember hearing some pretty eye-popping stories about the tricks that woman got up to. Not exactly your kindly grandmother-type, but a real viper. Wouldn't hurt just to have a chat with Adèle, see if she had anything interesting to say, thought Perrault.

"So for today, let's get outside, cover the village, look around, talk to anyone who'd like to talk. I think of a calm day like this as an opportunity to take the pulse of our village, and see if there's anything we've neglected that needs our attention. I'll see you both back here after lunch, unless I hear from you otherwise."

"Yes sir," said Perrault and Maron together. All three put on their coats and scarves and headed out in different directions.

❦

DUFORT WALKED the short block to the *Place*, the square in the middle of town. In the very center, an unremarkable monument to World War I dead stood surrounded by a bank of flowers in the summer, now bare ground. The Place was ringed with restaurants, the *Presse* where you could get newspapers, magazines, and cigarettes, as well as several banks and a number of shops. It was the heart of Castillac, where people congregated on market day and other days as well, but on a cold day in winter, it looked desolate and closed up.

Dufort wandered into *Chez Papa*, a bistro owned by his old friend Alphonse. No one was at the bar. In fact, it looked as though the restaurant was completely empty of staff as well as patrons, though Dufort could hear swing music coming from the back.

"Alphonse!" he shouted. "You here?"

The bartender Nico stuck his head around a corner. "Hey Ben," he said. "Hold on, I'll be right with you."

Dufort sat on a barstool and looked around. He couldn't help staring for a moment at the table by the door, where Vincent used to sit. He shook his head, thinking not for the first time that people were extremely difficult to understand. You just never know what's brewing underneath the surface, even people who outwardly seem perfectly pleasant and reasonable.

"Bonjour," Nico said, coming behind the bar and wiping his

hands on a towel. "Sorry, no one was coming in so I was in the back, trying to get the pantry organized. Coffee?"

Dufort paused. "All right, yes," he said. "*Petit, s'il te plaît.*"

Nico fussed with the machine, served Dufort his cup of espresso, and then made one for himself.

"Not much business this month?" asked Dufort.

Nico shrugged. "You know how it is. In December, everyone is huddled up next to their woodstoves, dreaming about spring. Alphonse has been talking about closing the place in January, maybe taking a trip to someplace warm."

Dufort shook his head. "Castillac without Chez Papa? Even for a month, hard to imagine."

The door opened with a gust of cold air, and a group of three people came in, followed by a couple.

"Perhaps Alphonse is being hasty," said Dufort with a smile, as Nico went to hand out menus. He thought he recognized the three as being related to Desrosiers, though he wasn't entirely clear on the family tree.

"I can't say I'm brokenhearted. She was an absolute horror, and I'll say it because it's true and so what if she is my aunt," the young man with brown hair falling into his face said.

"Oh now, Michel," said an older woman affectionately, perhaps his mother. "Some things are just better left unsaid."

Dufort slid off his stool and went to their table. "Bonjour, madame," he said to the older woman. "I am Benjamin Dufort of the Castillac *gendarmerie*. I'm sorry to intrude, but I believe you are related to the departed Madame Desrosiers?"

"She was my sister. I am Murielle Faure," she said, with a slight nod.

"I'm very sorry for your loss," said Dufort.

"Thank you, Chief Dufort. May I present my son, Michel, and daughter Adèle," said Murielle. Michel and Adèle showed their good manners by telling the chief they were pleased to meet him.

"Had your sister been ill? Of course it's always a shock, no matter how old a person is. I was just wondering if there had been any indication something was amiss, health-wise?"

"Oh no," said Madame Faure, brightening. "We always thought Josephine would live forever, didn't we children? Healthy as a horse. So yes, we're all quite shocked."

Michel's pinkie finger had a long nail, and he was sliding it along the edge of the menu, fraying it slightly. Dufort thought he saw Adèle kick her brother under the table, rather odd behavior for an adult.

"Well, again, my condolences. It is never easy to lose someone no matter the age."

Dufort went back to the bar and sipped his espresso. He thought about Madame Desrosiers lying on the bathroom tile at La Métairie, on her side as though taking a nap. He felt his throat start to close up.

But then he remembered someone once telling him that "dirt nap" was a term for death, and let out a guffaw before pulling himself together and leaving a few euros on the bar on his way back out into the cold.

Chapter Eight

M olly was an early riser and Frances a late one, so Molly got up and had coffee and breakfast by herself. She screwed up her courage for a phone call, still a difficult hurdle even though her French had improved dramatically over the months she had been in Castillac. There was something about that disembodied voice over the phone, with no facial expression or body language to help the communication along. Dread was not too strong a word for how Molly felt about phone calls in France.

She was calling a mason, recommended by her neighbor Madame Sabourin, who she hoped would be able to repair the external wall of the pigeonnier down in the orchard, the first necessary step toward turning the outbuilding into a habitation she could rent out.

"Bonjour, Monsieur Gault. I received your name from my neighborhood, pardon, my neighbor, Madame Sabourin. I wonder if...if...you have a moment to talk with me? I think of a project." She shook her head. Molly *liked* talking to people—adults, children, strangers, it didn't matter—and it made her very uncomfortable to come out with such stilted sentences. But the mason

understood well enough and said he would be out at the end of
the afternoon, if that was convenient.

Whew, glad that's out of the way.

"Molly!" shouted Frances as she came through the front door.
"I need coffee, stat!"

"Tell you what," said Molly, checking the big clock on the wall
that said it was a quarter to twelve. "Why don't we stroll into
town and eat at Chez Papa? The coffee is better than mine, for
sure, and I'll introduce you to another hot bartender. You up
for it?"

"Sure," Frances said. "I should probably take a day, or at least a
few hours, to get work done, at some point anyway. Not feeling
like it has to be this minute. You have a piano?"

"Actually," Molly said, with a slightly embarrassed grin, "I have
a music room. I'll show you." Frances followed Molly in the other
direction from the living room and into a room that contained
nothing but a dusty piano and a couple of chairs. "I feel silly
having this, because I don't play. But the piano came with the
house, and I don't need the room for anything else, so here
it sits."

"Awesome!" said Frances. She wrote jingles for a living—an
extremely good living—and needed to be able to noodle around
on a piano for ideas to come to her. She walked over and played a
few chords, pronounced it in tune, and said she was ready to go
into the village. "I'm starving. Last night's dinner seems like it was
a million years ago. And you know," she said thoughtfully, "I'm
sort of disappointed that I didn't get to see the body of the old
lady in the bathroom. I've never actually seen a real live dead
person before."

Molly started laughing and she laughed so hard she had to lean
on the wall for support, gasping for breath. Frances was puzzled
until Molly managed to choke out, "Real...live...dead person..." in
between gales of laughter.

"It's not that funny," said Frances, giving her hair one last comb before they went into the village. "Sometimes you can be so literal-minded."

Molly recovered herself and pulled on a coat. Both women looked in a long horizontal mirror on the foyer wall while they tied on scarves. "I saw a friend of my father's when I was a teenager," said Molly. "Open casket at the funeral. But that dead body looked sort of like a doll, even though it was an old man. His face was all waxy and he had on more makeup than I did. Madame Desrosiers...well, the way her body was, curled up on her side, I thought at first she was asleep or had passed out or something. But when I looked into her face..."

"You knew she was dead."

"Pretty much. Something about her eyes...they just didn't look like they were going to open again."

The day was bright and cold. Frances and Molly blinked at the sun and wished they had worn sunglasses. On the other side of *rue des Chênes*, almost at the village, was a small cemetery, and Frances walked more slowly, looking over the wall at the stone mausoleums and complicated ironwork of the gate.

"What does *Priez pour vos morts* mean?"

"'Pray for your dead'," answered Molly.

They walked on in silence, stomachs growling.

Walking into Chez Papa, Molly inhaled deeply, always appreciating the smell of coffee and humanity therein. Nico waved from the bar and a few tables were filled—nothing like the crowds and gaiety of summer, but still a welcoming, homey place.

"Nico, this is my American friend, Frances Milton."

"Very nice to meet you," said Nico.

Frances grinned at Nico and then gave Molly a sharp elbow to the ribs. "Look, Molls, it's that family from last night—"

And sure enough, there were Michel and Adèle, niece and nephew to the newly departed Madame Desrosiers, deep in conversation at a table nearby.

"*La bombe!*"

47

"Oh, brother," said Molly. Lapin Broussard swept into the room, waving at Nico and giving Molly a wink. "I'd love to stay and chat but I've got some business to do," he said, and continued on to the back room.

"Who's that? And what's a *bohmb?*" asked Frances.

"If you don't wanna find out, just keep your arms over your chest."

"Ha—one of those. So who is the guy, anyway?"

"Long story. Sort of decent, sort of a pain. He's a junk dealer."

"Such blasphemy! I deal in original antiques, Molly!" said Nico, imitating Lapin.

Frances ordered a *café grand*, and Molly had an espresso because why not, but she stopped talking to Frances and Nico, hoping to hear whatever Michel and Adèle were saying. As she sat on her stool, she hoped it wasn't obvious that her antennae were completely focused on the pair at the table, and she turned her head so that one ear was directly facing them.

"—what she did to that housekeeper from a few years ago? She was never right after that, I swear Michel. I think she had to move back in with her parents and hasn't had a job since. Nerves totally shattered."

Michel nodded. "I don't know what makes a person that twisted," he said, and then the next bit was garbled and Molly couldn't follow it.

"Hel-lo, Molly Sutton!" said Frances, annoyed. "I'm talking to you, Nico's talking to you, and you're sitting there with your eyes glazed not answering."

Something was up with that old lady, was what Molly was thinking. And now that she had that thought, she couldn't let it go.

🐌

MURIELLE FAURE GOT UP EARLY, as she usually did, and put on a pair of sturdy canvas pants and a heavy, man's flannel shirt. Over that, a workman's coat, then a wool scarf covering her head and tied around her neck. It was cold again, but she longed to be in her garden. She sat down on a bench beside her front door and bent one long, gangly leg up to tie her boot, and then the other.

It was beautiful outside. The sun was just peeking up over the trees and it cast a sharp glow where it hit: the crazy, wiggly branches of a Corylus avellana 'Contorta'; a six-foot Vitex agnus-castus with a few straggling leaves still hanging on; a bank of hydrangeas, the leaves long gone, but a few flower heads dead and shimmering with frost. Murielle stamped her feet to bring some blood to them, and walked down a garden path made of broken pieces of slate she had gotten at a discount from a building supply store, to the back garden where the fruit trees stood.

They too were bright in the early morning sun, every twig outlined in gold. She reflexively checked the bark for insect damage even though she had done so almost daily and it was not the season for insects anyway. She patted their trunks, considered where she would need to prune in the spring, and then, since it was barely dawn and none of her neighbors were early risers, she spoke to the trees out loud.

"You are my friends," said Murielle, reaching up and wrapping her bare palms around a cold branch. Now that her children were grown and out of the house, she was lonely and it was more difficult than ever for her to get through the winter while the garden was dormant. It was like having your husband sleep for four months straight, never saying a word, but lying next to you in bed with his back turned, his body cold.

She clapped her hands together for warmth and headed back to the house, thinking for the millionth time that if she only had a greenhouse, she would be able to accomplish amazing work. Next to the small house was a tiny shed containing her gardening tools, and nestled against the south wall was a cold frame where she nursed along several botanical experiments. In a neat row was a line of rose grafts, combinations of her seedlings and a stronger root, which she hoped would make quite a splash if they turned out the way she expected.

It was the day after Josephine died in the bathroom at La Métairie. Murielle did not miss her sister. She was a little surprised that she did not, since she imagined that sisters were supposed to miss each other when one died even if they did not get along, but that was how she felt and she did not dwell on it.

Chapter Nine

The day after his aunt died, Michel Faure sat in a café opposite her mansion, drinking coffee and pretending to read a novel. He had been out of work for months, and the small price of the coffee was money he should not have been spending, but he shrugged that knowledge off and spent the money anyway, feeling irritated.

Castillac in winter was a different place than in warmer months. He had no idea what people his age did with themselves, but they weren't out on the streets, that was for sure. The people-watching aspect of sitting in the café was more or less null, as the only passersby were an old lady walking very slowly with a cane, who Michel thought was a schoolmate's *grand-mère*, and the mailman.

He wanted a plate of cookies—this particular café was known for them, after all—but he had rules, whereby he was allowed to buy the coffee he couldn't afford, but not the cookies.

Forty minutes, and nobody but a granny and the mailman.

The mansion was imposing. Rising up behind an ornate but rusting gate, the house had four floors plus a cellar, and a carved wooden door painted a deep violet-blue with pots of topiary standing on either side. The long windows were shuttered, and Michel knew the curtains were drawn inside, thick brocade curtains, so thick they half-suffocated him just in the remembering.

He was waiting to see someone, watching, but she did not come. Maybe I've been wrong about her, Michel thought. But I don't think so.

He chewed on a fingernail, his eyes pinned to the grand building. His stomach didn't feel so hot.

He wondered when the will would be read. Wondered how long it would take before his aunt's things were handed out to whomever she had designated to receive them. Wondered if any of his efforts had paid off.

Michel Faure did not miss his aunt. He would have laughed at the suggestion that he might, as he believed her to have been one of the vilest creatures he had ever met. He had suffered from her as a young child, as she was the sort of aunt who pinched cheeks hard enough to cause bruising. The sort of aunt who insisted he memorize poetry and if he stumbled on a line would whip the backs of his legs with a cane.

Hateful bitch, he thought. He signaled the waiter for another cup, knowing it wouldn't do his stomach any favors, but wanting to spend the money if only because he shouldn't, and because Aunt Josephine would have lectured him about financial responsibility, and—thankfully, blessedly, gloriously—she was no longer able to do so.

MOLLY HESITATED. She thought Frances would probably like to see the Saturday market, but should she wake her up for it? It was cold, after all, and Frances did seem pretty devoted to getting a really good night's sleep. Molly dressed for the weather, put her basket under her arm and set off by herself.

She had lived at La Baraque nearly four months. Not long enough to feel as though it—or France—was home, not all the way. And not long enough that every single walk down rue des Chênes into Castillac didn't take her breath away in one way or another. That day, the world seemed muffled. The sky was cloudy and the limestone of the buildings didn't have that characteristic yellow glow, or at least the color was dulled. Thin wisps of smoke rose from chimneys. A dog barked.

The street was empty save for a small pickup that passed her heading away from the village. When she came to the cemetery, Molly ran her eyes over the inscription *"Priez pour vos morts,"* and she wondered if anyone was praying for Josephine Desrosiers.

She thought not.

She couldn't say exactly why, and if Dufort tried to pin her down she would have no way to describe it...but something about the tone of the conversation she had overheard at La Métairie made her think that it was possible the old lady's death was not as simple as Dufort seemed to think it was. It wasn't the words anyone said—and honestly, though her French had improved mightily, she hadn't been able to understand quite a few of them —it was the tone. Acid. Bitter. Plus the sense that the guests at the party were smiling when they faced Madame Desrosiers, but under their breaths, mutterings of resentment bubbled up.

On the other hand, she thought, kicking a pebble as she walked...as Frances said, plenty of families don't get along. Doesn't mean anyone gets killed. And besides, she hadn't seen anyone attend the old woman into the bathroom, or follow her in there either. Though of course, she had been eating a superb meal with her good friend, so she could easily have been distracted long enough for someone to leave the dining room without her noticing.

And surely there are ways to murder in which the murderer doesn't have to be present at the exact moment of death. Poison comes quickly to mind.

Oh please. Can't I just enjoy a simple walk into the village without looking under the bed for monsters?

She turned a corner and the Saturday market was there in its much-reduced winter glory. About half the usual vendors were present, all looking cold and rather depressed at the sparse number of customers.

"Manette!" said Molly, going up to her friend the vegetable seller and kissing both her cheeks.

"Bonjour, Molly! Nice to see you. I wondered if you might have fled once the weather turned."

"Oh no, I have no place to go!" said Molly laughing. "I am officially not a vacationer, not a summer person. Though I admit, I am finding the weather a little difficult."

"Not insulated, are you?"

"Afraid not."

Manette cut an orange into sections and handed a piece to Molly. "So tell me the news, I've been holed up cooking for my sick mother-in-law and have no idea what's going on."

Molly was so flattered to be asked that a blush crept up her neck and bloomed on her cheeks. "Well," she said, savoring the moment since she'd practically been an eye-witness, "did you know Madame Desrosiers? I was having dinner at La Métairie the other night, and she dropped dead in the bathroom."

"Really!" said Manette. "I must be the last to know. What did she die of?"

Molly paused. With some effort she chose not to ramble on about her theory of poisoning. "Probably a heart attack."

Manette nodded. "A grande dame of the village, or so she considered herself. Actually, she had perfectly humble beginnings —the daughter of a grocer, lived over by the railroad tracks. But she married an inventor who ended up making piles of money for some kind of transistor he thought up."

"Interesting. So she was really rich? Did she have any children?"

"No, no children. Wait, I think she did have one, but stillborn. Always sad. Her sister is Murielle Faure, who teaches at the *lycée*. She has two children, adults now. I can't say I know any of them, though they occasionally buy an eggplant or two from me." Manette winked at Molly and gestured to a neat pyramid of the purple vegetables. "Well, of course they're imported, it's December! But very good cut in thin strips and fried, with a marinara sauce."

Molly bought two. She was helpless in the face of Manette's selling techniques, but hardly minded since Manette did the work of figuring out what to make for dinner.

"Oh look," said Manette in a low voice. "Speak of the devils..."

"Bonjour!" sang out Murielle Faure to Manette.

"Hello, Molly," said Adèle, practicing her English. "It's nice to see you."

Molly grinned. There was something about Adèle that appealed to her, though she couldn't put her finger on what. She certainly dressed well. Her camel-hair coat looked freshly brushed, and her leather boots were classic without being in the least old-fashioned. "Nice bag," said Molly, noticing it was a different one than Adèle had carried at La Métairie.

"Thanks!" said Adèle brightly. "I just got it. I confess to a weakness for nice bags. I don't understand it, I don't even have anything that important to carry around with me, but I seem to care quite a lot about having the possibility of carrying all sorts of things."

"Maybe you have an explorer's spirit," said Molly. "You want to be ready at any moment if you get a call to head to the Arctic."

Adèle laughed. "That's generous of you. The truth is probably that I just want to carry something around that is beautiful, and that people will admire."

Molly cocked her head. She was impressed with Adèle's willingness to tell a truth that did not put herself in a flattering light.

"How is your family doing?" she asked. "I'm sure the other night must have been such a shock."

"Yes, it was," said Adèle. "I don't know if you have any deeply unpopular people in your family, Molly, but I think we all thought Aunt Josephine would live forever. An immortal tyrant. None of us can quite believe she's gone. And none of us are the least bit sad."

"Ah," said Molly, "I see what you mean. Was she horrible to all of you?"

"Well, that's one thing to say in her favor," laughed Adèle. "She was more or less equally horrible to anyone, friends or family, people in the street, anyone at all. An equal opportunity insulter. Made it easier not to take personally."

Molly nodded. "And—sorry if I'm asking too many questions —was there an autopsy? Did she die of a heart attack like Dufort thought?"

"*Merci et à bientôt*," said Manette to Madame Faure, who nodded at Molly and pulled Adèle by the arm.

"See you later," said Adèle, rolling her eyes toward her mother.

Molly watched the two of them walk away, Adèle limping slightly as though something wasn't right with her left leg. Her mother was dressed in a frumpy pair of trousers that had seen better days. Molly wondered if Adèle had a well-paying job that allowed her to buy such nice clothing and handbags, things her mother couldn't afford.

"Now let's discuss your Christmas menu," said Manette. "If there's something in particular you want, I'm going to need some notice, you know. Tell me, what bizarre things do people from Massachusetts eat for Christmas dinner?"

Molly reluctantly watched the Faures disappear around the corner of the church. She had so many questions, but the best ones were far too impolite to ask, even to Manette.

Chapter Ten

❦

Dufort hardly ever sat at his desk if he could avoid it, but that's where he was on Saturday morning, catching up on paperwork, when the coroner called.

"Bonjour, Ben," Florian Nagrand said in his deep voice, raspy from cigarettes. "I got some news on Desrosiers. Figured you'd want to know right away. Still waiting on some results, but it's not looking like a heart attack."

Dufort's eyebrows went up.

"She was poisoned. Sorry to toss this at you on the weekend. I'll know more when the lab sends me the results."

"Wait, poison? I'm...I wasn't expecting that at all. You're sure?"

"No, I won't be sure until the lab results are back of course. But the signs were not consistent with heart failure. Organs showed a pink lividity—didn't you notice her skin was reddish, far more so than any other corpse you've sent my way?"

"I did notice. I thought perhaps because I got there quickly... do you have ideas about what the poison is?"

"Cyanide. But again, Ben, patience. We should know in a day or two, maybe even later today."

"Can you tell me when she was poisoned? Right before she died? Last week? Can you narrow it down at all?"

"Gotta wait for the lab. Sorry."

They hung up. Dufort stood up and walked around his office. Why had he insisted the old lady had died a natural death? Simply because he wished it were so? A stunning lapse in judgment. He felt a wave of shame go over him and then he stood up straight, cleared his throat, and called Perrault to come into his office.

"Some news. Nagrand just called. He thinks Josephine Desrosiers was poisoned."

Perrault's eyes got bright and she grinned, and then mastered her emotions and made a neutral expression. "Is there any chance it was accidental?"

"It's possible. We'll know more when the lab tells us what kind of poison we're talking about. But we must act quickly even though we don't have all the information we need. I'm going to send Maron over to La Métairie. Perrault, you go over to the coroner's office and pester him for that lab report. I want it in our hands the instant it arrives."

Dufort reached Maron on his cell and told him the news. "Get over to La Métairie and talk to Nathalie Marchand. She manages the place. It's a longshot for sure, but ask if everything—plates, cutlery, even tablecloths and napkins—has been washed from Thursday night. We need to begin testing anything we can find for residue, working backward from the last moment Desrosiers was alive."

"If it was her birthday," said Perrault, "there were probably presents? Or maybe not. I know my *grand-mère* would not like opening things at a restaurant. But some people like to."

Dufort gave her a small smile and a nod. She was improving, Perrault. Her thinking was getting clearer. "Thank you," he said. "Now get over to the coroner's. If we don't keep an eye on him, he'll go home for a long lunch and not come back to the office. Babysit him until you get that report."

Perrault nodded. "Yes sir," she said, grabbing her heavy coat on her way to the door. "Chief? Is there any chance this is connected to the Boutillier and Martin cases?"

"Unfortunately for those of us who love logic and finding patterns, events in the world tend to be more disorganized and unconnected than we would like them to be. In other words: highly doubtful."

Perrault nodded and the door closed behind her.

A poisoning, thought Dufort, leaning back in his chair. Never been one in Castillac, not that he remembered as a child, and not since he'd arrived at the gendarmerie three years ago.

At least, not one we've known about.

&.

"YOU CAME HOME WITH *EGGPLANTS?* That's it? Jeez, Molly, I thought you had some sense of priorities."

"I know. And I was two steps away from Pâtisserie Bujold, too. In my defense, this has never happened before."

Frances took a long glug of her coffee. She looked disgruntled and her usually sleek hair was sticking up in back. "Eh, sorry Molls. I'm stuck on a jingle, and the deadline is two days from now."

Someone banged on the door and Frances jumped up to answer it. "It's the mason," said Frances, gesturing to him to come in. She said *bonjour* with an appalling accent, and then gesticulated in a way that she thought was a friendly greeting. "See you, Molls. I'm going to mess around on the piano and see if I can whip that stupid jingle off in the next hour."

The mason looked confused, no doubt in part because of Frances's continued waving of her arms and flapping of her hands.

"This way," said Molly to the mason, Pierre Gault. "As I was telling you, I'd like to convert my pigeonnier into a living space.

I've got some ideas and I'd like you to tell me if they're going to work."

Pierre nodded, relieved to be able to understand the American's French, which was a little disjointed but got her point across. His wife had been joking around and acting out scenes at breakfast in which Pierre was utterly lost while the American woman chattered away in French-sounding nonsense and then flew into a rage when he did not do what she asked.

But Molly was ignorant of Pierre's wife and her jokes, and walked with him out to the meadow where the pigeonnier stood, crumbling a bit on one side, thinking only that she hoped Pierre didn't charge too much for his services, since bookings had been nonexistent for over a month.

She did not think about the corpse she had found in the bathroom at La Métairie, nor of Benjamin Dufort, but the afternoon in the meadow with Pierre was the last time she was able to think about anything else for quite a while.

Chapter Eleven

Sabrina Lellouche pulled her scarf forward to hide her face as she quickly walked the last blocks before reaching the mansion of Madame Desrosiers. It was dusk on Saturday, and hardly anyone was on the streets. It was cold. She reached into her bag and drew out an old-fashioned key and let herself in through the kitchen door.

The shutters were closed and the house was dark. The heat was still on, so it was warm enough—too warm, Sabrina had always thought, but then old people probably got cold easily. She stood in the kitchen and inhaled the familiar smell of the house deep down into her lungs. It was strange to be in the house alone, but she had been going there for several years and it didn't feel right never to come again.

She could feel the presence of the old lady. Could feel her cruelty, her invasive personality, her evil, as though she were still alive, still upstairs pondering her next act of malice.

Whoever buys this house, thought Sabrina, will be affected by what happened here. How could they not be?

She could not imagine having enough money to afford to buy such a place. Castillac was not a village that attracted many tourists or expats, and the upper layer of Castillac society was not aristocratic or even especially rich, but even so, it had a level of wealth beyond what Sabrina could comprehend. Her family had moved there from Algeria nearly fifteen years earlier and they had been barely scraping by ever since. The Desrosiers mansion with its four floors and grand foyer and blue-purple door—Sabrina thought it might fetch a million euros.

A million euros.

She put her bag down on the metal table in the kitchen where she was used to chopping Madame Desrosiers's vegetables, and walked into the foyer. Peering upstairs, she looked for the old woman's face at the bannister, laughing down at her.

Of course she's not there, she's dead.

Sabrina knew very well she was dead, but some part of her resisted the knowledge, as though she was afraid of dropping her guard. But she started up the stairs, slowly and then running, up to the second floor. She had cleaned these rooms for years, but this was the first time she walked into them standing tall, taking her time, without dragging a vacuum cleaner or bucket and mop. All of it looked different—the ornate decoration no longer a series of cleaning tasks waiting for her attention, the paintings she could look at and consider at her leisure.

She pretended she was part of the family—Madame Desrosiers's daughter, perhaps—in the house alone, mourning for her mother. Drifting into the sitting room with the stuffed ostrich, Sabrina touched its feathers, which she hadn't dared to do with the old lady in the house. Madame was capable of swooping in out of nowhere to shriek at you if you touched anything the wrong way.

Her footsteps creaked on the floorboards and she kept stopping to listen as though expecting the shrieking to start up any minute, or to hear the television going on the third floor. But the house was silent except for an occasional sigh from the radiators.

Madame Desrosiers had always paid Sabrina in cash. Twice a

month and never missed, which was surprising in a way, considering how fond the old lady was of making people uncomfortable. Sabrina had to give her that—she paid on time. Of course, there was no knowing where the cash box was, if it was a box, but it must still be in the house, mustn't it? Somewhere? And aside from cash, surely there were other things...of interest?

Sabrina went back to the staircase and ran up another floor up to Madame Desrosiers's bedroom. The few times she had been allowed inside the room to clean, she had seen the jewelry box on the bureau. It was long and flat and Sabrina guessed there were rare and valuable necklaces inside.

Albert Desrosiers was famous in Castillac—both for the invention of the special transistor (whose use no one understood) and especially for the river of money that the invention had sent his way. She could remember schoolmates talking about him with reverence, a local man who had gotten rich just from having a good idea! And to think, that one good idea had made this house and this jewelry box possible. It sat on madame's dressing table, long and flat just as she remembered. Sabrina ran her hand along the velvet top. And then she took it in her hands and popped open the lid.

Inside was a string of pearls. Pretty enough, but not what Sabrina had been dreaming of. She had believed there would be diamonds, emeralds, perhaps sapphires, something with some flash. With disappointment she let the box drop back to the table, and began opening every drawer and box in Madame Desrosiers's room that she could find, searching for the treasure she was sure the old lady had hidden there.

❦

SUNDAY WAS WARMER BUT DREARY. "*La grisaille*," Molly said to Frances, pointing outside to the gray sky. "Maybe a day to read by the woodstove? Cold rain. Yuck."

"If I sit by the woodstove all day, I'm going to sink into a depressing heap," said Frances. "Come on, isn't there someplace we can go for brunch?"

"Brunch is not really a French thing."

"Well, we could go sit at the bar at Chez Papa and stare at Nico."

"And eat *frites*."

"Now you're talking."

They washed up their coffee cups and put on coats and hats. Once they were outside, Molly agreed that the air felt bracing in a good way, and didn't mind the light sprinkle of rain. It felt good to get out and breathe.

From far away they could see more traffic on rue des Chênes than usual. Cars parked on the road by the cemetery and black umbrellas were sprouting. When they got closer, they saw an old Citroën hearse pull up by the gates.

"Do you think they're planting the old lady?" said Frances, too loudly.

Molly shot Frances a look. She scanned the people climbing out of their cars and walking under umbrellas, looking for Adèle and her brother, but didn't see them.

The friends walked slowly, watching the hearse driver open up the back of the hearse, which was a thing of beauty, the elegant lines of the Citroën perfectly appropriate for a hearse. A few people stopped and looked in at the casket.

"I'm thinking it should say, 'Pray for the living'," said Frances, looking at the wrought-iron inscription over the gate. "I mean, we're the ones who could use some help. What good will praying do when we're already dead?"

"Hush," said Molly. "Talk to me about it when we're at Chez Papa." She thought it must be the funeral for Madame Desrosiers, and she didn't want to be distracted while she observed, just in case some sort of information dropped into her lap. She saw Rémy, the organic farmer, dressed in a dark suit, and wondered what his connection to the old lady was. And there was Pierre Gault, the mason, almost unrecognizable in a fedora and black suit. Also, the dark-haired young woman who had been at La Métairie, and her boyfriend or husband, his arm tight around her waist, just as it had been at dinner the other night.

Molly watched. She knew it was superstitious, but she had the idea that since she had found the body, she was responsible in some way for setting things right if, in fact, they were wrong. She had not even one tiny shred of evidence that anything *was* wrong. Desrosiers had most likely died of a heart attack, just like Dufort said.

But still.

The man with his arm around the dark-haired woman—he wasn't doing anything, he wasn't moving or talking, but Molly had the distinct impression that he was seething with anger. She could feel the waves of it as she stood thirty feet away.

What is he so furious about? And why was he always holding on to his wife like that, so protectively? Is he super jealous and controlling?

Then the sound of laughter came suddenly, like something alive being let out of a cage. Molly and Frances looked down the road and saw Adèle and Michel walking to the cemetery, their heads bare with no umbrella, and they were smiling and laughing as though on their way to the theater for a night of fun, almost as if they were a young couple.

Odd, thought Molly.

Don't blame 'em, thought Frances.

"Would it be horribly rude for us to go in for the ceremony?" whispered Molly.

"You *want* to go to a funeral?"

"Well, this one. Yes."

Frances looked at Molly like she had two heads. "Okay. You go ahead, enjoy yourself, you nutter. I'll trot on ahead to Chez Papa and dive into those frites. Nico will keep me company."

Molly nodded and Frances took off without a backward

glance. Adèle and Michel saw Molly and waved as they approached.

"Bonjour, Molly," said each of them, kissing cheeks with her.

"I was just walking into the village," she said hesitantly.

"We're going to our aunt's funeral," said Michel, grinning.

"Yes. I was wondering...would it be weird? Or impolite? I'd like to attend, if you wouldn't mind."

"Not at all!" said Michel. Adèle stared at him but he did not notice. "We'd love your company," he said, still grinning. He was wearing a very nice black wool suit that looked good on his slim frame. A lock of hair fell across his eyes as they walked on. So charming, thought Molly. Adorable really. Although maybe a little giddy for a funeral?

Through the gate and under the inscription, the three joined the cluster of people near the grave. Four men broke away from the group and went back to the hearse, lifted the casket, and walked back with Madame Desrosiers. The casket was ornately carved, a work of art that Molly couldn't help thinking was a shame to put in a grave. She was surprised to see that the casket was going in the ground and not being laid to rest in one of the mausoleums scattered about the cemetery, since from all accounts Madame Desrosiers had been a woman of means.

Rémy caught her eye and nodded. A blush crept up her neck, although their one date months ago had fizzled. She looked as closely as she could at the other mourners without staring. Michel and Adèle's mother was there, dabbing her eyes with a handkerchief. Her hair was scraped back into an unadorned ponytail, an unflattering hairstyle that was too severe. A couple of faces looked familiar from around Castillac, but she did not know their names or who they were.

When the priest began to speak, Molly observed the others. The dark-haired young woman buried her head in her husband's neck, and he glowered at the priest and then at the casket.

Michel and Adèle, on the other hand...the emotion Molly

picked up from them was all lightness, relief, even joy. Michel especially.

If you murdered someone, Molly was thinking, would you go to the funeral, if the person was someone you knew? She looked at each mourner in turn, trying to see some truth in their faces or the way they held themselves. At first she thought certainly yes, and then she thought perhaps it would feel like a trap, that going to the funeral would be exactly what a detective would expect and be waiting there with handcuffs.

She shook her head to brush such thoughts away. Really, sometimes her imagination got the best of her and she acted like she was living in an episode of Law & Order: *En France*. Heart attack makes the most sense. It was most certainly a heart attack.

Absolutely.

Chapter Twelve

Gilles Maron had never eaten a meal at La Métairie; the prices were completely out of reach for a junior gendarme with no money other than his salary. He was surprised to find that the inside of the restaurant was on the plain side, really. He had expected crystal chandeliers and gold leaf everywhere.

Nathalie met him at the door. She was dark and slender, practically no hips at all, just Maron's type. He had to make an effort to stay professional and not give her The Look. Her skin glowed, and her almost-black hair was glossy, pulled back from her face in a low ponytail that went down to her shoulder blades.

"Anything I can do to help," she said, as Maron came inside. "Let me take your coat." Maron slid out of his heavy coat and looked around at the dove-gray walls and carpet, and the painting of the sea. He didn't understand why everything was so subdued, and he didn't like not understanding.

"This situation has been very upsetting for us," said Nathalie, and Maron could see the strain in her face now that he observed her more carefully. "The chef...I know it sounds like a cliché, hell, it *is* a cliché—but he is a sensitive man. Temperamental. He was working on a new menu, we all had very high hopes for it, but now...now he comes in for the dinner service and goes home directly after. I don't believe he's even thinking about the new menu. Not that I mean to say a menu is more important than a person's life, I just mean—"

"I understand, and I'm sorry," said Maron, and he *was* sorry, sorry that anything could have caused trouble for this beautiful creature. He made an attempt to pull himself together. "I'm here to ask, first of all, if there is any chance that anything is left from the other night—any glasses, dishes, or the like. I will tell you in confidence," he said impulsively, "that Madame Desrosiers did not die of a heart attack as Chief Dufort first thought. No, it was poison," he said in a low voice though there was no one else around. He thoroughly enjoyed how Nathalie's eyes grew wide and her hand flew to her mouth when he spoke.

"Poison?" she said, not quite able to take it in.

"Yes. I'm here on the outside chance that anything, a wine glass, a plate, anything at all, might have escaped the dishwasher? We are trying to find how the poison was administered," he added, once again saying more than he should have.

"I'm afraid there's no chance of that," said Nathalie, brushing a strand of hair out of her face. "The party was days ago. Thursday night, was it? Everything has been washed multiple times since then. We don't keep dirty dishes hanging around in the kitchen," she said, almost laughing at the idea.

"I didn't think so," said Maron. "But we have to ask. Would you show me the dining room?"

"Certainly."

They walked down the short corridor to the dining room with its soothing gray monochrome, the small bar, the stack of folding stands that waiters sometimes used to hold large platters.

"May I get you a coffee?" asked Nathalie.

Maron shook his head, focused on his job. He walked around the tables, getting down on the floor at one point and looking at everything from down there. "It was a large party, yes? Can you show me how the tables would have been arranged, and approximately where Madame Desrosiers was sitting?"

Nathalie did as he asked. Maron wanted to get a clear and factual picture in his head of how the room had looked the night of the murder. "Do you know the names of the guests?" he asked.

"I'm afraid not, and the party was not so large. Five, maybe six? Her nephew, Michel Faure, made the reservation. He did the inviting as well, of course, since it was a surprise party. I must say he seemed like a very caring nephew, wanting to celebrate his aunt's birthday that way."

"And did Michel pay for the party?"

"Well, no. Actually, it was Madame Desrosiers who paid for it. I will tell you that it felt a little strange to run her Carte Bancaire through the machine, knowing that she was lying dead in the bathroom. But Michel had presented me with the card when they all arrived, and after what happened, I asked the family if I should cancel the charge, but they said no. Rather vehemently."

Maron nodded, unsurprised. "May I look around?"

"Of course. Let me know if there is anything at all I can help you with?"

Maron looked into Nathalie's warm, brown eyes, noticed her smooth cheeks, and had a sudden impulse to kiss her. "All right," he said, "thank you. You've been quite helpful. One more thing—can you show me where the garbage goes at the end of the night?"

"It's just around the back. There's a wooden fence blocking it from view, but if you go around the building you can't miss it."

Maron smiled at her, and she went back to her office. After giving the dining room one last look, he walked on the soft carpet to the bathroom, knocked, and entered the ladies' room. It was spotlessly clean and smelled of gardenias. He looked at the tiled floor, but there was no sign that anything had happened there, no sign of the last living moments of Josephine Desrosiers. Had she tried to call for help? Did she know what was happening to her?

Did she know who had poisoned her?

❧

MOLLY HAD BARELY GOTTEN SETTLED on a stool at the bar of Chez Papa when a text came in from her friend Lawrence Weebly:

heard JD poisoned. you on the case? xox

Molly stared at her phone. She blinked.

"The usual, Boston?" Nico asked.

Molly jerked her head up. "Not answering to that," she said, more sternly than she meant. "What the hell," she said, not to anyone.

"What's up?" asked Frances.

"A friend, my best friend in Castillac actually—I'm sorry you haven't met him, but he's been away. Thing is, here in the village, Lawrence always knows what's going on. Not a gossip exactly...just the kind of person who's always in the know. How, I can't say. Anyway, he just texted me to say that Madame Desrosiers was poisoned." Molly's eyes were wide and her mouth open, stunned.

Nico slid Molly's kir over to her and leaned back against a pillar. "So how's it going, then? Are you enjoying Castillac, Frances?"

"So far it's been nothing but corpses and funerals. Loving it."

Nico laughed.

"Have you heard anything in particular about Madame Desrosiers?" Molly asked him.

"Dead. That's all I know. And that you found her. I've heard of chick magnets, Boston, but you my friend are a corpse magnet!" and he guffawed at his own joke.

Molly wasn't laughing. "I just got a text from Lawrence saying she was poisoned."

"Honestly, I wouldn't be surprised. She was widely known as a bitch on wheels, pardon my language," he said, nodding and winking at Frances.

"I've been getting that impression," said Molly. She sipped her kir.

"How about a big plate of frites, handsome?" said Frances to Nico. He winked at her again and disappeared into the kitchen. "How come his English is so good?" she asked Molly.

"He studied in the US. He's practically a professor. Why he's bartending in a small village, I can't say. Don't know the backstory."

"I'll find out," Frances said, nonchalantly.

"No doubt," said Molly. "Just don't break his heart, okay? This place is too small for bad blood."

Chez Papa was empty but for Molly and Frances. The entire village was probably either at Sunday dinner with their families or at home recovering from Josephine Desrosiers's funeral. Alphonse kept the place open on Sunday mornings because he had a soft spot for people without families, who needed a place to go. Lapin was usually there, but he had kept more to himself after the Amy Bennett case.

Frances slid off her stool and drifted back to the kitchen to talk to Nico. Molly sat absently drinking her kir and drawing circles in a water droplet that had plopped off the bottom of her glass. She was thinking about poison and trying to sort out actual information from the perhaps less substantial gleanings she had stored away from random reading. It was the kind of subject that could grab her attention late at night when she should have turned off her computer and gone to bed—a perfect internet rabbithole when you're putting off sleep.

She wanted to go by the station and ask Dufort to fill her in, but of course that was out of the question. She wondered if Lawrence's contacts were good enough to find out what kind of poison? Because without that, without knowing if it was slow-acting or fast, she couldn't know whether the list of suspects was narrowed to the guests at La Métairie or not.

Could even have been a waiter, for that matter, she thought, taking care not to assume anything, and making notes in the new file that was taking shape in her head, with the title *Desrosiers: Murder*.

Chapter Thirteen

He had been feeling so much better lately. The long winter runs, the relative calm in Castillac, his dates with Marie-Claire...Dufort had not even been to see his herbalist in over a month. Anxiety was so low he had stopped noticing it.

And now, another death, and he was patting his pants pocket for his vial of tincture and feeling disappointed when it was not there. This death—it was nothing like the others. Not a young woman cut down and brutalized in her prime, not related to the unsolved Boutillier and Martin cases, but an elderly woman whom nobody liked. Nevertheless, the thought of her lying on her side on the tile bathroom of La Métairie made him feel queasy.

He had to wonder, even after so many years: am I in the wrong job? He knew other gendarmes with his experience had toughened up long before now. Had gained some resilience, some ways to compartmentalize, joke, anything to make death more bearable. But somehow he had not managed to acquire those skills even after ten years on the job.

Then Benjamin Dufort, chief gendarme of Castillac, pulled himself together and took a walk around the village before dawn.

He did not rush but observed the village in the lonely state of a frosty December morning. Life-sized Père Noëls emerged from chimneys, and decorated trees stood outside most of the shops. A huge snowflake that he remembered from his childhood hung from a wire across the main street, looking a little tattered around the edges.

Florian Nagrand, the coroner, had not called with the lab results, but Dufort knew what they were going to say. It was going to be cyanide, as doubtless he had known the minute he saw the flushed face of Josephine Desrosiers, her cheek pressed against the white bathroom tile. He had known but not wanted to face it. Why? Was it as simple as fear that he would not be able to find the murderer and fail at his job? Or was there more to it than that?

He saw the lights on at the station even though it was barely six in the morning and knew Perrault was inside, trying to find something to do. He envied her excitement about her job, and hoped that as the investigation went on, he caught some of her enthusiasm instead of feeling so morose about the state of humanity.

And himself.

"Salut, Perrault," he said, putting his heavy coat on a peg by the door. He could easily hide his emotional state, but was not sure that was actually a step forward.

"No results yet," she said, her mouth turned down.

"No matter," said Dufort. "I think I have a pretty good idea what they're going to say, now that I've given it some thought." He wanted to talk to Perrault, to tell her that he had avoided the idea of murder and couldn't understand why, but he knew it would not be an appropriate conversation to have with a subordinate officer. "We need to start talking to Desrosiers's family. You mentioned knowing the niece? That would be an excellent place to start. And—" he added, on his way into his office, "—early morning is often the best time to talk. People's defenses aren't all the way up yet. Especially before coffee," he said with a small smile.

"Yes, sir!" said Perrault. Not wanting to waste a minute, she slipped on her coat and took off for Adèle's apartment on rue Tartine, planning to hang around outside and knock the minute she saw the lights go on.

Dufort sat at his desk, his posture straight but his mind in turmoil. Florian must have thought me such a fool, he thought, feeling the unsettlement in his stomach that signaled shame.

§🐚

THE NEXT MORNING Molly was startled to wander into the kitchen and find Frances, already up and drinking coffee. "Morning!" she said, reaching for a mug.

"I'm awake," said Frances.

"I can see that," said Molly.

Molly was wearing a thick flannel shirt lined with fleece, sweatpants, and cozy slippers from L.L. Bean that she'd had for years. But she was still cold. She took a big sip of coffee, pleased that Frances made it strong, and turned her attention to the woodstove.

"Going for more wood," she said, and let herself out the French doors to the terrace. The first thought she'd had upon waking was about the Desrosiers murder—she had dreamed her new friend Adèle was guilty. Her second thought was *no, not Adèle*. If she could get the woodstove going and get warm, she wanted to close her eyes and think it all through, go over every moment of the other night in the restaurant, as well as the other times she'd seen the brother and sister.

The morning was frosty, and she paused for a moment to notice the beauty of the white-tipped branches and blades of grass before shivering and walking quickly to the woodpile. She stacked three logs on her arm and turned back for the house, wondering whether she should stop Pierre Gault from working on the pigeonnier in favor of spending the money on a different heating system or some insulation in the main house. Extra bookings won't matter if I expire of cold, she thought.

"So I dreamed last night that Adèle killed her aunt," Molly told Frances, while shoving a new log in the woodstove and shivering.

"Interesting. Do you think you're psychic, or was that just your brain throwing sparks?"

"I don't think I've ever had a dream like that before. My dreams are usually crazy, incoherent nonsense. Maybe this one was too." Molly stood, watching the fire, then squatted down and poked another piece of kindling under the log. "I don't want it to be Adèle, that's for sure."

Frances pulled a blanket around her and sipped her coffee. "Well, we know something bad was happening in that family. The aunt was a tyrant, okay, but what's the rest of the story?"

"Yeah," said Molly, her voice flat. "The thing is, she and Michel seem so normal, when you hang out with them. They feel like...like people I already know, somehow. Familiar, in a way."

France hummed the *Twilight Zone* theme song.

"I know in the U.S., you're way more likely to be murdered by a family member than a stranger," said Molly. "Think that's true in France, too?"

"Families," Frances said in a disgusted tone. "*Ugh*. This is a horrible thing to say, but in some ways, you're lucky."

Molly just nodded. She had a younger brother and an assortment of cousins, but that was more or less it for family. Her father had died in a nursing home the year before she moved to France, but in the haze of Alzheimer's, he had not been able to recognize her for at least three years before that. Her mother had died in a car accident fifteen years ago. Molly's relationship with them had been decent, if not especially close, and even though her grief at their deaths had long mellowed into some other, less-painful emotion that was difficult to describe, still, she never forgot she was an orphan.

And she knew that people who were not orphans, like Frances, were unable to understand what it was like. No matter how old you were or even how close you had been. No matter that it was the natural order of things to lose your parents eventually.

"I dread spending Christmas with my family," said Frances. "It's just one long dreary event with a lot of commentary about how my hair is all wrong, how could I possibly have divorced my second husband because he was *so nice*, and lots of other special Hallmark moments."

Molly laughed. "Do you doubt my ability to put together a Christmas that will beat anything you could have at home? Franny, listen: I've got pastry, I've got duck, I've got *Pascal*. By the time this celebration is done, you're never going to want to leave."

"You've got Pascal? Can you be more specific please?"

Molly laughed. "I mean I can invite him over. That's all you need to work your magic, right?"

Frances looked up at the ceiling and a slow smile broke out. "That'll do," she said. "Crap, it's cold in here! Can't you turn up the heat?"

"This *is* the heat," said Molly, gesturing sadly to the wood-stove, where the fresh log had failed to catch. "I'm going to have to take the logs out and start over. Please remind me to bring the kindling in at night so I have something dry to start the fire with?"

"Hey, that little electric heater in the cottage works fine, why don't we go over there?"

Molly poured the rest of the coffee into a thermos, and the two friends walked arm in arm to the cottage, where Molly talked about what to plant in the front garden in spring, and Frances talked about how she had recently discovered that lemonade helped her write better jingles, and no one brought up poison or toxic family ties or anything else that might derail their buoyed-up moods.

Chapter Fourteen

"I waited outside her place practically all day," Perrault was telling Dufort. "No sign of her. I thought maybe she'd moved or something, but I checked with some friends, and they said Adèle definitely lives there. Apartment in a converted house on rue Tartine.

"I just asked you to talk to her, I didn't mean for you to set up a stakeout," said Dufort with a slight smile.

"You don't think she's a suspect? I was figuring anyone related to Desrosiers is on the list until we can cross them off. Who knows how much she might stand to inherit, right?"

"I applaud your persistence," Dufort said. "Since Desrosiers had no children, there is no *légitime*, the portion that the law insists go to each child. Nevertheless, she would not have been able to leave every penny to whomever she wanted—the extended family will get something. Of course, we will have to find the will, if there is one.

"We will begin by addressing this puzzle from the other end, however. Not looking at motive first off, but opportunity, because the timing of her death is limiting, happily for us. Has the lab report come in yet?"

Perrault looked chastened and ran off to check. "Why in the world would they send it by snail mail?" she shouted from the other room, where Maron's and her desks stood, and where the basket for the mail delivery was.

"Perhaps Monsieur Nagrand thought he had given me enough of a head's up," said Dufort. He tore open the envelope and scanned Florian's note and then the lab report. "As I thought. Cyanide." He was about to put the papers on his desk when the last bit caught his eye. "Well, this is interesting. The usual routes for cyanide poisoning are swallowing, or even more quickly fatal, breathing cyanide gas, as the Nazis well knew. I had already discounted gas as a possibility because there would be no way for Desrosiers alone to have breathed it in a crowded restaurant. I assumed her food had been doctored, either at La Métairie or sometime earlier in the day.

"But it appears that the coroner's opinion is that the cyanide exposure was on her skin. Her face, actually."

"Hmm," said Perrault. "Did someone give her some face cream for her birthday?"

"Perrault, I believe you have the makings of a real detective," said Dufort. "Face cream is an excellent place to start."

Perrault beamed. She thought she was improving too, and it felt wonderful to hear her boss say it. "Would Nagrand be able to tell us how quickly cyanide in face cream would act? Could she have put it on before coming to the restaurant?"

"I will call him to discuss that very thing. Now where is Maron? I'm hoping he will have found something at the restaurant. Not residue on a glass, we'd never be so lucky to find something like that this many days later, not at a ship-shape place like La Métairie. But perhaps he will have found gift cards so we could find out who brought presents," said Dufort, thinking out loud.

"If there were presents, I wonder what happened to them?" Perrault took a small pad from her back pocket and began to scribble notes of things to ask Adèle when she found her.

Dufort pulled out his cell to check the time. "Let's get over to the Desrosiers house now. We need to take a look around before the family goes in there and wreaks havoc."

They took their coats from the pegs and put them on while heading outside. Madame Desrosiers's house was not far from the station, an easy walk, and Dufort was happy as always to stretch his legs. Now that the investigation was underway and cyanide was confirmed, he felt robust and optimistic, as though his feet were solidly under him again.

"It's a little weird to kill someone that old," said Perrault, as they headed down the street.

"Because you think she already had one foot in the grave? Spoken like a young person," he said, affectionately. "Seventy two is old, yes, but not very old. There are people in Castillac decades older than that. Madame Gervais, who lives in that tiny house down by the shop that sells old lamps? She's well over a hundred. Hundred and two, I believe."

Perrault shook her head, unable to imagine lasting that long.

"What, so you like to think you'll flame out at your peak, or some such romantic nonsense?" said Dufort, teasing.

"Nah. And I wasn't talking so much about her being almost dead as that I usually think of old ladies as harmless. I mean, my *grand-mère* will have a fit if you don't wash the lettuce properly— you'll hear about it for weeks if she bites into a little sand. And I guess sometimes they tell the same story six hundred times a day. But obviously I have not been driven to the point of murder."

"Perrault, as I have told you before, your life and experiences will be of value to you in your work, so I do not want to sound as though I am diminishing them. But at the same time, you must strive for some objectivity. Just because your *grand-mère* is a pleasant person does not mean that all women her age are. You cannot generalize from one specific example in that way."

"Yes sir," said Perrault, telling herself once again to think before she spoke.

They passed through the gate and arrived at the front door. "Quite a place," said Dufort, gazing up at the huge mansion. "You know about Albert Desrosiers?"

"Everybody knows about Albert Desrosiers. He's like the one semi-famous person ever born in all of Castillac."

"Some kind of resistor, or transistor? I don't know what was so special about it, science was never one of my strengths."

"All of school wasn't one of my strengths," laughed Perrault. "So how can we get in?"

"Well, before you start breaking any windows, let's try knocking. Possibly a housekeeper might be inside. You do that, and I'll take a look around, see if there's a gardener or anybody in the back garden."

Perrault thought to herself that gardening must not be one of Dufort's strengths either, since it was December and freezing, and gardeners were likely to be inside drinking something warm instead of hanging around an iced-over garden with nothing to do. She used the brass knocker several times and listened, but could hear no one inside the house. The windows were shuttered though it was afternoon, so if anybody was inside, they would have to put lights on to see. Perrault craned her neck trying to see if any light was coming from under the bottom of the shutters, but she could see nothing.

Dufort had better luck. As he came around the side of the house he thought he heard the sound of a door closing. He was just tall enough to see over the stone wall surrounding the garden, and a dark-haired woman leaving by the back door, carrying several large plastic bags.

❧

IN THE AFTERNOON, Molly left Frances alone at the piano where she hoped to write a lucrative new jingle. All Frances asked for was a glass of very tart lemonade and a stack of napkins, which she claimed were the best for writing down ideas and snatches of lyrics.

Molly told Frances she was heading into the village to get a few almond croissants (of course) as well as pick up a bottle of wine at the *épicerie*, and a steak at the butcher's. And she did plan to do those things—along with as much snooping as she could fit in while Frances was occupied. It wasn't that Frances disapproved of her nosiness, exactly; more that she wanted Molly's attention for herself at the moment, and quickly got tired of having conversations with her friend during which Molly's eyes would glaze over as she got distracted by thoughts of poison and motives and death.

Out on rue des Chênes, Molly pulled her coat collar up against the bitter wind. It wasn't half as cold as it had been in Massachusetts, but she was acclimated to the Dordogne now, and her measurements for what was cold and what was comfortable had shifted considerably. At any rate, it was cold enough that villagers were mostly inside, except for a farmer going slowly past on a tractor. Molly could hear someone splitting wood in the distance, the easy rhythm as the axe lifted up and then came down with a mighty *thwock* into the log.

First question, she thought, getting her thoughts organized. Did the poisoner kill Desrosiers for her money, or for some other reason? It hadn't been a happy birthday party, that was for sure. The tension and resentment had been palpable. She wondered if Dufort was going to question her. Surely he would want to know her impressions, wouldn't he? Going around the table, place by place, Molly tried to remember everyone who had been there. She stopped and dug in her bag for her phone, and tapped in a few notes:

Desrosiers
Michel
dark-haired woman and her angry husband
Adèle's mom

Adèle

another old lady, white bun

She could check with Frances to see if she remembered anyone else. Now all she had to do was find out something about each of the participants and figure out which one had done the deed. She did realize she was acting as though it was all nothing but an interesting puzzle to solve, when in fact a person had died. And the killer, unless the poison turned out to be a long-acting variety, had been in that dining room, sitting near Molly and Frances, on Thursday night.

That was no television show. It was no joke.

Molly had never thought of herself as having an especially strong sense of justice, at least no stronger than any other typical, law-abiding person. But perhaps she had been wrong about that. She felt a sort of outrage when she thought about a murderer sitting in the dove-gray dining room at La Métairie, deciding for her- or himself who should live and who should die. The arrogance was unspeakable. Molly wanted to see the smug expression on the murderer's face fall as he or she was marched off to prison.

With a start, Molly realized she had gotten all the way to the épicerie without seeing where she was walking. She went in, grateful for the heat, and picked out a couple of bottles of red wine. She added a handful of caramels at the cash register, but did no conversing because the young woman at checkout had a funny accent and Molly couldn't understand a word she said. Was it a speech impediment or a regional accent that made her sound as though her mouth was full of marshmallows?

What she wanted was a villager to talk to her about the guests at the party. But where would she find anyone on a cold Monday afternoon? All of Castillac was holed up someplace warm, out of sight. There was no market, no public gathering place in December. While she waited for an idea, Molly left the épicerie and headed, as though on a track, to Pâtisserie Bujold. It was toasty inside and it felt as though the heavenly aromas were almost solid, wrapping her up in a delicious vanilla blanket.

"Bonjour, monsieur," she mumbled to the proprietor, who as usual stared delightedly at her chest instead of making eye contact.

"Madame Sutton! It makes me very happy to see you today. Would you like your usual?"

She wasn't sure whether to be happy or sad that she had a "usual" at the pâtisserie. She did make a pig of herself, it was true. But these almond croissants, today—these were strictly medicinal. She had a murder to solve but no way to find anyone she needed to talk to. Surely an almond croissant would help.

Then, after so many rambling thoughts, Molly had a moment of clarity: it was Adèle Faure she needed to talk to.

But how to find her?

Chapter Fifteen

1969

Josephine had studied the fashion magazines carefully and put in plenty of time practicing at her vanity table. She had it now, lining her eyelids with the perfect cat's-eye technique, the black line thickening and swooping up as it went past the outer end of her eyelid—a confident, unwavering line, the epitome of modern. She was wearing a pair of silk bikini underwear Albert had sent her when he was off on a business trip, with a silk bra to match, all in the most flattering rosy peach color. She stood and walked to her bedroom door, then whirled around to catch herself in the vanity mirror—yes, she was practically Jean Shrimpton. How could he resist?

Josephine slipped a clingy Pucci dress on. Her feet were bare, and her chestnut hair was tied in a cascading topknot just like the model's on the cover of that month's *Vogue*. She went barefoot because she had gotten the idea that Albert liked her feet. Padding downstairs to his office, she paused for a moment on the stairs, watching herself as though she were in a movie: seeing herself glide down the wide stairs, her legs shapely, her makeup perfect. Seeing herself go to her husband's door, and slowly open it.

Transfixed by her vision, she imagined Albert leaping up from his desk, his face turning red from desire just at the sight of her, screws and wires and bolts dropping to the floor in his haste to come to her.

Josephine approached his office, her steps quiet. Still, it was as though a camera were going, as though she were not one person but rather several, one of whom was always observing. She was always her own audience and never fully whole.

"Albert," she said, as sweetly as she could.

Albert did not look up.

"Give me a moment, if you would," he said. On his desk was a magnifying apparatus and he was looking through it at something vanishingly tiny on his deck. Keeping the rest of his body as still as possible, he reached in with a minuscule pair of tweezers and then pulled them back, resting his hand on the edge of his desk, staring intently into the apparatus.

"Albert!" said Josephine, her fantasy breaking up, feeling as though the jagged bits and pieces of it swirled around her head and into her mouth, threatening to choke her. "You won't so much as look up when I come in? You won't stop your work for just one single solitary instant?" For a moment she stood trembling, jaw clenched. And then in her rage she reached over to his desk and picked up a musty-smelling book. "This is what I think of you and your stupid work!" She threw the book directly at the magnifying apparatus, knocking it to the floor, although Albert had moved quickly and put his hands over the circuitry he was working on, and it remained safe.

After that, Josephine was unable to make any more unannounced appearances in Albert's office, because he locked the door. A different sort of man might have divorced his violent wife, even though of course divorce was far less common then than it is now, and on top of that it would have killed his deeply Catholic mother. But Albert Desrosiers was a man who carried through with his commitments, even if those commitments turned out to be horrible mistakes, and so Josephine and Albert lived all the years of their marriage in separate forms of abject misery.

Though they *were* rich, which for Josephine at least, provided nearly enough compensation for the rest of it.

Chapter Sixteen

✿

2005

"My Sabrina worked for her two years. I tell you, Desrosiers was a devil," Jean-François said to his friend at the bar of Chez Papa. The friend nodded and drank his beer.

"You saw how my girl has to wear a splint on her hand? That old shrew set rat traps out, trying to hurt her!"

"Maybe the house had rats?"

"No! And the trap that got Sabrina was in a bucket, who sets a trap in a bucket? I'm telling you, it gave that harpy pleasure to hurt her. She knew Sabrina really needed that job. It's not easy for immigrants to find decent work, you know that. Too many of our women end up having to clean for the capitalists!"

"Well, the old lady's out of the picture anyway," said the friend, with a sideways look at Jean-François. "So you gonna marry Sabrina now?"

"Pft. Sabrina and I, we are soul-mates. Documents from the state or the church, these do not matter to us. This is something you do not understand."

"Oh, I think I do. I know, I know, hardly anyone gets married anymore. But all I'm saying, Jean-François, is that chicks like it when you ask them to get married. I don't care how political they are. Socialists, communists, doesn't matter. They can be anarchists to the marrow—they still like it."

"You only say that because your mother is more religious than the Virgin Mary."

"No, Jean-François, not at all. I say it because it's true."

"And you speak from your long experience of asking women to marry you? You are single, you crétin!"

The friend smirked and drank his beer.

"Another?" asked Nico, coming to their end of the bar.

"He's already drunk," said Jean-François, pointing at his friend. "Spouting more nonsense than you can believe."

Nico drifted away back to the other end, where a good-looking Dutch woman was flirting with him.

Jean-François's face darkened. "I love Sabrina more than life itself," he said. "Why do you think I work so hard for the cause? It's because I want a better life for my girl. This is love, yes?"

"Well, no, not in my book. But eh," said the friend, shrugging and giving another sideways look. Jean-François loved to argue politics and always had, and could use it to justify anything he wanted to do or not do. "Anyway, Desrosiers crapped out from a heart attack, that's what I heard. So who's Sabrina going to for work now? A bad job is a whole lot better than no job."

"Ah, no," said Nico from down the bar, having heard that last remark. "What I heard was poison. Not heart attack after all."

Jean-François did not look surprised. "Well, poison is a woman's weapon. I can tell you right now that no man with any balls is going to poison someone, especially a weak old woman." He thought for a moment. "Not that she didn't deserve it."

❧

MOLLY WAS JUST COMING out of Pâtisserie Bujold with a bit of powdered sugar on her upper lip when far down the street she saw a woman in a chic trench coat, walking with a bit of a limp. That's got to be Adèle, she thought, and hurried along, grateful that in a village where people walked almost everywhere it was possible to run into someone you were looking for. Molly's legs were not long but Adèle was walking slowly, almost meditatively, and Molly had no trouble catching up with her.

"Oh my," Molly said, out of breath. "I saw you——"

"Salut," said Adèle, amused at Molly's gasping for breath. "Are you training for some sort of event?"

"Yes. The fifty-yard dash while holding a bag of almond croissants," she said.

Adèle smiled, but Molly stopped, her eyes wide. "Okay, I know that was not the best joke on earth. It was not even funny. But I think it may be the first joke I ever made in French, without thinking about it. I mean, the words just came out the way English words do. Or used to, I find I can't really speak English all that well anymore, but that's a different thing."

Adèle applauded lightly and said, "Félicitations! My English is not the best and I agree that jokes are the most difficult. Which is quite a shame, since jokes—I mean, you know, laughing together, humor—that is the joy in life, isn't it?"

"It is," Molly agreed. They walked part of a block in silence, Molly trying to figure out a way to ask Adèle about the guests at her aunt's birthday party without seeming like a terrific busybody. Even though she admitted to herself that's exactly what she was.

"So Adèle, I know we've really barely met, and it's sort of a delicate subject to talk about, but I heard the news about your aunt."

Adèle looked at Molly in surprise. "What?" she said, confused.

"I know, it does seem like there's an underground or even magical communication system in Castillac where people instantly find out the news about everyone else. I'm not a part of it, myself, really—but I have a friend...anyway, I'm sure your family is shocked. I know I was," she added, disingenuously. She felt quite proud at having thought of poison before hearing about it, but she couldn't exactly tell Adèle that.

Adèle stopped. "I'm sorry. I don't understand you. I...I mean, I understand the words you're saying, but not the meaning?"

"Shall I speak in English then?"

"I don't think that would improve matters," said Adèle. She started walking again. "Oh, look, I adore this little boutique. The woman who owns it has impeccable taste, don't you think? Look at those hats!" she said, pointing at the display in the window.

Molly wasn't sure whether she had been brushed off or hadn't been making sense. Both equally possible. In that moment Adèle seemed like the answer to everything—she would have history and details about everyone at the party. But how to get her to talk?

Molly made agreeable noises about the hats without paying them any attention. Then she pulled out her phone to check the time. "Oh look, it's after five. Wait, let me think...it's after seventeen. Is that right?"

Adèle smiled. She liked this woman who tried so hard to take on everything about French life—look at her with her market basket, her scarf, and now using the 24-hour clock. The sweatpants not so much, but Adèle was willing to give her a pass this once.

"Would you like to go somewhere for a kir?" Molly asked.

"*Bon*," said Adèle with a nod, and steered Molly down a street she hadn't seen before, and into a small bar with no sign outside.

"Sort of mysterious," said Molly. "Interesting." Which meant, *What the hell kind of place is this?*

The place was dark with purple lighting. The tables, the bar, even the napkins were black. It felt rebellious and young and to

Molly's mind did not fit with the well-dressed, mature Adèle. Clearly she needed to get to know her better.

"So here's a typical American's question," she said as they waited for their drinks. "But I don't mean it to be rude. What kind of work do you do?"

"Ah yes," said Adèle, motioning to the bartender.

"Wait, no—let me guess. Is it anything to do with fashion?"

Adèle laughed, "Not even a tiny bit. Why in the world would you guess that?"

Molly shrugged. "You're always so well put together. Your clothes are really, really nice."

"That's habit more than anything else. It was important to my mother, when I was growing up, that my appearance was...that it had a certain polish. Which is a bit odd, actually, because she doesn't care a fig about clothes or her own looks. As you might have noticed!" she added, laughing.

Molly laughed too, a little nervously because how early in a friendship can you have a good laugh over how dowdy the other person's mother is? Back in America, she would have had a feel for it, but here in Castillac, she wasn't so sure. "Well, whatever the reason, every time I see you, I adore your outfit."

God, do I sound like the most ridiculous suck-up?

"I am confused about what you said earlier," said Adèle. She smoothed her wool skirt with both hands. "You mentioned something about getting the news of my aunt. What do you mean? You were the one who discovered her, after all."

"Oh, I mean the new news," said Molly, wondering how Adèle had not heard of the poisoning. Had Dufort not even told the family yet? Or did the family not talk to each other? "Um, no one has said anything about...?" Molly sent a pleading look to the bartender to hurry up with the kirs, but she was leaning on her elbows in deep conversation with a man with six ear piercings. "Okay, well, this is awkward. But I heard that your aunt was poisoned."

Adèle sat very still. Her eyes widened and she looked away from Molly. Molly saw that she was breathing rapidly and her nostrils flared.

It certainly looked like Adèle was surprised, but the main feeling Molly sensed in her new friend was fear.

Chapter Seventeen

"**P**oisoned?" said Adèle, almost too quietly for Molly to hear.

Molly nodded. "Yes. I'm...I'm so sorry. It's sort of scary to think that whoever did it was probably at that birthday party. Your aunt seemed fine earlier in the evening, right?"

"We always said she'd outlive us all." Adèle was holding on to the bar with both hands. "I'm sorry," she said. "I'm...I'm in shock, to be honest. You did say poisoned?"

"I know! I mean, who would want to kill a little old lady?"

"That's the thing, Molly. With Aunt Josephine...possibly a lot of people."

"Not the most popular?"

"No. I don't think she had any friends. Michel said he was scraping the barrel to come up with guests for her surprise party. As far as family, Maman is her only sibling and they couldn't be more different. Maman is hardworking and uncomplaining. She hasn't been a perfect mother, but then who has? She raised Michel and me by herself, and we turned out all right—she adopted Michel when he was just a baby, because she likes kids so much. But Josephine?" Adèle shook her head and let out a bitter chuckle. "Her whole life has been about trying to get under other people's skin. At best, she was an annoyance. At worst…at worst something approaching sadistic. No, not approaching. Absolutely sadistic. The poor people who have worked for her have really gotten it bad these last few years. She goes through housekeepers and gardeners at a pretty good clip, as you might imagine."

Molly was listening intently, hoping she would elaborate. Finally she said, "Like…what kind of stuff did she do?"

"Well…" Adèle closed her eyes for a moment, remembering. "How about the time she switched all the gardening chemicals around? She emptied everything out of bottles and boxes—and believe me, we're not talking about non-toxic organic stuff, either —and then she put everything back but all in the wrong containers. The gardener thought he was using a solution of fish meal but got muriatic acid instead. He was in the hospital for a month with disfiguring burns from that little trick."

"Wow," said Molly, searching for what to say when someone's just announced her relative is a monster. "Did she get arrested or anything for that?"

"No way. The gardener just wanted to heal up and get as far away from her as possible. People were scared of her, Molly. I know it seems crazy, she looked harmless enough. But Aunt Josephine was anything but harmless. She lived to hurt people and she didn't just daydream about it, she acted on her horrible twisted impulses—and the gardening chemical story is just an example of something I knew about. I hate to think of what she pulled off that no one ever found out." Adèle shivered and tossed back the rest of her kir.

The bartender broke away from the guy she was talking to and came over. "Want another?" she said, scooping up a small bowl of chips from a bin under the bar and putting it in front of Adèle.

"Yes," said Adèle. "Please."

"Did she ever hurt you?" Molly asked gently.

Adèle swung her long blonde hair onto her back. "Not really. Nothing like what she did to the people who worked for her. She didn't like me—she glowered at me, pinched me when I was a little girl to make me cry, always quick with a cutting remark...but luckily for Michel and me, our family did not get together with Aunt Josephine all that often. Brief events at holidays, that sort of thing. Months would go by without our seeing her."

Molly sipped her kir, wishing she had asked for a hot chocolate instead, something homey and comforting. She tucked her hands under her scarf and crossed her fingers. "Would you mind talking to me about the other guests? That night when you all came in, I was so curious about how everyone was related."

No, I don't mind," said Adèle, a little woodenly. "It wasn't a large party, as you could see. Aunt Josephine used to talk about how all her friends were dead, but the truth is, I don't think she ever had many friends. She...she was difficult, you understand, not just as an old person, but going way back."

Molly nodded.

A long pause while Adèle turned on her barstool and looked out a grimy window to the street, and Molly felt tense, wondering how to get the conversation moving along a little faster.

"There was a dark-haired woman there? Frankly, not looking too happy. With a guy?"

"Sabrina. That's what I mean about Michel having a tough time coming up with enough guests. She's the housekeeper, been working for Josephine for a couple of years, which must be a record. The guy is Jean-François, her boyfriend. He was the gardener there briefly, but he was not one to put up with Josephine's treatment, I don't think he lasted a week. Talented with plants, so it was too bad. Not that Josephine was spending any time in the garden anymore anyway. Michel said she barely even came downstairs, and kept the shutters closed all day. Like a mausoleum in there, he said."

"Hmm," said Molly. "Do you think...I mean, Jean-François looked *really* angry—I'm sorry," she said, trying to laugh gracefully. "I don't want to sound like I was stalking all of you. But I like people, I like parties—and I couldn't help looking over that night, and wondering how everyone fit together."

"Very awkwardly," said Adèle with a faint smile. "It's just starting to sink in what you're getting at. You're saying...somebody at that table, at La Métairie, killed my aunt?"

Molly shrugged. "It seems so, but I'm no expert. Maybe she was poisoned with something long-acting, that she took hours or even days earlier. But she seemed fine at first, yes?"

"Yes," said Adèle slowly. "And then, suddenly...not. We had our first courses, and then she opened a few presents. And I remember looking down at her end of the table and seeing that her face had gotten red, which it used to do when she got really angry about something, and I said to myself I was lucky to be all the way at the other end, out of gunfire range. Not long after that, she got up to go to the bathroom. Our mains had been served, but we hadn't gotten that far with them."

"Did anyone offer to go to the bathroom with her?"

"Go to the *toilette* with Aunt Josephine? Ha! Not if you wanted to escape insults coming at you like a swarm of hornets for the rest of the evening! Josephine did not take it at all well if her age or frailty was ever alluded to. Not that she *was* frail—like I said, we all thought she was strong as an ox."

"I guess somebody got impatient."

"It's terrible to say, and we barely know each other, I shouldn't burden you with such confidences," said Adèle. "But to tell you the truth, I was happy when I heard she was dead. Happy! And Michel—he was about to burst into song!"

Molly couldn't help smiling, but then her expression turned serious. She felt protective of Adèle somehow. "Do you either of you stand to benefit from her death? I don't want to tell you your business, but if you are going to, maybe dancing in the streets might give the wrong impression?"

"You don't understand," said Adèle. "Having Josephine in the family meant that we were forced to think about impressions constantly. I think that is why my mother always dressed me so nicely—far beyond her budget, no doubt. Because it gave Aunt Josephine one less thing to criticize. Even though we saw her infrequently, we walked on eggshells, not wanting to incur her rage. Once I wore something a little racy to school—I was a teenager and I bought a red mini-skirt with money I had earned. Josephine heard about it and made me come over so she could rant and rave over the damage I had done to the family's reputation.

"Josephine's death means we don't have to worry anymore. No more having to keep up this false front just to keep her off our backs. No more dreading holidays and being forced to endure her vicious insults. We feel free, Molly," said Adèle intently, taking Molly's hands and squeezing them, a beatific smile on her beautifully made-up face.

CLAUDETTE MERCIER SPENT most of every Tuesday morning at the market in Bergerac. Of course she went to the Castillac market on Saturdays, but there were some particular things she could only get in Bergerac, and even though she felt it was an imposition, she wanted those things so badly she allowed the teenage son of her next-door neighbor to drive her. He was a nice boy and dropped her off on his way to school and picked her up during his lunchtime. She paid him in cherry tarts, which he loved with a passion, thus thoroughly winning her over.

Some of the particular things were mushrooms, *cèpes* and *girolles* especially. There were no mushrooms in December, but Claudette had gotten into the habit of the Tuesday market in Bergerac, she had friends there to talk to, and so the Tuesday after her old schoolmate Josephine Desrosiers died, Claudette went as usual. Marc was a careful driver, and it occurred to her that really, she hadn't a care in the world—she looked forward to a chat and then coming home to a glass of sherry in the afternoon, and it had the makings of an excellent day.

The market was lovely, if cold. Afterward, Marc was on time to pick her up as he almost always was, and she was thinking about that sherry as they arrived home. Claudette waved goodbye to Marc and unlocked her front door. She walked inside. She stood still, her mouth gaping. A barely audible peep came out of her. The basket dropped to the floor. Her living room, always neat as a pin, looked as though a hurricane had gone through it. Sofa cushions on the floor, lampshades awry, papers dumped out of drawers and lying on the rug.

Her first impulse was to get down on her hands and knees and begin to clean up the mess. But then she had the frightening thought that whoever was responsible could still be in her house, possibly lying in wait! Slowly, she backed out the front door and scurried as quickly she could to the next-door neighbor's. Only Marc was there, but he called the emergency number and even made her a cup of tea.

Gilles Maron received the call and got on his new scooter. He had convinced Dufort to spend the money on it, saying that one police vehicle was not enough and with Castillac growing as it was —not quickly but steadily—

+the force needed to update if they wanted to be responsive to the village's needs. Maron could read Dufort well enough to know that words like "responsive" were likely to have an effect, and in the end, he got his scooter.

He drove straight to Claudette's house after receiving the call. Finding the door open, he walked in, alert and listening. A plump tabby cat was curled up in an armchair, sleeping. An antique clock was ticking. The living room floor was covered with papers, clothing, a tangled knitting project, and knickknacks. He stepped carefully over the mess and went down the hallway to the kitchen, obviously the heart of this house, the pans well scrubbed and shining, everything neatly put away, not ransacked as the living room had been. He walked to the bedroom of the small house and saw that the night table had been overturned, a lamp broken, bureau drawers pulled out and rummaged through, but no one was in the closet or under the bed.

The bedroom window had been jimmied open and a cold breeze swept through.

Maron went to the next-door neighbor's and knocked on the door.

"Bonjour, madame," he said to Claudette, who stood partly behind Marc. "I am Officer Maron. You're all right? Did you catch a glimpse of anyone when you entered your house?"

"Oh no," said Claudette. "I didn't want to see anyone. I ran straight here, to the neighbor's!"

"Whoever it was is gone now. But I ask that you give me a few moments to look for evidence before returning."

"Of course! Thank you for coming so quickly," said Claudette, trying to muster a smile. "Who would do such a thing? I've never had anything like this happen in my whole life. It's terribly upsetting."

"*Oui*, madame, I understand," said Maron, though his tone was not warm. "I'm afraid your house is not the first. In the last month, we have had two other similar cases. May I ask you a few questions?"

"Please, come in," said Marc, who was secretly thrilled at the idea of a burglar breaking in right next door, in broad daylight.

The temperature had risen some but the wind was still biting. Maron nodded and came inside. "First, do you have anything valuable in your house that anyone knows of?"

"Heavens, no. Not unless you mean my collection of copper pans? I know they're worth an awful lot now, I've been adding to them slowly over the years, you know. I just got a lovely little one-quart saucepan last month to replace one that the handle wasn't as nice, how it felt in my hand, you know."

"I believe the kitchen was untouched," said Maron, sighing

inwardly. Why hadn't Perrault taken this call? "No family heir-looms, nothing like that, that people might know about?"

"No. I don't go in for frippery, monsieur. My father used to buy me necklaces and things of that sort, but I told him to stop, I didn't like it. What I wanted was a Sabatier cleaver instead. He was very disappointed in me."

Marc looked at his neighbor with new admiration. He thought cleavers were awesome.

"All right, Madame Mercier. I'd like to walk through the house with you after I'm done, and perhaps you can tell me if anything appears to be missing. The thief was most likely after items that are easy to sell—televisions, computers, things of that sort."

"Well, I do have a little television. There are so many cooking shows on now, you wouldn't believe it! I have several of those I keep up with. Have you seen that Gordon Ramsay? Such language! And of course he's not French, but I believe he does know how to cook. My English isn't all that good and I can't follow it all. But still, I watch." She shrugged, and gave Maron a mischievous smile. "But no computer, oh no. I'm too old for that foolishness."

Marc snickered and then patted Madame Mercier on the shoulder.

"My next question: do you have a predictable schedule? Are you out regularly on Tuesday mornings, for example?"

"Well, of course I have a schedule. Who doesn't? On Tuesdays, Marc drives me to the market in Bergerac. The man who sells walnuts on the north side of the church has the best walnuts in the Dordogne. I try not to miss a Tuesday market. And thank-fully, even though as you may have noticed I am not young, I still have my health, and so it is quite rare that I have to call Marc and tell him I can't make it. I hope someday to drop dead of a heart attack, like Josephine Desrosiers did—here one minute, gone the next! That's the way to do it, don't you think, Officer Maron?"

Maron nodded slowly. He noticed how Madame Mercier's

expression lit up when she mentioned the death of Desrosiers, like it was the happiest news she had heard in a very long time.

"All right, thank you, madame. I will step back over to your house and see if I can find anything helpful to the investigation. If you would please stay here for the moment, I thank you for your patience." Maron turned and went back to the Mercier house.

He was pretty sure the burglar was an addict, looking for something to sell to make money for drugs, and hoping maybe to find a bundle of cash under an old lady's mattress. It was not a crime that called for forensics; it wasn't even clear that anything had been stolen. Castillac had not seen much drug activity over the years, but there had been those two other similar break-ins, and based on his experience in the Paris suburbs, all of them felt like drug money burglaries—sloppy and not very successful.

Maron squatted down in the living room and picked through some of the papers on the floor. He looked around the room, trying not to look for anything in particular but letting his eyes roam, trusting that they would pick out any anomalies.

The room was so typical it verged on cliché: lace antimacassars on the chairs and sofa arms, the dozing cat, the ticking clock, the small framed family photograph on a side table. It looked like a room where nothing exciting had ever happened. He stood up, ready to return to the station and make his report. Glancing back at the mess on the floor, his eyes fell on an envelope of heavy stationery, lying on some papers. He picked it up and saw that it had a recent postmark. He told himself that it might give a clue about the break-in, though he knew that was unlikely.

He pulled the letter from the envelope and read it. His eyes widened as he read the caustic, threatening words. The letter was short and unsigned, but there was no doubt the writer bore Claudette Mercier a great deal of ill will.

Well then, thought Maron, maybe there is more to this break-in than I thought. And maybe something *has* happened in this stuffy little room after all.

Chapter Eighteen

"Sorry Chief, I don't think you can just dismiss this," said Maron, who was back at the station, having shown to Dufort and Perrault the letter he found at Claudette's.

"It's a nasty piece of business, no question about that," said Dufort. "So what are you saying, that you think the burglar wrote the letter? On what basis? Perhaps your intuition?" he said, teasing Maron because in fact Maron would never, ever use the word "intuition" without a sneer.

"Mercier has been the victim of two acts of violence, one physical and one emotional. It's not a huge reach to think that they might be connected. *Might*," Maron added, with some vehemence. "But actually, it's not the attempted burglary I'm wondering about. There's a connection between Mercier and Desrosiers. Turns out Mercier was at the birthday party. All I found at La Métairie was a note card, on the ground outside near the dumpster. Looks like it was on a birthday gift?" He went to his coat pocket and brought it out, a small rectangle of thin cardboard with some purple flowers decorating the top. 'From your friend, Claudette'."

"Claudette Mercier was at the party?" said Dufort, looking up quickly.

"Yes," said Maron. "Some coincidence, huh? And actually she mentioned Desrosiers—said she wanted to drop dead of a heart attack too, when the time came."

"They were around the same age, probably in school together," said Perrault. "They both grew up in Castillac, right?"

"Yes," said Dufort. "The Merciers used to own a hardware store in the center of the village. They were quite a prosperous family, still are as far as I know."

"Don't you think it's meaningful that one lady gets offed, and then another one from the same party has her house broken into *and* was receiving anonymous bullying letters?"

"We can't say whether it's meaningful or not," said Dufort. "Let me caution you both against trying to make order where there is none. All three events might be unconnected, and we are still in the preliminary stages of the investigation, Maron. At the moment, it is looking as though Desrosiers was roundly despised by everyone who knew her—at least by family and the people who worked for her. Any of them could have killed her. Mercier may have been her only friend."

"Maybe the rest of her friends are all dead. She was seventy-two, after all."

"As I told Perrault, seventy-two is not that old. You must both make an effort not to view everything through the lens of your own youth. Perhaps...she didn't have any friends. It does happen, you know. Although not usually because someone is odious to every single person they come across; usually it is a matter of some mental illness getting in the way, high social anxiety or something of that sort."

"Desrosiers hated other people," said Perrault.

"Who knows what happened to twist her personality that way? There are mysteries we'll never unravel, not without much more understanding of the mind and the things that affect it. Desrosiers's sister isn't cut from the same cloth?" asked Dufort.

"No," said Perrault. "I asked around. She's a respected science teacher at the lycée, leads an upstanding life as far as I can tell. Raised two children by herself with little support from her rich relatives."

Maron said, "Back to Mercier—I'm just saying that looks can be deceiving. She looks like a gentle old lady, sure, but she did something to enrage that letter-writer. I don't see how we have any actual evidence to eliminate her from the list of suspects."

"All right then, look into it, you're like a dog with a bone. Go talk to her again. But don't blame her for getting those letters. As far as we know, she's the victim, not the perpetrator." Dufort shrugged. "It sure hasn't been the best week for the seventy-two-year-old ladies of Castillac. Now, on the other matter, Perrault and I caught Sabrina Lellouche coming out of Desrosiers's house yesterday, carrying some bags. I questioned her; she said she had come back to the house one last time to pick up a few things that were hers, as well as some things Desrosiers had given her."

"If she's lying, she's a really good liar," said Perrault.

"She was quite cool and collected," agreed Dufort. "I asked her what was in the bags, and she offered to dump them on the sidewalk, but I told her that wasn't necessary. She may be a useful witness to us later on, and I don't want her to think she's under suspicion. According to her, the bags were filled with a bunch of old clothes, hand-me-downs Desrosiers had given her, that's all. I asked if there was a key to the house, and she told me there's an extra under a flowerpot in the back garden. We were interrupted by a call from Madame Vargas, but Perrault and I will head over there again to look for the will and see what we can find. Perhaps more letters!" he said, teasing Maron again. There was something about a person who took himself so seriously that tempted Dufort to poke him. He did not admire this quality in himself.

Maron leaned against Dufort's desk. His dark eyebrows looked heavier and darker than usual, knitting together as he stared at the floor. Dufort felt a twinge of remorse. "So Maron, nothing else to report from La Métairie? My hopes aren't high," he said.

"Not much," said Maron, his face not brightening. "All the plates, glasses, cutlery—that had been washed and put away, then used for another service. Any trace of cyanide that might have been in Desrosiers's glass, for example, would have been long gone, not that there was any way to distinguish which items she had used. No birthday presents left behind."

Dufort nodded. "We could use a break," he said. "All right then, we need to find the will, to see who will inherit. Could be a lot of money involved. No children, so presumably the larger portion will be split by her sister and niece and nephew, although there may be more distant relatives we aren't aware of, with some claim. At any rate, for now, that definitely puts the Faure family top of the list."

"Adèle and my sister used to hang out," said Perrault. "They were way older than me, but I always thought she was one of the really cool girls. I mean, she stood out, you know? Dressed to the nines, but with that limp."

Dufort cocked his head, picturing Adèle walking down a school corridor, head held high.

"She had this...this disability that she never let slow her down. I guess...a lot of times when people have something like that, they don't want to attract attention to themselves, you know? But Adèle didn't let that bad foot slow her down. You have to admire her for that."

"Do you know what's wrong with her foot, Perrault? Clubfeet are rarely seen anymore because they fix that. Perrault, find out if it is a clubfoot and whether or not she was treated."

"Awkward," said Perrault, hanging her head for a moment. But then she got a look of determination on her open, freckled face, and said she would get the information.

"We'll need to look into the brother and the mother as well."

"Michel is out of work, last I heard," said Perrault.

"Out of work means an inheritance might be timely," said Maron.

"And beyond the Faures, who else have we got? Maron, go back to La Métairie and a get a list of guests at the birthday party. Anyone present had opportunity, if it turns out the poison could have acted that quickly. I know you already asked, but press Nathalie. She may simply be reluctant to give any names. I'll drop in on Molly Sutton. She was at the restaurant the night of the murder; perhaps she saw something."

Dufort's cell rang. "*Oui?*" He nodded his head. Perrault and Maron could hear a rasping voice on the other end and knew it to be Florian Nagrand, the coroner.

Dufort said thank you and hung up. "He was calling only to confirm that we understand what was in the report. Cyanide. Route of entry was the skin on her face, which was slightly abraded allowing for quick penetration. It killed her quickly."

"Definitely someone at the party," said Maron.

"Or the restaurant, anyway," said Perrault.

Maron shot her a cold glance, thinking she was criticizing him.

"Let's get to it," said Dufort. "Perrault, find Adèle and wring every last drop of information out of her. I want to know what was going on in that family—I want to know why Michel isn't working, I want to know how well Murielle and her sister got along. And—I know you know this, but I will mention it all the same—Adèle is no longer the cool girl who's a friend of your sister. She is a possible murder suspect. Don't let that slip your mind."

Perrault said "Yes, sir," taking the reminder to heart, but wishing he hadn't felt the need to say it.

"Maron, you're off to La Métairie again. I'm not convinced Nathalie doesn't remember perfectly well who was there. Find out who waited on them; since it was a large party it might have been more than one person. Names and numbers, of course."

Dufort felt energized and confident. They knew the murder weapon, they knew when it had been utilized, and they had a room with a reasonably small number of people in it who could have committed the crime, and witnesses galore.

How hard could the rest be?

ADÈLE SPENT that Tuesday night at her mother's house. She didn't think about why, it was simply something she did whenever she felt unsettled, even now when she was thirty-nine years old, an officer at the bank, and had had her own apartment for years. It was inconvenient because the bank where she worked was on the other side of the village, and in December, it wasn't always a pleasant walk. It made her foot hurt and she had to get up very early in order to get there on time. But still, a few times a year, she came to her mother's anyway, because her old room was the same as when she was a child, and it was comforting to sleep on that narrow bed with the familiar duvet, and see the branches outside her bedroom window in what seemed like the exact same pattern as when she was ten.

Murielle always got up early. In the dark days of December that meant long before sunrise, and she would make coffee and read scientific journals and gardening magazines until it was time to go to the lycée where she had taught for over thirty years.

"Bonjour, Maman," said Adèle, padding down to the small kitchen in her nightgown and robe. "Did you sleep well?"

"Of course not," said her mother. "When you get to be my age, no one sleeps well. Not unless they drug themselves, which many choose to do. There's coffee," she added, and went back to reading her journal.

Adèle helped herself to coffee, adding a big splash of cream and two spoonfuls of sugar.

"You know that sugar is devoid of nutrition," said Murielle.

"Yes, Maman, you've mentioned that once or twice. Listen, I want to talk to you about Michel."

Murielle's head jerked up from her journal. "What about him?" she demanded.

"Well, I just...the whole business with Aunt Josephine..."

"What about it, Adèle? Speak up."

"Do you think he's all right? I mean, *really* all right?"

"He's as right as he's ever been. As right as he was the day I picked him up at the hospital as a baby. I don't think for one minute that Josephine's death will have any sort of bad effect on him, if that's what you're saying."

"Not exactly, Maman. It's that—didn't the police tell you? Aunt Josephine was poisoned. And if that's true, then Michel..."

"That sounds like rubbish," Murielle said. "Who in the world would want to poison Josephine?"

Adèle laughed. "Half the village?"

"Adèle!"

"Sorry, Maman. Well, I heard from what I think is a reliable source that she was definitely poisoned. And probably by someone at the birthday party. And so, I was wondering...I wanted to talk to you about...it couldn't be...you're *sure* it wasn't... not Michel? Tell me you don't think it could have been Michel."

Murielle stared at her. "Why would you say something like that? Why would you even think it? Of course Michel did no such thing. He hasn't got his feet under him yet, that's true. But he couldn't hurt a fly. Michel, a *murderer*?" Murielle shook her head decisively.

"Of course I don't think he could do it," said Adèle, feeling better. "But I just worried, because of the money..."

Murielle shook her head again and looked out of the window

at the gray morning, her expression doleful. Adèle wondered if she felt more grief at losing her sister than she was admitting.

"Maman, you mentioned picking Michel up at the hospital. I don't think you've ever really told that story, Maman, I mean of Michel's adoption. I'm very glad you did adopt him, it's wonderful to have a brother I'm so close to. But what made you decide to take him?"

Murielle looked as though she was trying to decide what to say. "You were lonely," she said finally. "You were a vivacious little girl and honestly, I wasn't enough company for you."

Adèle laughed. "You could have just gotten me a dog."

Murielle shrugged. "And also—I got a call, from a lawyer I used to know. He said there'd been a birth, the mother was young and unmarried, the family was Catholic and not at all pleased, and would I consider..." she trailed off, looking out of the window, remembering. "You have to understand, in those days, being an unwed mother was considered a scandalous, shameful thing. It wasn't easy to get through."

"You managed, Maman," Adèle said softly, for the first time really understanding that her birth had caused her mother real difficulty, even pain.

Murielle did not respond at first but kept looking out of the window. "Michel came from Bergerac, not a village family," she said finally. "I've forgotten the name."

Adèle was not sure she believed her. "Well, it was good of you to do it. I know it wasn't easy with the two of us and not much money."

"And no husband. Not that I wanted one. More trouble than they're worth."

Adèle nodded. She herself had never been much interested in marriage, or having children either, for that matter. She drank her coffee. Her mother went back to her journal. After fifteen quiet minutes, Adèle went upstairs and dressed carefully for work in clothes hanging in the armoire in her old room. The fabric of the wool skirt was very fine, and the sweater cashmere.

"À bientôt, Maman," she said as she left, kissing her on both cheeks. Leaving her coat unzipped as the weather had warmed considerably during the night, Adèle made her way through the cobblestone streets of Castillac, thinking not about murder but about her first tasks at the bank that morning, and wondering again about her mother and the adopting of Michel. She hadn't given it much thought before, but all of a sudden it was something that nagged her. It was just a feeling, nonetheless she felt confident that there was more to that story than her mother had just told her.

Chapter Nineteen

Dufort walked back to his house from the station so that he could drive his own car to Molly's. The police car was available, but he preferred a more low-key approach, having found that showing up in an official car—even without sirens and lights flashing—tended to put people ill at ease. Even people who were not guilty of anything. Even someone like Molly, who he guessed would be eager to help with the case.

He knocked on the door and stood waiting, looking around at the property of La Baraque. It was a mess, really—the front garden still had tall frozen stalks of something or other leaning this way and that. A woodpile lay in disarray near the side of the house. The lawn needed raking. Yet the place gave him a good feeling; it didn't seem neglected so much as a lot going on at once. He saw a cart with a load of stone, and a giant metal toolbox next to it. Probably Pierre Gault, he guessed correctly.

He knocked again, more loudly, and heard rustling inside. The door opened and a striking woman with a black pageboy and pale skin opened the door.

"You're not Molly," said Dufort, drily.

"I have no idea what you just said," said Frances. "But hey, I like a man in uniform as much as the next girl. Want to come in? Molly is back in the meadow talking with the mason guy."

Dufort considered making an effort in English, but she was distractingly pretty, and he couldn't stand how he mangled the language. So he simply nodded and smiled and came inside. Frances went to the French doors and shouted to Molly that someone was there, and the two of them sat in the cold living room, uncomfortable without the grease of small talk to make things less awkward.

Molly came in shortly, not wearing a coat, her cheeks flushed from the cold, and her red hair flying up in a curly cloud around her head. "Ben!" she said with a grin, striding over to kiss cheeks. Ben gripped her arms firmly and smiled back.

"So you two met?" Molly switched to English. "Frances, this is Ben Dufort, our chief gendarme. Ben, this is my old friend, Frances Milton."

"Are you from Massachusetts also?" he ventured in English.

"*Oui,*" said Frances, but that was the end of her French, and she smiled and excused herself. Dufort and Molly heard her tinkling on the piano in the music room.

"Police business?" asked Molly, hoping hard that it was.

"Well, I'm just here informally. Can we sit? There are a few things I'd like to talk to you about."

They walked to the sofas facing the woodstove and sat down. "Is it about Madame Desrosiers?"

"Yes. You were at the restaurant, of course, and there are a few things I'd like to nail down, if you have a moment to talk."

"Of course! I was just out with Pierre Gault, the mason. You know him? Of course you do. He's going to rebuild my pigeonnier so I can rent it out. Hoping to be done by early summer, fingers crossed." Molly blathered on about the cost of stone and dry-stack walls, wondering at the same time why she was delaying getting to the subject that had been consuming her. It was a bit like saving a fat wedge of chocolate cake to eat in bed at the very end of the day.

Dufort was wondering the same thing. Did she know something she didn't want to tell him? Curious, he decided to let her babble on.

Finally Molly said, "So about the other night. Frances was there too. She kept getting mad at me for watching the birthday party. You know I'm incorrigibly nosy. So anyway, what can I tell you?"

"First, the guests at the party," he began.

"Yes, I've been giving that some thought," Molly jumped in. "Okay, there was Desrosiers, of course, at the head of the table. Michel right beside her, on her left. They were there before anyone else."

"How did they seem together? Did you notice any...unhappiness between them?"

"None. He seemed like a pretty devoted nephew, to be honest. Even though Desrosiers looked like someone who was hard to please."

"By all accounts," said Dufort. "Next?"

"Next to Michel was his mother—I keep forgetting her name—"

"Murielle Faure."

"Yes. She was next. She seemed pleasant enough. One of the few people at the table who wasn't either angry or looking like a wolf caught in a trap who would happily chew off a leg to escape."

Dufort laughed.

"Next to Murielle was Adèle. Then coming around the other side of the table were Sabrina and her boyfriend, Jean-Francois."

"You figured all this out just by sitting at the next table?"

"Well, not exactly. I also went out for a drink with Adèle."

Dufort raised his eyebrows but said nothing at first.

"Would you like some coffee or anything? Excuse me for being a terrible hostess," said Molly, jumping up and going into the open kitchen.

"No, no thank you. Do you mind telling me why you went out with Adèle? Is it because you were engaged in some, uh, some amateur sleuthing?"

Molly bustled around in the kitchen getting herself some coffee. "Well, not exactly, Ben. I mean, yes, it's true that I had some questions. I *am* curious about a few things. But also—I like Adèle. We have things in common." She shrugged, not specifying that she was thinking about their taste in handbags.

"May I ask if you talk with her in French, for the most part? I must add that yours has improved rather dramatically since I first met you."

Molly beamed. "Thank you! Of course I'm learning more every day. But the main thing is, I got over my fear of making mistakes. I just make them and keep on going, and paradoxically, that means I make fewer of them."

Dufort nodded. "I wish I could say the same about my English."

"People back home think they will be crucified if they make a mistake, trying to speak French in France. But aside from a few snickers and the occasional belly laugh at my mistakes, I've found people to be extraordinarily patient about it. Sometimes my genders get corrected, but that seems like more of a reflex correction than anyone trying to be overbearing and critical."

Molly settled back on the sofa and took a long sip of her coffee. "All right, now be straight with me, Ben. I'm picking something up in your tone...are you thinking Adèle was responsible for poisoning her aunt? Or is there someone else you're looking at?"

Dufort considered brushing her off, telling her "police business *blah blah blah*." But he was still grateful to her for her invaluable help in that earlier case. He liked her. And he wanted to see her reaction to what he had to say.

Chapter Twenty

"I haven't said anything to Perrault and Maron yet," said Dufort. "But looking at the usuals of means, motive, and opportunity —the person who comes at the top of the list is not Adèle, but her brother, Michel Faure." He watched Molly carefully.

She sipped her coffee and narrowed her eyes, thinking.

"We have no physical evidence—not yet. But Michel ticks all the boxes. Number one, he arranged the party," said Dufort, "which I believe is an important point. If you're going to poison your aunt with face cream—that is how we believe it was done— then it's clever to invite as many people as you can so you have a crowd to blend into. If he had simply taken the cream to her house, the list of suspects would narrow to him and Sabrina, the housekeeper. Madame Desrosiers did not have other visitors, and she very rarely left the house.

"Michel's family stands to inherit the money, since Desrosiers had no living children—and who knows, perhaps he had managed to persuade her to favor him with a large share. Arranging birthday parties for her might be kindness, or perhaps he was trying to curry favor, you see?

"Perrault is at the house now searching for the will, and I've got an accountant working on Desrosiers's books. We're still waiting to hear how much she's worth, but possibly in the neighborhood of five to ten million euros. Not in the same category as your American tech billionaires," he said with an ironic smile. "But for a young man with no work, no career, and no money? More than adequate."

"I think for most of us," said Molly. She felt herself pulling away from Dufort, not wanting to be convinced by his theory. She *liked* the Faures. She remembered the siblings coming down the road on their way to the funeral, laughing and walking in the light rain—Molly had interpreted that moment as innocent joy, not guilt.

But she also knew she had a bit of a weakness for charm. Her ex-husband being Exhibit A.

Not that charm was all bad. What she wanted was for the charm to *mean* something. For Michel and his lovely suits and good humor to be her actual friend, not just a man looking for a momentary audience. And certainly not the cover of someone capable of killing an old woman, no matter how unpleasant she was.

For his part, Dufort was not as decided about Michel as he pretended to be. He wanted to see Molly's reaction, see if she could be convinced. Especially now that she appeared to be making friends with Michel and his sister.

"Well?" he said, breaking a long silence. They heard some rather frantic piano coming from the music room.

"I...I don't know. I'll tell you, I noticed immediately that something was off at that party. People were tense and unhappy. And it did occur to me, probably because of that and my sometimes out of control imagination, that she had been murdered. Once I found her, I mean. But now that you're presenting me with who might have done it, my brain is resisting and rejecting the idea as hard as it can. I don't want it to be Michel. Or Adèle. Honestly, Ben, I think they're lovely."

Dufort shrugged. "I don't have to tell you that lovely people can commit murder. People who appear lovely, I should say, but I think you understand what I mean."

Molly nodded. Intellectually she agreed with him, and she knew that there were serial killers who were known to be especially charismatic and engaging...Ted Bundy, right?

"I hear what you're saying. I'm afraid I've got nothing, no evidence or conversation to report, that would steer you in Michel's direction or away from it." She sighed. "I have some questions, if you don't mind my asking?"

"I believe that's supposed to be my job," he said, amused.

She grinned at him. "Well, I'm just wondering if money is the only motive you're considering. I know it's a pretty good one, I'm not saying otherwise. But what about...what about revenge? What if Desrosiers had been absolutely horrible to the maid, for instance, and the maid snapped? She wouldn't inherit, obviously, but we're not talking about a well-thought-out crime with a jackpot at the end. We're talking about the satisfaction of hurting someone who has made your life a misery."

Dufort nodded. "Of course. For the right person, certainly revenge could be motive enough," he agreed. "Was there anything about Sabrina's behavior at the party that would lead you to believe she would capable of seeking it?"

"Well, no. No one behaved badly, at least that I saw. But she really did look like if she had to stay there one more second it might kill her. And her boyfriend was trying to soothe her, but she was having none of it."

"What do you mean, 'soothe'?"

"Oh, he was stroking her arm and occasionally nuzzling her—I think at one point Desrosiers snapped at him for it. But the whole time Sabrina just looked like she was in agony. But...I guess that could be about anything, right? Like maybe something in her life that had nothing to do with Desrosiers was making her so upset?"

"Could be," said Dufort. "And was Jean-Francois the last guest?" he asked, knowing he was not.

"Nope. Another old lady was next to him. Beautiful white hair in a braided bun. No idea who she is, though."

"Claudette Mercier," said Dufort. "A classmate of Desrosiers's. Did you happen to overhear any conversation between her and Madame Desrosiers?"

"I'm afraid not," said Molly. "I mean, I wasn't paying attention to the table every single second, but I'm not sure they ever spoke to each other."

She and Dufort sat in silence for some time, blocking out the tinkling of the piano in order to think about the case, but neither of them had the slightest bit of inspiration.

"I hope it's not Michel," said Molly in a quiet voice.

But Dufort only pressed his lips together, and said nothing.

Chapter Twenty-One

Thérèse Perrault left the station in high spirits. The job Dufort had given her was probably not going to be that exciting, she was telling herself, but she was thrilled that he had chosen her to do it, and by herself for once. Especially after she had not managed to find Adèle or find out anything about her bad foot. She grinned at a young boy coming out of the épicerie clutching a package of Haribo gummies. She nodded to a mother pushing a stroller, and then to a workman going into a *boulangerie* to get some bread to take home for lunch. Her stomach growled.

Just a few blocks away, the Desrosiers mansion loomed up, a floor or two higher than the other houses on the block. The shutters and door were violet-blue; twin topiaries on the front landing had started to look scruffy. Thérèse went around back to look under flowerpots for the key, and found it easily.

It wasn't until she was inside the house that she got the creeps. She couldn't stop thinking that the house belonged to a dead woman, a murdered woman, and the thought made her startle at any little sound, a pop of the radiator or a bird chirping outside.

Um, old houses have belonged to heaps of dead people, you idiot. Loads of them. And she wasn't murdered here, anyway.

Taking a deep breath—and unaware that she was imitating Chief Dufort, who used breathing exercises all the time to calm his stress—Thérèse pulled herself together and explored the house. First she looked around the big kitchen, which looked as though a real meal hadn't been cooked in it for some time. Then not much more than a glance in the laundry room, storeroom, broom closet, butler's pantry. The front of the house had a salon on either side of the front door, and she walked through them, looking for anything of interest, but there was little to see. Nothing but furniture, and in one salon, a decanter and some fragile-looking glasses.

No magazines, books, or the usual signs of habitation. The rooms were almost sterile.

Up to the next floor. Therese's eyes widened when she turned on the light and saw the stuffed ostrich. She turned on a table lamp and saw a delicate desk that had one central drawer and several smaller ones on the sides. Here we go, she thought, sliding down into the leather-padded chair in front of it. Methodically, she opened the drawers, starting at the top left and moving down. Two empty ones. Another with pencils and pens and nubs of eraser. The wide central drawer, however, was crammed with papers, so crammed that many were bent up against the bottom of the desktop. Carefully she pulled out the ones on top and placed them on the desk, looking for a lawyer's letterhead or any indication of a will.

She drew out another handful and made a pile. It was odd for anyone to store their valuable papers like this, Thérèse thought, using her hand to flatten one especially wrinkled paper out. The drawer empty, she riffled through the pile. The deed for the house was there, as well as a note she assumed had been written by Desrosiers listing the hymns she wanted sung at her funeral, grocery lists, and thirty-year-old receipts from Chanel.

But no will.

The top drawer on the right side was filled with letters. Packets of them, tied in ribbon. Expensive, heavy stationery with no address. Thérèse took the top one out from under the ribbon and opened the letter.

Ma Belle, it began. She skimmed the rest. Well, she may have been a miserable old woman, thought Thérèse, but maybe that's because she'd lost a husband who was devoted to her.

The other drawers were empty.

She got up and searched the other rooms on that floor: an informal room with a loveseat and armchairs less nice than ones in other rooms, and a large mirror and several armoires and chests, all filled with clothing; a vast bathroom with an enormous porcelain tub with lion's feet; a stark bedroom with a single bed and a plain bureau, another room with nothing in it at all.

Up to the third floor. There was no mistaking Desrosiers's bedroom—it was the only room in the entire house that felt as though anyone had spent any time in it for the last ten years. Her dressing table had makeup open on top of it, as though she had just gotten up to leave the room for a moment or two in the middle of getting ready to go out. A dress had been flung across an armchair, and a pair of shoes stood next to the bed, one shoe on its side.

Thérèse could imagine the old woman putting on the dress and deciding it wasn't right, didn't fit the way she wanted, and tossing it aside for the housekeeper to deal with later. She could see her slipping off her shoes as she climbed into bed. She could sense Josephine Desrosiers in this room. Not just the obvious signs of her physical presence; there was something else too, something about her personality was in the air: her dissatisfaction and unhappiness, perhaps even desolation.

A good detective sees what is not present as well as what is, and Thérèse *was* good. Where is the jewelry box, she wondered? Surely the old lady had some jewelry, and she probably spent some time sitting at the dressing table looking at herself wearing them; Thérèse was correct about this. She looked in the bottom drawers of the mirrored armoire, she looked under the bed, she looked everywhere in that room where a jewelry box might be hidden, but she did not find one.

However, in a shoebox that was tucked into a storage area under a window seat, she did find a brown envelope with a lawyer's office as the return address—Blaise and Descartes, of Paris—and she sat right down on the old lady's bed and read it straight through.

"So, did the copper tell you who poisoned the old lady?" asked Frances, as she and Molly made lunch.

"He doesn't know who did it," said Molly.

"Does he think you know?"

"Nah, he was just asking a bunch of questions about the other night at La Métairie. Sometimes people see things, you know, and they don't know what they're seeing is important."

"Right, Nancy Drew," teased Frances.

Molly chopped a head of romaine, lost in thought. "I don't agree with him, though. I just don't think..."

Frances waited a moment for Molly to finish her sentence. "Um, so...are you talking to yourself or to me?"

Molly shook her head. "Sorry! It's just that—Ben thinks Michel did it. Do you think that's possible? Doesn't he seem like a totally nice guy? Maybe not an alpha, Mr. Successful—but decent, even good-hearted?"

Frances cocked her head while she sliced up radishes. "Yeah, to us he seems that way. But we're not his family. Who knows what kind of crazy stuff has been going on behind the scenes."

"Secret babies! Insane first wives hidden in the attic!"

"Well, exactly," laughed Frances. "Family members can be incredibly vicious to each other. And secretive."

"You know how much I wanted kids," said Molly quietly. "But maybe that's because the picture in my mind is all rosy, like we'd get along like gangbusters and have nothing but laughs and fun together. And the truth is, the little tots might have grown up and wanted to poison me, or I'd get so annoyed I'd want to disown them."

"No doubt. But I'm pretty sure neither of you would actually do those things. It's not *wanting* to do it that makes you crazy, it's following through on it."

Molly nodded.

"So does the copper always let you in on police business? And have you let him visit your office of internal affairs?" Frances waggled her eyebrows at Molly.

"Shut up," laughed Molly. "It's nothing like that. Only that I helped with that last case, so he's...and also he actually listens to people, which as you know isn't all that common. Anyway, he listens to what I have to say, and if you ask me, that's a pretty wonderful quality. Doesn't mean I want to go out with him."

Frances nodded, not completely believing her friend. "Got any cheese to put in the salad? Mind if I throw some sardines in there?"

"Not at all," said Molly. "There's some goat cheese in the refrigerator door, got it at the market on Saturday. Damn! I just realized that when I was talking to Adèle about the guests at the surprise party, I never got around to asking her about the white-haired lady."

"The one sitting closest to our table? You think she was up to something? I'm not sure white-haired old ladies are prime murder suspects."

"I don't think you can exclude people based on hair color."

"Maybe not," said Frances, chewing on a radish. "But realistically? Do you really think that sweet-looking old lady offed her friend? They've probably known each other since they were kids."

"It's possible. Ben said the poison was on her face, they're thinking maybe a birthday present of face cream. Doesn't poison face cream seem like the way a sweet-looking seventy-two-year-old lady would murder someone, if she were going to do it?"

"There's a fallacy in there somewhere, I just don't know what to call it. I would say it's highly unlikely—and by that I mean freaking impossible—that the lady with the braided bun killed anybody. Just no. It's way, way more possible that your boy Michel did it. Probably he buttered up the old battle-axe so she left him everything."

"But I don't want it to be Michel," said Molly, almost whining.

"He's cute, I'll give you that. Pass the salt."

Molly poured them each a glass of wine, and they dug into their gigantic salads.

Someone was banging on the door.

"Probably the murderer," said Frances drily.

Molly jumped up and thwacked her friend lightly on the back of the head. She opened the door, letting a frigid breeze in, and there was Constance, jumping up and down on the doormat.

"Hiya," said Constance, using the one American word she had picked up from Molly. She stepped inside, rubbing her arms. "Look, Molly, hey it's good to see you—and hello to you whoever you are—" she said in Frances's direction. "Listen, I know I should have called first like you asked, but I dropped my phone on the street and it nicked the curb just so and the whole thing shattered into bits. So I'm totally incommunicado except for in person, which really I like better even though I know that makes me sound totally Amish.

"Anyway—Molly! I'm dropping by because Thomas and I are dying to go to this concert in Toulouse. There's gonna be like four bands and we love all of them with a complete passion, but the thing is, we're broke as all hell and can't afford the gas to drive down there. So I was wondering, hoping actually, really really hoping, that you could afford to have me clean today. I know your bookings have been off with the cold weather and all, but this concert, it's like our dream, the best dream of my entire life, it really is. So what do you say?"

Frances was smirking, able to guess more or less what Constance was saying just by the tone of her voice, and knowing that whatever it was she wanted Molly to do, she was going to get her way.

"Constance, this is my friend Frances," said Molly, trying to buy some time.

The two women smiled at each other, unsure of what other greeting they should do.

"Oh, all right," said Molly, unable to say no. "Just make sure you mop the cottage really well?"

Constance rushed into Molly's arms. "Thank you so much, Molly, you're the best! I'll make that place shine! And maybe I'll work so hard you'll want to give me an extra tip. Gas is ridiculous lately."

"Pushover," said Frances, when Molly sat back down at the table.

"Eh, she's young and she wants to work. Why not support that?"

Frances shrugged. "All the great detectives have a cold-hearted side," she said. "Fearlessly objective, something like that. You, my friend, are a marshmallow."

Molly threw a hunk of bread at Frances and hit her on the forehead. There was a slight pause as both of them considered regressing all the way back to having a real food fight, but in the end they decided they were more interested in eating the food, which they did with much gusto, continuing to talk over the details of the Desrosiers murder but getting absolutely nowhere.

Chapter Twenty-Two

꧁❀꧂

After lunch Frances went to take a nap in the bedroom next to Molly's, since Constance was noisily cleaning the cottage. Molly was restless. She was reading a good book but kept getting up and finding chores to do, and finally she gave up and walked into the village, wanting to stretch her legs and possibly procure a few pastries for Frances and herself to eat in late afternoon. Yes, it was gluttonous to have pastries twice in one day, but it was cold and wintry and her best friend was visiting and...well, she could come up with reasons for pastry all day long. It was a real talent, and one she was grateful for.

Castillac looked sad to her in mid-December. Hardly anyone was on the street, for one thing, and the Christmas decorations looked droopy and half-hearted. But her own preparations for Christmas hadn't even begun, she realized with a little panic. Hurrying to Pâtisserie Bujold, she spoke to the proprietor about reserving a *bûche de Noël* (that most scrumptious of holiday desserts, a rolled cake made to look like a log), which he reassured her he was glad to do. So distracted by worrying about Michel and wondering how she could help him, Molly didn't even notice Monsieur Nugent's usual staring, leaving with a waxed bag of afternoon delights—a Napoléon, two cream puffs, and a straw-berry tart.

She nibbled on one of the cream puffs as she wandered around the center of Castillac. Ben had told her Josephine Desrosiers was one of the wealthiest people in the village, and had described her house to Molly, a house she recognized since it was the grandest mansion in the village and a commanding presence on rue Simenon, one of the main streets of the village. Without meaning to, she drifted toward it until she was standing directly outside. The shutters and door were the perfect color blue, Molly thought, although she wanted badly to get at those topiaries with a pair of shears.

She wondered what had made Josephine so mean. Or maybe that was irrelevant. The question was, what had made someone want to kill her? Was it just about the money? Or was it rage? Or something else altogether, something no one will never know?

Molly ducked into a café right across the street and sat at a table where she could look at the house. She felt as though seeing the house was helping her understand Josephine somehow, as though some of secrets were hidden within it. She would possibly have given up her bag of pastries to get inside for a look around.

A waiter brought her a petit café and she smiled at the plea-sure of her first sip. The coffee was very strong and bitter, the perfect accompaniment to the sweet and fluffy creampuff, which she ate surreptitiously since she guessed correctly that the café manager wouldn't be thrilled about her eating food she had brought from somewhere else. Her eyes were turned to the house but she wasn't really seeing it. Lost in the sort of random thoughts that slosh through our minds when we're alone, thinking about everything and nothing, looping around and around, murder/coffee/topiary/murder/cream puff...

At first she didn't notice what she was seeing. Another sip of coffee jolted her into the present, and she realized there was a man at the front door of the mansion, his back to her, who seemed to be using a key. He was dressed in blues, a workman's overalls, and he was carrying a plastic bag with something heavy in it. She wanted to whistle, to call out, anything to make the man turn around so she could get a positive ID. He looked like Jean-Francois, Sabrina's boyfriend. She was almost certain it was him.

The man finally got the door open, and walked inside without turning around until just at the last second, when he closed the door, Molly saw his profile against the darkness inside. It was Jean-Francois all right.

Molly jumped up from the table with an impulse to do something, but once she was standing, she had no idea what. She couldn't go running over and let herself in the Desrosiers house... could she? If Jean-Francois was up to something, that could be dangerous. Besides, she had no standing to go in there, no matter who was inside. No connection to Josephine Desrosiers except finding her dead on the tiled bathroom floor of La Métairie and the beginnings of a friendship with her niece and nephew, which even with Molly's skills at rationalization did not add up to letting herself into the old lady's house without an invitation.

Even if Josephine were still alive and Sabrina was working there, it would be strange for her boyfriend to have a key to the house, wouldn't it? thought Molly. Yes, it would. If he came to pick her up from work, he should knock. And if Josephine was the type of woman Molly thought she was, he would be knocking on the back door and not the front.

Molly paid her bill and crossed the street. The shutters to the house were all closed so there was no way to catch a glimpse of Jean-Francois inside. She walked along the side of the house toward the back, peering over the wall to the garden. It was a little difficult to tell in winter, but it looked as though once upon a time it had been a beautiful place. Molly could see an espaliered tree on the back wall of the house, and two circular goldfish ponds, the edges rimmed in tile the same violet-blue as the shutters and front door.

I bet he's stealing or destroying evidence, Molly said to herself, continuing down the block and turning toward home. But what? And how in the world can I figure it out?

⁂

BENJAMIN DUFORT WAS in a sprightly mood. First of all, after Perrault showed him the will, he was eighty-five percent sure Michel Faure had killed his aunt to inherit her money, and all that remained was finding enough evidence first to arrest and then to convict him. And second, he was going over to Marie-Claire's for dinner. He wasn't miserable leading his bachelor's life, but he appreciated a meal cooked by someone else, especially someone with as much talent in the kitchen as Marie-Claire had. And of course, he very much enjoyed *her*, apart from the food—her intelligence and forth-rightness, and the sexy-librarian way she dressed.

After praising Perrault for her good work finding Desrosiers's will, he left the station for the day, wanting to pick up some odds and ends at the épicerie and possibly drop by the florist's to see if there was anything he could take to Marie-Claire. He whistled on his way down the street. He stopped to chat with the woman behind the register at the épicerie, and the delivery boy. He kept whistling on his way to the florist's, which was a little out of his way.

"Salut, Ben!" said Madame Langevin, the tiny woman who had run the florist shop for as long as Dufort had been buying flowers. "Have you caught the murderer yet? I can't believe someone killed poor Josephine! Of course, I say 'poor Josephine' only in the way you would speak of the dead, no matter who it was. Because mon Dieu, that woman was execrable! Oh now Ben, you should not look away when someone is telling you the truth!"

Dufort smiled and shook his head. "It is not my job to slander the victim, Madame Langevin."

"Slander? Who said anything about slander? Slander is untruth, yes? Listen to me. I had dealings with Josephine Desrosiers for years. Years! She was fussy—I didn't mind that. *I'm* fussy. Things ought to be just so, I understand that entirely. But Ben, she would keep a bouquet for several days, and then return it! Return it, complaining that it did not look fresh. Well, everyone in the world understands that flowers aren't going to stay fresh into eternity. Their impermanence is their glory, as I'm sure you understand. Madame Desrosiers understood it perfectly well too. But that didn't stop her from trying to get her money back.

"I'm not talking about once, Ben, or even twice. I am telling you she behaved this way for many years, off and on. I would have refused to sell to her, but then she would hit a good patch and all would be well for a few months. As you might know, my business has its ups and downs; sometimes people can afford flowers, and in leaner times, they cannot. I couldn't afford to lose her business, even though I despised her and barely made any profit from her at all."

"You're going to put yourself on the list of suspects if you keep talking like that," said Dufort with a faint smile.

"Oh, I *should* be on it," said Madame Langevin, "In fact, it would give me pleasure to be on it!" She collapsed with laughter on the stainless steel counter where she arranged flowers.

Dufort was glad that Desrosiers had been rich enough for someone to kill her for money; if she had been much poorer, the suspect list would have gotten completely out of hand.

He selected a white poinsettia, even though he didn't like them much. Madame Langevin was waiting on a delivery and didn't have much else in stock besides some sad-looking carnations. Dufort paid and said goodbye, leaving Madame Langevin wondering whom the poinsettia was for, because she knew quite well that Dufort's mother was allergic to them so that crossed her off the list of possibilities.

Dufort reached his place in the gendarmerie and went inside to put his odds and ends away and to shower and change before going to Marie-Claire's. In the shower, allowing himself some extravagance with the hot water, he felt a pang of uncertainty. He often did his best thinking in the shower and had learned to pay attention when anything occurred to him while the water was beating down on him.

Michel may want the money, but is there any particular reason why he couldn't simply wait? True, she was not that old, as Dufort kept reminding Perrault and Maron. But still, another ten or fifteen years maximum, and Michel would have gotten the whole eight million euros without taking any risk at all. He was out of work, but he could get by on social services and he has a supportive family. It's not like he was living on the street with nothing to eat.

Some people can't wait, Dufort thought as he toweled himself off, struggling to understand a man who could take the life of an old woman, even a tremendously disagreeable one, simply to make his own life more comfortable.

Chapter Twenty-Three

1967

Albert Desrosiers slammed his desk drawer shut and stood up suddenly, scowling. I've been a fool, he thought. A ridiculous, damned fool.

He had been working on one project for the last two years, and it was nearly finished. If he managed to pull it off, it would make him a very rich man, no question about that. There had been problems, of course—delays, many times pursuing a path that turned out to be fruitless, brick walls that took him a week or even months to find a way around—but Albert had every confidence he would succeed. Even though his invention did not yet exist, he could physically feel it somehow, the shape of it was so clear in his mind. Its essence was alive to him, and all he had to do was make it concrete with wires and solder, and investors would be falling over themselves trying to get a piece of it. Money was never his prime objective and it was not his focus then either, although he did find himself thinking of things he would be able to buy that he had never been able to before. Instruments, mostly.

And also, perhaps, the right piece of jewelry might bring her around?

Albert strode to the window and opened the shutters, looking out at the sidewalk in front of his modest house.

Where is she? Why does she not speak to me? Ma belle, I need you...

With a shuddering sigh, he went back to his desk and picked up his tiny pliers and swiveled his magnifier back into place and went to work. He needed to have tremendous control over his body to do the work because it was so painstaking, and the slightest jiggle would wreck the whole enterprise. Over time, he had trained himself to be still, to keep from trembling, but a large part of the secret to doing that was maintaining an emotional equilibrium that for the last few hours had been impossible.

I bring her flowers but she looks away from me. Are the flowers the wrong ones? Is it hopeless?

Albert was thirty-six years old. Too old to be so much in love, he believed. Too old to be chasing after a woman who was never going to relent.

Chapter Twenty-Four

2005

The Castillac police force was in Dufort's office on Thursday morning, having looked at everything Perrault had brought back from the Desrosiers mansion: the will, a stack of letters, a stuffed bear.

"Nice work, Perrault, although I don't see the significance of the bear."

"Well, me neither," said Perrault. "I'm not saying it means anything. It's just that it was propped up on a pillow on her bed, and I got the feeling it was important to the deceased, so I brought it along."

Dufort gave the small bear a quick inspection, palpating it to see if anything was inside besides stuffing, and then put it on a shelf. "He can be our mascot for the duration of the case," he said.

Maron rolled his eyes when Dufort's back was turned, and then bent back to the pile of letters, reading with no comment.

"Since she bequeaths nearly everything to Michel Faure, obviously he's our top guy," said Dufort.

Perrault nodded. When she had sat on Desrosiers's bed and

read the will, and saw that Michel was the major beneficiary, a flash of heat had gone through her. The fact that she found him charming and attractive made him seem all the guiltier, though she did not share that thought with her boss.

Maron had put the letters aside and was studying the final page of the will. "Hey now," he said, going to his desk and pulling out the letter he had taken from Claudette Mercier's living room floor and not yet entered into evidence. "Look at this." He smoothed the handwritten letter out on Dufort's desk, and put the last page of the will right beside it. "I can't call myself an expert, but I did take a handwriting analysis course when I was in Paris," Maron said. "Look at the capital 'D' here, and here," he said pointing to places in each document. "And also the small 's'— see how on each one there's a slight squiggle on the bottom, as though the writer's hand hesitated for a moment?"

"You're saying Desrosiers wrote the poison pen letter to Mercier?" said Perrault breathlessly.

"It sure looks like it," said Maron, trying not altogether successfully to keep his feelings of smugness out of his voice. "They knew each other well—don't forget, Mercier was at the birthday party."

"I thought people quit doing that kind of crap in middle school. Gave me chills when I read it."

"Maybe it gave Mercier chills too, or worse," said Maron.

"Why would Desrosiers write a letter like that by hand, anyway? Everybody knows handwriting can be matched, don't they?"

"I can't see her sitting at a computer," said Maron. "That generation, you know it's hit or miss when it comes to computer skills. And typewriters, who even has those around anymore?" He paused, looking back and forth from will to letter. "There's definitely something here."

Perrault studied the note, then added, "And listen to this part: 'you're lucky you didn't end up a scullery maid'. Either the writer is good at throwing false clues or it's someone old. Who even knows what a 'scullery maid' is anymore?"

Dufort asked, "If Desrosiers hated Mercier enough to write the letters, why was Mercier at the party?"

"Michel did the inviting," said Perrault. "It was a surprise party, not something Desrosiers planned. Maybe she was horrified to see Mercier there?"

"Or maybe Mercier got herself invited, so she could bring a very special present," said Maron.

"Maron likes Claudette Mercier for the murder," said Dufort, grinning, unable to help himself. What was it about Maron that brought on such an urge to tease?

"It's not a ridiculous idea," said Maron. "Poisoning is a woman's weapon, after all."

"Oh, please," said Perrault, rolling her eyes. "Where did you get that stupid idea? Maybe from your misogynist handbook?"

"Actually that is incorrect, Maron," said Dufort. "A quick glance at the history will show you that more men have been convicted for poisoning than women. Men kill vastly more often than women, no matter what method is employed. Over ninety percent."

"Okay, fine. Let me say it this way: if Desrosiers was bullying and threatening Mercier, and Mercier got pushed to the breaking point and wanted to kill her, how do you think she would do it? I don't think she's going to go over to the Desrosiers mansion and strangle her, do you? Do you really picture the two of them grappling in the salon, a fight to the death? No. No, she's going to use poison. It's more genteel, it's something she can physically manage.

"And just because men are more likely killers, that doesn't mean that every murder was done by a man, as you both well know."

"But seventy-two-year-old women are generally not the first cohort one suspects," said Dufort.

"Agreed," said Maron. "But I still say we shouldn't count Mercier out. You're being sexist, really," said Maron, drawing himself up. "You're making generalizations about her because of her gender and age, and I think that's wrong." And he left Dufort's office and went to sit at his desk.

Perrault and Dufort exchanged glances. "How about you?" asked Dufort. "How do you see this murder happening? Have you got any ideas other than Michel?"

Perrault thought a moment. "To me, it's got to be about the money. It's easy for people to lose their heads over an inheritance, you know? Especially one that big. They might do something that in the rest of their lives would be unthinkable. And in the Desrosiers case, a killer would have the easy rationalization that by getting rid of a horrid old woman, he was doing the world a favor. A favor he would profit from, but still."

Dufort nodded. "What if the contents of the will were unknown to everyone—are there other family members who might have believed they would get something if Desrosiers died?"

"I don't think there's much family left. It was only the two girls, Murielle and Josephine. Their parents of course are long dead. I've looked for extended family and found none so far besides a couple of cousins up in Franche-Comté."

Dufort walked to the window and looked out. It was gray and drizzling, perfect for a run. Perhaps he would leave work early and get another one in before dark. Sometimes he had better ideas when running than he did in uniform.

"I know it's not a horse race," said Perrault. "But if I were betting? I'd put my money on Michel. Even if he didn't know about the will."

Dufort agreed. "He had opportunity. As for means, cyanide is not something you can buy at the épicerie, but it is not so terribly difficult to get hold of. As I've said, his organizing the party is definitely a strike against him—it looks as though he wanted to plump up the list of possible suspects."

"Exactly," said Perrault. "And plus, he's been out of work for a long time. Never really got going in any job, from what I can find out. He might have been looking at his aunt like she was a fat goose, prime for the slaughter."

"No, of course this isn't an arrest," Dufort was saying to Michel Faure, whom he had found having coffee at Chez Papa. "I'd just like you to walk over to the station with me so we can talk about a few things. If you have a moment?"

Michel cocked his head. He had never met Dufort before and he wasn't at all sure what to make of him.

"I think you might be able to give us some important help in the matter of your aunt," Dufort added, his expression pleasant.

Michel nodded and slid off his stool. "All right then, I'm free just now." He tossed some coins on the bar—not quite enough for his bill, never mind the tip—and followed Dufort out to the street. It was cold, and both men wrapped their coats tighter and raised their shoulders up.

"You've lived in Castillac all your life?" Dufort asked Michel as they walked.

"Yes. Well, I don't actually know for sure, but I think so. I was adopted just after being born, but I have no reason to think that I was born anywhere other than Castillac."

"Ah," said Dufort. "So, you're not a blood relative of the Faures or Desrosiers then?"

"No." Michel shot the gendarme a glance, wondering if Dufort knew something he didn't. What he had been thinking about constantly—but didn't dare ask—was whether or not Aunt Josephine's will had been found. All those dinners he had endured with her, all those Dubonnets poured into the tiny glasses while he went thirsty, all the criticism and abuse he'd allowed her to heap upon him...had it paid off? Was he named in the will, even if not as the main beneficiary? Please God?

Michel kept his eyes on the pavement. His coat was thin and he was shivering, and one shoe had a hole in it that he kept putting off getting fixed.

"I'm going to speak plainly," said Dufort. "Your aunt was not a great favorite of anyone, have I understood that correctly?"

Michel laughed. "Spot on," he said. "A nasty bit of business, she was."

Dufort thought Michel was perhaps being clever by owning up to his distaste for the woman he had murdered, because what murderer would admit such a thing?

Michel noticed that they had turned down rue Simenon, going away from the station, but he didn't want to ask why. He could see his aunt's mansion looming up farther down the street, and felt a strong desire not to have to go inside, especially not with Dufort watching him like a hawk. Maybe a dull-witted hawk, Michel wasn't sure about that, but in any case, he fervently wished he were in a bar somewhere with Adèle, having a drink and a laugh...or anywhere, really, but there.

They stopped in front of the mansion. The violet-blue shutters were closed as they had been for years.

"I do not want to go in," said Michel, the words coming out before he could stop them.

"Any particular reason?"

"No. Well, yes." Michel looked up at the house, his eyes moving over it. The slate roof was whitened with frost and he thought the mansion exuded a kind of chill that was way worse than the weather. "Don't you feel it? Can't you tell just standing out here that the place has some bad juju?" He ran his hand through his hair.

"It's a house," said Dufort, shrugging. "Quite a nice house, perhaps the nicest in the village. Early nineteenth century, isn't it? Can you describe the inside for me?"

Michel rubbed his arms in a futile attempt to warm them. He desperately wanted to go someplace heated but was trying his best to seem amenable to whatever plan Dufort had. "Um, all right, I can do that, I suppose. It's rather grand inside, with two salons facing the street and a wide foyer between them. Wide staircase with a wrought-iron baluster comes down to the foyer. The kitchen is quite large with an old wood-fired stove as well as a gas stove. I don't think I was ever served a meal from that kitchen after my uncle died, back when Adèle and I were kids. There are several other rooms downstairs—a laundry, a pantry, and maybe more. I don't really remember. I can't tell you about upstairs because I never saw it.

"My aunt was a bit reclusive. As far as I know, over the last five years or so, she never went out unless I took her. The house-keeper, Sabrina—she came every day, cleaned and cooked for her, although I don't think my aunt ate very much. Anyway, I came to visit her because she didn't have friends and the rest of the family avoided her as much as possible, and I felt sorry for her."

Dufort raised his eyebrows as if to say, "Do you really think me that gullible?"

"Did she give you money?" Dufort asked, his tone friendly and conversational.

Michel just smiled. "Oh, not usually. A five-euro note if I was lucky. She did pay for dinner if we went out, but it's not like we were dining at La Métairie all the time—just the once, actually. Usually she wanted me to get her a bowl of paella from the guy who sets up in the Place on Tuesday nights. Or she'd ask me to run over to the *boulangerie* and get her a fresh baguette, and some cheese from the épicerie. She wouldn't eat it in front of me. I got the idea she would hide that food in her room and then refuse to eat what Sabrina was making for her. Aunt Josephine was like that, she spent all her time cooking up ways to make other people unhappy, from what I could see. 'Drama queen' was a term invented for her, but with a mean sort of twist, if you see what I mean?"

"She doesn't sound like a very pleasant person," said Dufort, thinking that was the understatement of the week. "And did you have any sense that she was unhappy? That perhaps these acts of hers were an indication that she was tired of life, tired of...of whatever her existence had turned out to be? I don't mean to suggest suicide, I am only wondering if it is possible that the person who killed her might have believed he was doing her a favor in a way."

"Doing the rest of the world a favor, I should say," said Michel, laughing.

Dufort ended the informal interview soon after, making an excuse that he had someone to see. He hurried off down the street and circled back to observe Michel surreptitiously. What Michel did was stand outside the mansion looking from shutter to shutter, stamping his feet from time to time, and then he turned away and did not look back, pulling out his phone and disappearing into the café across the street.

Maybe yes, maybe no, thought Dufort. Now I want to find his sister, and see what she has to say for herself—and for her brother.

Chapter Twenty-Five

O n rue Simenon, about two blocks from the Desrosiers mansion, Lucas Arbogast was getting ready to serve dinner to his elderly mother. She was seated at the table, freshly bathed and dressed. On her plate, he put four slices of duck breast, cut thin the way she liked it, and carried the plate to the table along with a basket of bread. Then he stopped. The bread basket dropped to the floor in his rush to put down the plate and see to his mother, who was suddenly gasping for breath and very agitated.

"Maman!" shouted Lucas who, luckily for Madame Arbogast, was a nurse at the local hospital. The old woman anxiously got up from the table, still gasping, moving with purpose as though she had somewhere to go that second. Then for a moment she stood up straight, her eyes blinking and unfocused.

"Maman! What is the matter? Sit down and let me check your vitals," said Lucas, trying to ease her back into her chair. He leaned down, for he was considerably taller, put an arm around her, and she collapsed, sinking into the chair like a rag doll.

Lucas was stunned, since he had just talked to his mother an hour before and she had been the picture of health. But his training helped him put his shock to one side as he pulled the chair away from the table and worked his arms under her, picking her up and settling her on the sofa. Her head rolled back; she was unconscious.

Lucas bent his head down close to her face, and it was then that he got a whiff of the characteristic smell of bitter almonds, which he had smelled only once before, in the unit on poisons, which he had found to be one of the most interesting in all of nursing school.

Immediately, he pulled out his mobile and called the hospital. He made sure his mother was breathing and adjusted her legs to make her more comfortable. Then he ran upstairs to her room, looking for anything that could tell him whether he was correct about an exposure to cyanide.

It couldn't be gas, he reasoned, because she wouldn't have made it downstairs. Cyanide gas kills quickly, he remembered that quite clearly. It couldn't have been in food or drink, because his mother never, ever ate or drank anything outside of mealtimes, and besides, he himself was preparing the meals. In any case, she had not taken a single bite since lunch.

Lucas found nothing out of order in her room. He checked under the bed, opened the drawers to her dressing table—everything looked the same as usual, as far as he could tell. It felt important to know where the cyanide was coming from, but he didn't have time for a proper search, not when his dear Maman was slipping into a coma.

As he ran back downstairs to check on her, he thought, wait a minute. Hold on. How in the world is Maman getting cyanide poisoning when she has barely left the house all day, if at all? Is this even an accident?

Lucas shook his head, unable to believe anyone in Castillac could possibly do such a thing, or have any reason for it either.

Maman was still unconscious. Her gasping was very hard to witness. Her skin was turning a bright cherry-red, which for an instant he thought meant she was doing better before he remembered it was a symptom of cyanide poisoning. He bent his head to her again, and sniffed noisily. Yes—he flared his nostrils and breathed in again, catching the scent.

His mother had a mild obsession with rejuvenating creams and lotions, demulcents and emollients of all types—perhaps the poison was on her skin, from a contaminated batch? If it *was* in a cream, then he could do something for her before the ambulance got there. And if it wasn't, washing her face wasn't going to cause any harm. He darted into the kitchen and got a bowl of water, a bar of soap, and a couple of rags, and then he kneeled beside her, dipping the rag in the soapy water and wiping her old, wrinkled, beloved face.

"Maman," he whispered hoarsely, "you're going to be all right. I just need to get this stuff off your skin. I think it's the cream, Maman, you know I've told you before, you don't know what they put in that stuff—"

Lucas was thorough. He wiped her down completely, then got a bowl of fresh water and new rags, and wiped her off again, going down to her collarbones. He repeated the process a third time. The gasping became less frequent. Her skin was reddened where he had been rubbing, but otherwise her color appeared to be returning to normal.

Lucas was thirty-eight years old and had never lived anywhere but home, except for the three years when he had to go to a larger town to study nursing. He and his mother were very close. They liked the same sorts of television programs, the same food, the same books. Even though his mother was old, he had never really contemplated the fact that he was likely to lose her at some point in the future—obviously he was aware it would happen, but that reality had never penetrated his consciousness but rather skated along the surface, with no attention paid to it. This close call— impossible to ignore—rattled him so much he could barely speak.

He stayed kneeling beside her, holding her hand and

murmuring to her, and getting up to change the water in the bowl and get yet more clean rags to wipe her down, until at long last—where was that ambulance?—Madame Arbogast whispered to her son to cut it out before he wiped her face right off.

The bell rang, and laughing and tremendously relieved, Lucas went to answer the door. He knew the driver and the medic, and quickly told them what had happened. Madame Arbogast was sitting up on the sofa now, asking for a glass of brandy, and was going to be fine.

"I went ahead and called the police on the way over, Lucas. With a suspicious poisoning, that's the protocol, as you know."

Lucas nodded. "I took a quick look around, trying to figure out where the stuff came from, but I had to stay with Maman so I didn't take the time for a real search. I knew she hadn't eaten anything I hadn't prepared for her, so I was thinking it must be some kind of face cream or something. Sure enough, cleaning her up brought her around quickly."

"You did good," said the medic, gesturing to Madame Arbogast who was feeling well enough to be flirting with the ambulance driver. "How'd you know it was cyanide?"

"Smelled it," said Lucas, laughing again and feeling a little giddy.

"You're lucky then. Not everybody can smell that smell—not even fifty percent, if I remember right."

Lucas shook his head slowly and let out a long breath. "What a close one. She goes a little crazy with the face cream." He paused. "But why in the world would her face cream have cyanide in it?"

"Yeah, that's the question right there," said the ambulance driver, who usually wasn't very interested in the patients he drove to see, but poison? Now that makes a good story for the folks at the bar after work.

A firm rapping on the door, and Lucas let in Thérèse Perrault, who was the officer in charge that Saturday evening. "Hello,

Lucas, Madame Arbogast," said Thérèse, who knew them. "Suspected poisoning, that's the word I got?"

"Yes. She's all right now, thank God. But it was a close thing. I was lucky and smelled that bitter almond scent when I got close to her face, so I cleaned her up and she rallied. But wow, for a little while there, I thought I was gonna lose her." He reached down and gave his Maman a pat on the shoulder. She poured herself another finger of brandy.

"What do you mean, 'cleaned her up'?"

"When the poisoning exposure is to the skin, as this was, the best antidote is just to get it off," said Lucas. "So I washed her face with soap and water a bunch of times, and she perked right up. She was unconscious for about ten minutes, I'd say. Had the cherry-red skin that's symptomatic of cyanide exposure as well."

"Well, lucky for her you know your stuff," said Perrault. "May I go upstairs and have a look in her bedroom?"

"Of course," said Lucas, making no move to leave his mother.

The ambulance driver would have liked to go search for poison too, but knew he had no believable reason to join Perrault.

It didn't take her long to find something suspicious. She put on her gloves and picked up a jar of face cream, unmarked, no label at all. She called downstairs to ask for a cardboard box, and just to be thorough, put all of the lotions and creams from Madame Arbogast's dressing table in it, to take to the lab. A second old lady assailed by cyanide-laced face cream.

Did Castillac have a serial killer on its hands?

Thérèse felt a thrill run through her body, and chastised herself for feeling so happy when people were suffering and dying.

Chapter Twenty-Six

"I don't care how cold it is," said Frances. "I've been cooped up all day, I think I just wrote a jingle that every person in the United States is going to be cursing me for—massive earworm, haha—and so anyway, I'd like to look at something besides your sweet face."

"Nico or Pascal, I'm guessing you have in mind?" said Molly, putting away the last dishes from the dishwasher.

"They *are* easy on the eyes," said Frances, grinning. She was standing in front of the mirror in the foyer, trying to tie her scarf in that chic way Frenchwomen seemed to manage so effortlessly. "Holy smokes, Molls, how do they do it?" she said, frustrated, whipping the end over, under and around, and looking half-strangled.

"I think it's genetic," said Molly. She stood next to her friend and swooped hers around her neck, up and through, and came out looking better, if a little cockeyed.

"Sometimes when I look at you, I want to push Donnie out a window," said Frances, looking sideways at Molly's chest.

"When you look at *me?*""

"Those fake boobs he talked you into. And it's not just Donnie I'm mad at. Also you, for agreeing to that nonsense."

Molly thought about what Frances said. "I guess I used to be mad at myself too. I know it was a really bad decision to have surgery just to make someone else happy. So dumb. Someday when I have some extra money, I'll get rid of them. But you know, Frances? The whole thing was years ago now. I've let it go. So maybe you can let it go, too."

"Okay, but I'm still gonna push him out of a window if I ever get the chance."

"Understood," said Molly cheerfully. "So, is Chez Papa okay with you? I'm sorry Lawrence has been out of town during your whole visit. He definitely brightens things up when he's around."

"Yep, sure, anyplace is all right with me. Let me just..." she rummaged in a makeup bag and brought out a stubby pencil and made a smoky, smudgy line around her dark brown eyes. They looked enormous and faintly forbidding. Then she fished out a tiny bottle of perfume and spritzed into the air in front of her, and walked into the mist.

"You're irresistible," Molly said drily.

Putting on their heaviest coats and hats, the friends walked quickly into the village in search of company and kirs.

"The Pales!" said Nico as they came inside with a whoosh of cold air.

"Wha—?" said Frances, looking at Molly.

Molly shrugged. "I was in here the other day while you were working. Nico was asking how we met and all that, and I may have told a few stories about our early years."

"And you went to the same college, too? I went to a university in America for two years," said Nico. "I know all about the crazy stuff you college students do." He winked at Frances, and she hopped on a barstool and smiled at him flirtatiously.

"Gracious goodness, I was an *angel*," she said, and Molly and Nico laughed.

Just as Nico put kirs in front of them both, Molly's phone went off, the text sound of a chirping robin. She pulled it out of her pocket and looked at the screen, her eyes wide.

"It's Lawrence..."

"Hi Larry," said Nico, waving at Molly's phone.

"This is unbelievable," said Molly. She stared at the screen hard, as though she must have misread what was there.

"Well?" said Frances, her eyes on Nico as he made a cup of espresso for a middle-aged man at the other end of the bar.

"He says there's been another poisoning. A woman on Madame Desrosiers's street. Cyanide again, but she survived."

"Good heavens! Is it someone you know?"

"I'm...I'm having a hard time believing...maybe Lawrence is just messing with my head."

"Does he like doing that?"

"Well..." Molly thought about it. He did like to tease, but this wasn't exactly teasing. It would be an unfunny practical joke, if he were making it up. "I wish I could call Ben and ask him what's going on."

"What's up, my beauties?" said Nico, having served his coffee and sensing a good story.

"Molly just heard there's been another poisoning," said Frances.

"Larry told you?"

"Yes. How in the world does he always know everything? And when he's in Morocco?"

Nico shrugged. "Who was it? Is she okay?"

"How did you know it was a 'she'?" said Molly, narrowing her eyes at him.

"Don't turn those detective eyes on me," said Nico. "Look, I had a fifty percent chance, it was just a lucky guess."

"Call up Ben!" said Frances. "You know he's sweet on you."

"Do you know that half your expressions come straight out of *Gone With The Wind*? We're not getting ready to go to a barbeque with the Tarleton boys at Twelve Oaks." Molly stood up. She took a sip of her kir. "This is serious. A second woman with cyanide poisoning within a week? Could we have a *serial killer* on our hands?"

"Just call the cop," said Frances. "You're not going to be able to think of anything else until you know the deets, so just call him!"

"I don't think civilians can just call up gendarmes and ask for the latest gossip."

"It's not *gossip*, Molly. You're worried about your safety and the safety of your houseguest who is tremendously important to you. Right?"

"Nico? What's your vote?"

"Call him. What's the worst that can happen? He'll say it's none of your business, see you later."

Molly took out her phone and almost tapped in the number to the station. After some frightening events earlier in the year, she had put his home number in her contacts as well, but she didn't feel like she could call it unless it was an emergency. And while finding out exactly what happened felt like an emergency, she understood that it was not.

But oh, how she wanted to know what was going on! First she texted Lawrence back, asking for more information.

"Let's have one more kir," said Frances. "Will you join us, Nico?"

"I never drink on the job," he said. "But hmm, it's almost empty in here except for you lot...Alphonse is home with a bad cold...okay, never except just this once," said Nico, grinning and reaching for a bottle of schnapps and pouring himself a shot.

"Okay, I'm calling," said Molly. "But I'm going in the back room to do it. I get twitchy if I think anyone is listening to my phone conversations."

Frances waved as Molly walked away. "Pour me another, Nico," she purred. "Did you go to the U.S. to act? You look like you could be in movies."

Nico laughed. "You are such a bullshitter," he said. "And quite entertaining. Go on..."

"I have plenty of questions I want to ask you," she said, smiling at him. "Which university you went to, how your English got so perfect, stuff like that. But while Molly's in the other room, let me ask you this: what do you make of Ben Dufort, anyway? Is he a good guy?"

"Yeah, he's a good guy. I can't say I know him very deep down, you know what I mean?"

"You don't know what makes him tick?"

"Ha, I don't think I know what makes anyone tick."

"Yeah," said Frances. "That's profound, you know that?"

Nico just shook his head and poured himself another shot.

DUFORT TOSSED his cell on his desk, irritated. He stood up and paced back and forth in front of the window, staring at the floor. The evening before, he had called up Marie-Claire to invite her to dinner, and she had refused. Told him she was fond of him and would like to be friends. Only friends.

Well, he could admit to himself that he wasn't in love with Marie-Claire, much as he liked her. But it was still a conclusion he would rather have reached on his own, and it stung.

And then this morning, the lab report had come in—no cyanide in the unmarked jar of face cream. He had been so sure that was the source and was pleased that Perrault had brought it in. Had been hoping for prints, and maybe if they were really lucky, the pharmacy in the village would remember the killer coming in to buy an empty jar, along with face cream.

But they were not lucky.

Dufort passed his hand over his face and squeezed his eyes

tight. Patting his pockets, he found the vial of tincture and let five drops splash under his tongue, not caring if the other officers saw him. All right, he thought, pulling himself together, either Michel has poisoned someone else to throw us off the trail, or it is not Michel. And if it is not, we are nowhere. And if we are nowhere, the killer will keep going and more people will die.

He called for Perrault and Maron, who hustled in, hearing bad news in his tone. "The Arbogast case—either the nurse was wrong about its being cyanide, or she was poisoned some other way. The unmarked jar is clean."

"Damn it," said Perrault.

"All right, this is only a setback," said Dufort. But we move forward. Maron, go interview Arbogast's son. Maybe it's Munchausen by proxy, or maybe he tried to kill his mother but failed. Nose around and see what you think. Perrault, you knock on doors and talk to the neighbors. Ask if they saw anyone unusual coming to the Arbogast's door. And then go to both pharmacies and ask about anyone buying face cream and empty glass jars. You'll need to get phone numbers of everyone who's not at work when you're there, and interview them over the phone."

"It's unlikely that the two poisonings are unrelated, isn't it?" asked Perrault, her head cocked.

"I just told you, the lab says no cyanide. Pay attention, Perrault. Maybe she was poisoned another way, but we will need to talk to the medic to see if he corroborates the son's report of his mother's symptoms. And we proceed with inferences only when we have more facts. Is that clear?"

"Yes sir," said Perrault, feeling tears welling up and sternly ordering them to go away.

"Do you think it could be a serial killer?" asked Maron.

Dufort held his palms in the air. "I don't know," he said. "The two of you—get going. Be meticulous. This is a precarious moment in the investigation—we're dealing with someone who is extremely dangerous, especially since we don't know the motive and are in the dark to stop him. I won't be surprised to get a report of another poisoning quite soon."

Perrault and Maron took off, their expressions serious. Dufort took five more drops, then five more, and then threw the bottle against the wall.

Chapter Twenty-Seven

Michel spent the morning cleaning his small apartment. He was very thorough, taking books off the bookshelf and dusting each one before putting it back on a clean shelf. Everything under the bed was pulled out and dusted as well, and the two windows opened despite the cold to freshen the air in his one-room-with-kitchenette. When there was nothing left to straighten or clean, he put on his thin coat and a scarf and went for a walk.

He wandered aimlessly through Castillac, but the Desrosiers mansion exerted magnetic force on him, pulling him closer when he had had no thought of going anywhere near it. He cut through an alley to get there more quickly, then jumped over a fence and trotted through someone's yard. The streets were relatively crowded with people walking home from the market, and Michel nodded to one or two as they passed, finally coming to his aunt's house. He grasped the freezing iron bars of the gate and looked up at it.

Nothing had changed. The same violet-blue shutters, closed, making the house look blind. The same tattered topiary, the same frost on the roof slates. He thought he saw a strip of light under one of the shutters upstairs, but when he looked more closely he decided he was mistaken. He kept walking, still without any intention to go one place over another, just wanting to be out of his cramped apartment, and always hoping he would run into someone who would take him to lunch or at least buy him a cup of good coffee.

Michel was hungry. Impulsively, he went into a specialty shop, the kind of place that sells fancy chocolates, imported delicacies, and in this case, truffles and foie gras. All foods he adored but had not had the opportunity to taste in a very long time. "Bonjour, madame!" he said warmly to the middle-aged woman behind the counter.

"Bonjour, monsieur," she answered, noticing his thin coat, and also the charming way he smiled at her.

"I'm wondering—your shop is full of the most divine things," he said, after a moment's perusal. "Do you think you could tell me where I might find some oysters?"

"You mean fresh oysters? For those you'll have to go across town to Bedin's place. He gets deliveries from the coast every Saturday morning so this would be a good time to go."

Michel was nodding and smiling. A lock of hair fell into his eyes.

"And if you want smoked oysters? Just at the end of the aisle you're standing in, monsieur."

"Thank you so much," said Michel. He walked slowly down the aisle, looking at all the bottles and cans, his mouth watering. At the end of the aisle, he deftly slipped a tin of smoked oysters into his pocket, then walked slowly up the next aisle. "I believe I will go over to Bedin's right now, thank you again," he said, smiling brilliantly on his way out the door.

"THIS IS SORT OF A TRICKY INVITATION," Molly was saying to Frances as they stood in the foyer as usual, trying to knot their scarves. "It's not every day you go to dinner with someone who's under suspicion for murder."

"Well, do you think they'll speak English? Because if not, I'm just going to be sitting there like a dummy."

"Maybe not. They both speak English with me, but I don't know about their mother. You're sure you want to come?"

"Yeah, yeah, I don't mind being a dummy. Maybe I can come up with a distraction so you can search the house for evidence."

They left La Baraque, Molly locking up behind them. "There's no evidence there," she said, "because I don't for one second think Michel had anything to do with it. Do you?"

"Honestly? Yes. Maybe. I do think it's possible. Five million is a lot of euros, you know?"

Molly felt irritated. In the dark they walked without speaking all the way down rue des Chênes, and then down an alley and a narrow street, more turns and then more until Frances was utterly lost, on the way to Murielle Faure's small house on the other side of the village. It was neat and orderly and drab. Molly knocked on the door, forcing a smile at Frances that she did not feel.

A pause, then the door swung open and Murielle welcomed them inside. "So happy you could come!" she said. "Michel and Adèle have been talking nonstop about the interesting Americans who have come to Castillac. May I get you both a kir?"

Molly and Frances both gratefully said yes, and they came into a small living room where Michel and Adèle were waiting.

"As usual, love your clothes," said Molly as she and Adèle kissed cheeks.

Adèle was wearing a short wool skirt, thick tights, and boots with a shearling lining. "Merci, Molly," she said. "It's good to see you again." Adèle and Michel greeted Frances with interest and Frances performed her gesticulations that she thought communicated good spirits and friendly feelings, and the siblings laughed.

"Oh, Maman, I brought something for us to have before dinner, do you have any little toasts to go with them?" Michel reached into a knapsack and brought out the tin of smoked oysters and handed it to his mother.

"Michel, how wonderful!" she exclaimed, putting an arm around him and giving him a squeeze. "Always full of surprises, my dear. Can you imagine how many frogs he brought me when he was a little boy?" she said to the guests, who laughed politely.

Molly saw Adèle giving Michel a hard look. She tried to read it: was she jealous of her mother's attention? Wishing she had something to offer too? Doesn't like oysters?

And then, seemingly from nowhere, the most dreaded circumstance of any dinner party: a long, uncomfortable moment that stretched longer and longer. All of them were suddenly at a complete loss for words, and the feeling was compounded the longer the silence went on. All Molly could think about was dead Aunt Josephine lying on the bathroom floor, and then of her fears for Michel, but of course she couldn't mention any of that, and not being able to mention it meant she could think of nothing else. Murielle gave Michel's shoulders another squeeze, then left without a word and went into the kitchen. Adèle walked to the window and pretended to look outside, and Michel smiled ruefully and shook his head.

"I'm afraid we are all thinking about the same thing," he said. "So I suppose it is up to me to say it out loud. It's true, Dufort has been talking with me. Nothing formal—not yet anyway. But it is pretty plain that he considers me a suspect, possibly even the prime suspect. He came around to my place this morning, in fact, after talking to me yesterday afternoon. According to him, it turns out I am going to inherit Aunt Josephine's fortune, which would be lovely if it didn't put a noose around my neck."

Adèle made a humorless chuckle and shook her head. "If Dufort knew anything, he would know you are incapable of hurting anyone. It's just not in Michel's nature to do something so...so aggressive."

"Congratulations—and I'm so sorry," said Molly. "Do you understand?" Molly asked Frances, since everyone had spoken in French.

"Of course not," said Frances cheerfully.

Molly translated for her. "Well, I don't know," Frances said. "Can we really say that anyone—and I'm including myself, absolutely—wouldn't ever be capable of murder? Not *ever*? I'm kinda on the side of everyone might do it, if the conditions were all met. Some of us have more conditions than others, yeah sure, but unless you believe in angels..." She shrugged.

Molly translated for the others. Adèle gave Frances a frosty look. Michel smiled at her. "Actually, I agree with you, Frances," he said in well-accented English. "I did not poison my aunt. But I cannot say that I would never kill anyone, no matter what. And I am a bit affronted that you think me such a placid soul, incapable of action!" he said, still smiling, to his sister.

"I don't think you should joke that way," Adèle said softly.

Murielle returned with kirs and a small plate heaped with toasts, and a saucer of the smoked oysters in the center. "These are very good for your love life, I've always heard," she said, looking at Michel.

"To love!" said Michel, lifting his glass and rolling his eyes.

Molly watched Adèle. Her face had a sort of frozen look, with the plastic smile you see on television newsreaders. The four of them struggled to make conversation, whereas every time they had been together before, they had chattered away so easily. Molly looked around the room, which was almost entirely devoid of decoration except for a bouquet of dried flowers in one corner. Nothing on the walls. Just a sofa and four chairs wedged into the small space, a dim lamp, and a hooked rug. Everything spotlessly clean.

Frances ate most of the oysters. Finally, since the other three were barely speaking, she began talking in English, telling stories about her eccentric mother who believed cars were evil and thus only rode her bicycle everywhere, and rambling about which pastries she and Molly liked the best and why. Molly finally began to talk about the work being done on the pigeonnier, but since Pierre Gault was doing a perfectly good job, it didn't make much of a story. Adèle kept giving Michel looks until finally he shifted in his chair so that his back was toward her.

"*À table!*" called Murielle, and with relief the four went into the kitchen and sat down at a rough wooden table.

"I must warn you," said Michel with a twinkle in his eye, "Maman is a very talented woman, but perhaps not so much in the kitchen."

"I dare you to say that in French," said Adèle, laughing, her expression unfreezing for a moment.

Murielle put two baguettes on the table along with a pot of sweet butter and another of country pâté. Molly and Frances, feeling awkward, dove into the food with gusto.

Once Murielle was seated at the table too, conversation revived somewhat. At least they were able to muster up some chitchat about the weather, and various other topics with no emotional or intellectual complication. Frances pressed on Molly's toe under the table and Molly pressed back, a method of communication they had developed in childhood in which the first said, "Can you believe this?" and the second responded, "I know! It's crazy!"

Dinner was lamb stew. The meat was tough and the sauce bland, but Molly and Frances did their duty and ate it up, making compliments to Murielle. They were not offered coffee or anything to drink after dinner, for which they were grateful, and after a few moments of kissing goodbye and effusive thanks, they were back outside in the cold and dark, walking quickly back to La Baraque.

"Well, that was excruciating," said Molly.

"I'm starting to understand your sleuthing a little more," said Frances, as she would her scarf up over her head to protect her ears. "Something is off in that house, for sure. I'm super curious about what it is."

"Me too," said Molly. "And I'm going to find out somehow."

Chapter Twenty-Eight

1966

It was a hot spring night, the village quiet enough that the cuckoo asserting its territory could be plainly heard. Josephine had dressed carefully in white, shiny, imitation Courrèges boots and a dress so short she was barely covered. Her hair was piled up on her head with curling tendrils falling around her face, which was made up so that she imagined she looked practically like Jean Shrimpton, whom she admired more than any other model.

She had to look perfect. She had to entice him, to lure him, to tempt him.

Josephine had paid attention to his schedule, and he was a man of regular habits so it was not difficult to guess when he might be walking by the park on his way home from work. She waited behind a thick shrubbery breathing in the thick, complicated smells of the spring air, trembling from excitement, knowing her life was about to change.

He was a dull man, really, an electrician—probably the most tiresome occupation a man could have. Josephine did not understand herself well enough to know why she was choosing him, of all people, a man who inspired contempt more than love. She heard footsteps and held her breath. Pushing a branch to one side, she looked to make sure it was him, and then stepped out onto the sidewalk in his path.

"Josephine! How funny to see you!" Albert stopped suddenly so as to avoid running into her. He looked down at her, unable to help noticing her curvy body in the slight dress, and her legs so dramatically on display. He would never in a million years have told anyone, but he had a thing for women in boots.

"I'm *so* glad I ran into you," said Josephine, smiling up at him through her mascaraed lashes. "You're *exactly* the man I was hoping to see. Do you think you might—I know I'm imposing, but—if you could humor me, just a little? It won't take a moment."

Albert's expression softened. "I would be happy to help," he said, not allowing himself to look at her legs and the hem of her scandalously short dress. "You know I think of your family quite warmly."

Josephine's face hardened for a moment and then the moment passed. She glanced at Albert coquettishly. "I'm being silly, really," she said. "But would you come into the park with me, just for a few minutes? I used to love the swings when I was a child—it was my favorite, happiest thing to fly way up high. And so..." she looked down and moved the toe of her boot in a circle around her.

"You want me to push you?" said Albert, happy that he understood. "Of course I will!"

Josephine felt awash in gratification that he had taken her hints with such enthusiasm. They went through the gate and down the gravel path to the playground section of the park. It was hidden from the street by a wide bank of viburnums, newly leafed out. It was almost as though they were alone in the countryside, surrounded by greenery, even though they were practically in the center of Castillac.

Josephine settled herself in the swing, her underwear almost showing in front because her dress was so short. Albert put his hands on her back. He could feel the strap of her brassière, and he swallowed and squeezed his eyes shut, trying not to think about her body even as he had his hands firmly against her.

"Push me," said Josephine, sounding at once like a child and a queen, and Albert pushed.

She flew higher and higher, turning her face to the sky and seeing the stars spread out over the village. "Harder!" she shouted to him, and shrieked with happiness when he pushed her even higher. Eventually his hands drifted south, and did not push on her back but lower down, and finally on the swell of her bottom. He allowed Josephine's swinging to wind down, slower and slower, and when she had stopped altogether and she was thanking him breathily, Albert came around to face her. He lifted Josephine from the swing and kissed her, more ardently than he had thought himself capable of.

There was an equipment shed not far from the swings, and before long, Josephine was pressed against that shed as Albert kissed her neck, her lips, her forehead. And when he lifted her dress, she did not protest but leaned her head back, looked at the stars and smiled, having gotten precisely what she had planned for.

Chapter Twenty-Nine

2005

The Sunday morning routine had become coffee at Chez Papa followed by frites, and Molly and Frances wasted no time getting there, still feeling a bit hungover from the awkward dinner party at the Faure's.

"Bonjour, my beauties!" said Nico, when they walked in and began unpeeling their winter clothes.

Frances gave him a crooked smile and reached across the bar to touch his arm. "We should have had dinner with you last night," she said.

"An excellent idea," said Nico. "Were you bored?"

"It wasn't that," said Molly, settling on a stool. "Coffee, stat. Please. We went over to Adèle and Michel's—"

"Did Dufort crash through the door and arrest him?"

"Not funny, Nico."

Nico winked at Frances, who laughed.

"Anyway," said Molly, "it just...I don't know why, but you know how it sometimes happens: you go to someone's house for dinner and it just falls flat. The conversation...lagged."

"I'll say," said Frances. "Of course, I couldn't understand it anyway. I'm just glad to be here now. Much better view," she said, looking at Nico and winking back.

"Good Lord," said Molly, rolling her eyes. She sat staring at a fleck of dust on the bar, thinking.

A gust of cold hit their backs as two men came in. "Beer!" one shouted to Nico, and they sat at a table close to the bar. "He is always making the most dramatic gesture he can think of," said one man to his friend. "And now, he can enjoy all the attention that a night in jail—if he's lucky—will bring!" the two men laughed uproariously, one of them slapping the table repeatedly.

"What's up?" said Nico, delivering two frosty glasses of beer to their table.

"Just Jean-François cooling his heels in jail, that's all." They cracked up again.

"What'd he do?"

"We were at the demonstration yesterday in Périgueux. The garbage collectors were on strike. It's horrible, the working conditions they endure! They had plenty of support, students coming out, and all kinds of workers...and Jean-François, he gets so worked up that he throws a brick through the window of a shop. Glass everywhere! A gendarme saw the whole thing and carted him off in seconds, Jean-François yelling the whole time about *liberté* and *fraternité*. What a crétin!" His friend was holding his belly, which hurt from laughing so hard.

"Maybe that's exactly who Dufort should be looking at, instead of Michel," said Molly to Frances, surreptitiously pointing behind her.

"Who? You know I can't understand a word they're saying."

Molly leaned her mouth next to Frances's ear. "Jean-François is in jail. Threw a brick at a demonstration. You know the guy—he's Sabrina's boyfriend. The type who's always pissed off about something."

"Does he have a record?" Molly said to Nico in a low voice.

"Jean-François?" Nico laughed. "A mile long, I'd guess. He's been to every demonstration within three hundred kilometers for the last ten years. He usually does his best to get arrested—might get his picture in the paper that way."

"Hmm," said Molly. "You know, I saw him going back into the mansion, after Desrosiers was killed. He was carrying a sack with him. Now, you know something's not right about that."

"His girlfriend worked there, right? He could have been going to get her things. Probably left a sweater there or something. Hey, let's have some frites," said Frances, never losing sight of the best reason to come to Chez Papa on Sunday mornings. "And tell me, Nico—does the chef make his own mayonnaise? Because if so, bring some out with the frites, will ya?"

"Your wish is my command, Princess," said Nico with a smirk as he disappeared into the kitchen.

"Don't even," said Frances as Molly was about to speak. "I know you're going to blather on about how Michel didn't kill his dear Aunt Josephine and blah blah blah. The fact is, Molly, you're attracted to him. And that's blinding you to reality."

"So it's case closed as far as you're concerned? Some detective you are. You just go along with what Dufort says and don't question anything?"

"I didn't say anything about case closed. All I'm saying is that you, dear friend, have lost your objectivity. And you know, Michel does remind me of Donnie, just the tiniest bit…"

"Who's Donnie?" asked Nico, putting his elbows on the bar and stretching his back.

"Never mind," said Molly.

"Molly's ex," said Frances. "Total crétin," she added. "Hey…did you hear me speaking French right there?"

Molly wasn't laughing. Maybe because Frances had hit on some truth, and she had been too willing to give Michel a pass. And also, why in the world would she think that the lock of hair falling into his eyes was charming anyway? It's just a dumb hank of hair. Means absolutely nothing.

"So about Adèle and Michel—have I got this right, that no one knows who their father is?" Molly said to Nico.

Nico looked up at the ceiling and thought this over. "I guess not. Honestly, I'm not the best person to ask. My parents always had their noses in books and didn't spend any time talking about other villagers, so I missed out on a lot of gossip."

"I'm so sorry," said Frances.

Nico laughed. "You're a trip," he said.

Molly could see where this was going. She wasn't at all sure it was a good idea, but she was sure it was none of her business, so she spent the next half hour not listening to Nico and Frances flirting, and trying to come up with a plan to shift suspicion off Michel.

Chapter Thirty

Maron waited until Sunday afternoon to stop by Claudette Mercier's, guessing correctly that she was at church in the morning. He also thought she would probably be having Sunday dinner at someone's house, since she had a large family in Castillac, but on that particular Sunday, Claudette had felt a cold coming on and stayed home once church was over. Maron knocked on her door, ready with a list of questions.

"Why, Officer Maron, bonjour!" said Claudette, opening the door for him. "What a surprise! I was just making some soup. I've got that tickly feeling in my nose like I'm right on the verge of catching a cold, you know how that is? I hope you've made progress. Did you catch the burglar, is that why you're here? Shall I come to the station for a lineup?" she asked, her eyes bright.

"No, I'm afraid I haven't made any headway on your case," said Maron. "I've got my eye out, though, you can count on that."

"Oh, I'm so glad to hear it. You know, it isn't easy living alone, a woman of my age. I never minded being alone when I was young; in fact, I liked it, to be honest. Never one for the boys and such, except for my Declan. I miss him terribly, as you might imagine. And now, you know, it can feel awfully...awfully vulnerable, being here by myself. I don't think Diderot would do much to protect me," she said, pointing her elbow at the tabby cat, which was stretched out on the back of the sofa, sound asleep.

"I would agree with you there," said Maron, inwardly sighing. Old people made him want to yawn, even this one, whom he thought might be Desrosiers's killer. *Might*, he added to himself, defending himself against Dufort.

"May I get you a coffee? I'm afraid I don't have much else to offer besides a bit of toast and jam. Declan liked a big breakfast—a lot of men do, I'm sure. The soup won't be ready for at least another hour."

"I'm fine, Madame Mercier. I was hoping to talk to you about a few things, if you are feeling up to it."

"Oh, I'm not sick yet," she said, winking at him, which made him tense. "Ask away, young man!" She gestured to a high-backed chair with velvet upholstery. "And make yourself comfortable."

Maron sat gingerly in the velvet chair. The room made him feel slightly claustrophobic. "Let's start with Anne Arbogast. Do you know her or her son Lucas?"

"Not well," said Claudette, wiggling into the sofa cushion. "She was younger than I by a few years. I know her to say hello in the street but not anything more."

Maron nodded. "You know she nearly died from cyanide poisoning a few days ago?"

Claudette's eyes widened and she shook her head. What was happening to her sweet little village?

"How about Josephine Desrosiers. You were schoolmates, is that right?"

"Yes, but Officer Maron, I thought you had questions about the break-in."

"I'll get to that," Maron lied. "What was your relationship with Josephine like, when you were young?"

Claudette looked hard at Maron. She found him difficult to read, nothing at all like Declan, or any of the men in her family for that matter, who were all rather genial and liked to laugh. This officer looked as though he hadn't had a giggle in months.

"Well," she said, "We were good friends, as children. Went to the same school, of course. At least, we were good friends for a while."

"And then?"

Claudette shrugged. She said nothing. She looked at the front door as though wishing someone would come in and interrupt the conversation, then trailed a hand along Diderot's back, waking him up. "You know how it is in the schoolyard. Children can be vicious, really. The situation was that my family was prosperous—my father owned a big hardware store in the village, and oh my, he did quite a business, I'll tell you—but Josephine's family...was rather hard up. Her parents ran an épicerie but I believe it was a faltering business. You know how it is, Officer Maron—some people's personalities are suited to sales, and some are not. My father was helpful and popular, and people wanted to buy from him. Josephine's father, well, he was a sour kind of man. Who wants to buy their jam from someone who glowers at them, you know?"

"And this inequality of finances, it came between you?"

"I certainly didn't care. It wasn't important to me, although I suppose that's easy for me to say, when I never had to go without. My interest was always food. I wanted to be in the kitchen all the time, learning how to make everything! So finery and such—that was what Josephine cared about, but not me. Eventually her envy..."

Maron waited.

"Well, she became bitter and unpleasant toward me, and we stopped spending time together."

"And how old were you when this rift occurred?"

"Oh, I don't know. This was all a very long time ago, Officer Maron! Before lycée, I would guess. Twelve, thirteen years old, something like that."

Maron nodded. "And Madame Desrosiers was not well off until her marriage?"

"Well, not even then, not right off. Albert didn't have any money at all when they married. I was shocked, actually, that she married him—always thought she would go after someone rich. She was that kind of person."

Maron noted a hint of coldness that came into Madame Mercier's voice.

"But of course, there was the baby," she said, shrugging, and giving Maron a meaningful look.

"Baby?"

"Oh, yes. Now, let me assure you that I don't judge them. You might not think it to look at me now, but I understand passion, Officer Maron. Declan and I—well, to get back to Josephine, yes, she seemed to be pregnant right off the bat, if you catch my meaning."

Maron wasn't sure that he did. "But Madame Desrosiers has no children. Am I mistaken? Or did something happen?"

Claudette stood up, frustrated with Maron who was rather trying to talk to. "I'm afraid the baby was stillborn," said Claudette, "but that is not my point. What I'm saying is that it was plain to everyone in the village that Josephine was pregnant before marriage."

Maron just stared, unable to see why this mattered to the case.

"She would never have married Albert otherwise, don't you see? In those days, the only option in that circumstance was marriage, if you wanted to escape the condemnation of nearly everyone in the village. Josephine wanted to be admired; she had no tolerance at all for being shunned or thought badly of. But even more to the point—Albert was poor, and she wanted money! She was always so envious of me because my Papa was generous and gave me pretty things. And yet—as I'm sure you know, Albert ended up inventing something or other and making truckloads of money after all. Josephine always was the luckiest woman ever."

"Not so lucky to end up poisoned on the bathroom floor of a restaurant," said Maron, watching for her reaction.

But Claudette just shrugged again. "Eh, who knows. What you young people can't understand is that there are worse things than death." She stood up, having had enough of talking about the past. "I'm sorry, but I feel that cold coming on and I'd like to have a rest. Thank you for coming to see me, and do let me know if there's a break in the case."

Maron quickly made his escape, noting that Mercier did not specify which case she was talking about, and thinking that nothing she said made him any less inclined to believe she was capable of murder.

Chapter Thirty-One

Now that's more like it, Dufort said to himself when the next lab report came in. The chemist had tested all of the jars of face cream Perrault had brought in, including the commercial ones that appeared to be either unopened or barely used. The unmarked jar had indeed tested clear of any poisons (though in Dufort's opinion, cosmetics and lotions were usually loaded with all kinds of less-than-salubrious chemicals, but at least they were legal and not immediately lethal). One of the barely used jars was Chanel, a monstrously expensive beauty product in a small glass jar: the Chanel cream had been replaced with dimethyl sulfoxide, which had been loaded with cyanide. The chemist pointed out that dimethyl sulfoxide was readily available to anyone and would allow for very efficient absorption of the poison into the skin. Madame Arbogast could easily have stepped from her bath and moisturized with the adulterated cream, and exhibited symptoms within fifteen minutes, as her son stated.

In a side note, the chemist said that upon further testing he found that none of the jars held what their labels promised. The Chanel cream was in a Guerlain jar, mixed with lye; the Guerlain cream was in the unmarked jar, mixed with naphthalene from crushed mothballs. Neither of these was likely to be fatal, but Madame Arbogast would possibly have had unpleasant symptoms if she had applied either of the creams to her face.

So: two poisonings, both older women. Unrelated to each other, and possibly unknown to each other even though they lived on the same street, given how reclusive Desrosiers had been. Curious that not one but an array of poisons had been used—and why the mixing up of containers? But of course the important question, thought Dufort, is whether one or both of the victims were selected on purpose, or were simply the unlucky casualties of someone who wanted to cause random destruction and mayhem.

Maron and Perrault came in on time, and Dufort got them up to date on the lab report. "And what do the two of you have for me?"

Perrault shrugged. "None of the neighbors saw anything. But if we're thinking the murderer is someone from Castillac— someone the neighbors might know—then they might have seen him and not paid any attention. Also, I went to the hospital and talked to the medic. He says Arbogast's symptoms had pretty much faded by the time they got there. She was conscious, not gasping, and her skin was ruddy but not abnormally so. He reports that she did look as though she had been through some-thing—her hair was in disarray, and she was sweating—but overall, she was right as rain, and enjoying a nip of brandy."

"There's no reason to think the son was involved," said Maron. "I talked to some of the neighbors as well, and he appears to be devoted to his mother, and genuinely relieved that she is all right. No reports of fighting or falling out or anything like that. He's upset that she's always spending money on these ridiculous creams that promise to make you look like Deneuve, and he says now maybe she'll listen to him.

"However," Maron continued, steeling himself, "I also dropped by Claudette Mercier's—"

Dufort looked exasperated. "So you think she poisoned both

of them? Did Mercier and Arbogast know each other? Is there any evidence of a motive or have you promoted the poor woman to full-on serial killer now?" Dufort's tone was biting, and it was clear his questions were rhetorical only.

"You have another way this went down?" said Maron, barely able to keep the contempt out of his voice.

Dufort gave him a long, level look. Maron glanced away. Dufort stalked around the side of his desk and then back again. "All right. Michel Faure could have dropped a bag of face creams off at the Arbogast house. Perhaps with a note saying You've Won a Grand Prize! or some sort of nonsense like that. He rings the bell and walks away. The son is at work and Madame Arbogast comes to the door, sees the bag sitting on her front step—maybe it's a fancy bag too, from Chanel—and inside is her favorite indulgence and fancy, expensive ones at that. She can't wait to take her bath that evening and try out her new goodies. Then we have a second cyanide murder, unconnected with Desrosiers as far as we know, and suspicion moves away from the family and toward some nut choosing random victims."

He walked to the window and raised his arms up, stretching to one side and then the other. "Well? Is it plausible?"

"I think so," said Perrault. "Although unless Michel knows the Arbogasts, he wouldn't have known that she was nuts for face cream. But really, what woman wouldn't try a little Chanel, if it dropped out of the sky? The stuff probably goes for close to 300 euros a jar."

"That little thing?" said Maron, disbelieving.

"Fantasy can be expensive," said Dufort. "All right then. Maron, first make some calls and put the word out that no one in Castillac should use any face cream they did not buy themselves. And they should check any jars bought recently for signs of tampering. Get that on the radio and the internet. Then go find Michel. If he'll let you into his apartment, so much the better. Ask him his whereabouts on Saturday, see if anyone can corroborate. Perrault, you and I are going to see if we can figure out where the source of the cyanide is. There are some factories on the edge of Périgueux, we're going to drive up and have a look around, ask some questions. Someone is either being paid to hand over a quantity of the poison, or it's being stolen." Dufort was already at the door with his coat on. "Come on, let's move," he said, his voice still hard. "It's Monday. I'd like to have someone in custody by the end of the week, not next year."

Maron and Perrault exchanged a rare glance of comradeship, as Dufort was almost never this testy.

Chapter Thirty-Two

"Yes, I'm aware that it's none of my business. Also that I'm in no position to offer advice about romance. All I'm saying, Franny—all I'm saying is—don't break the poor man's heart."

"Oh, you're funny. Nico's not any more serious than I am. Gracious goodness, we're just going to hang out tonight and have a good time together, not elope and have a pack of love children," said Frances. "Do you have any good eyeliner? The stupid security person at the airport confiscated mine and this stuff I picked up isn't doing the job. I think he was trying to flirt with me or something because eyeliner is hardly a weapon."

"In your hands, it sort of is," said Molly, snorting into her coffee.

The orange cat suddenly appeared from nowhere and jumped up on the kitchen counter.

"Well, hello!" said Frances. "I didn't know you had a cat. Where have you been hiding, pretty girl?" she said, stepping over to pet it.

"No!" shouted Molly. "It bites! And I don't know where that hell-fiend came from. I haven't seen it in over a month. But it is *not* my cat. It just shows up occasionally to bite me and run away laughing."

"I'm a cat person," said Frances. She rubbed the cat's lips and the cat fell over onto its back, purring. "See? She knows I'm on her side."

"I was on her side too until she bit me."

"Just give it up and get a dog, Molls. You can't make yourself be a cat person when you're not one on the inside. Cats can tell."

Molly snickered. "I do want to get a dog. I've been sort of thinking one would just show up."

"Since when do you just sit back and cross your fingers? You're a go-git-'em kinda girl, Molly Sutton! Is there a shelter anywhere nearby?"

"No idea. I'm not ready to take that on right now. Anyway, today I'm going to paint the hallway, finally. The terrible paint job the last owners did has finally pushed me over the edge. I can't stand looking at those wavery lines one more second. Plus I got a little crazy and bought mango-orange paint."

"What, no sleuthing today? Are you feeling okay?"

"Yep. Fine. Well, maybe a little dejected."

Frances waited for an explanation but Molly got up and went to her bedroom to change into old clothes she could paint in. "Dejected about what?" Frances said, following her. "Are you really upset about my date with Nico?"

Molly cracked up. "God, no, it's not that. I just…I'm afraid for Michel. I get the feeling Dufort has made up his mind, and the inheritance thing seems so damning. I really really in my heart of hearts believe he's innocent, but what can I do to prove that? Nothing. I'm just praying the cops don't find a way to tie him to that second poisoning. That would really cook his goose."

"But Molls, if he's tied to the second poisoning, his goose *should* be cooked."

Molly shrugged. "Here's my eyeliner. Listen, you haven't bought any face cream since you've been here, have you? Just on the off chance the poisoner is like that Tylenol murderer back home, we should probably be careful about what we're putting on our faces."

"Check," said Frances. "So, give me the lowdown on Nico. Other girlfriends? Other jobs? I know he studied in the U.S., but he won't say much about it."

"I know nothing. That's all going to be up to you to find out."

"Some detective you are."

"You know, I knew a private investigator once. Most of his work was stakeouts trying to catch cheating spouses."

"I bet he had plenty of work."

"Sure did. Either people are really suspicious or cheating a lot."

"Or both."

Dressed in her painting clothes, Molly went to the closet where she'd stashed the paint and supplies and started to get everything arranged in the hallway: drop cloth, paint can opener, paddle to stir up the paint, brushes, roller, and paint tray. Frances talked about Nico, about the time when she and Molly were kids and they had made a magic potion by mixing all of Molly's mother's makeup together in a bowl, and about her ideas for a new jingle. Molly dipped the roller in the tray, smoothed it along the bottom, and lifted it to the wall.

"Painting is maybe my favorite job," she said, just as Frances was waving her arms talking about the jingle and stepped into the paint tray, flipping it over. Mango-orange paint flew everywhere, including all over Frances's pants and in Molly's hair.

"Oh!" said Molly, wanting to laugh, but feeling too depressed about the river of paint oozing over the edge of the dropcloth and onto the floor.

After a flood of apologies, Frances went back to the cottage to change and Molly began to clean up. But as she wiped up the paint with a sponge and squeezed it out into a bucket of water, it finally, blessedly hit her: what had Manette said the other day about Josephine Desrosiers having a stillborn baby? Molly was sure she remembered that French law required a substantial share of an estate to go to any children. If that baby wasn't actually still-born, and was alive somewhere, then Michel couldn't be the main beneficiary. Wouldn't that be enough to move him out from under the cloud of suspicion?

Was this a brilliant idea, the lead of a lifetime—or had she watched too many soaps as a teenager?

For a moment, Molly was giddy thinking of the possibilities. A moment later, crestfallen (and covered with paint), she realized that to save him from Dufort, Michel would have to have known about the child. Otherwise he would still have a solid motive, even if it was due to his ignorance of the true situation. But she couldn't worry about that now. The first thing was to make abso-lutely sure that Josephine Desrosiers was as childless as everyone thought.

Molly had no ideas about how to do that. But as she swooped the roller up and down the hallway walls, she felt pretty sure something would occur to her. At long last, she had a lead to follow, and all she had to do was follow it.

Chapter Thirty-Three

I t was late when Dufort and Perrault finished up at the factories outside Périgueux. They didn't speak on the drive home, both of them dispirited by an afternoon of dead ends. Managers at all three places had been defensive and uncooperative, insisting that the cyanide at their plants was used solely for electroplating/film development/textile production. They bristled at the idea that any of their workers could be trying to make a few euros on the side by selling the poison to anyone, saying that the material was tightly controlled and all was accounted for.

There was no way to link the cyanide in the face creams to the cyanide at the plants; Dufort had ruled that out with the chemist before making the trip. His only hope had been finding someone who had noticed something suspicious, and was willing to come forward. He had no evidence that the managers were lying and no reason not to believe them.

Cyanide is found naturally, after all—in apple seeds, cassava roots, cigarettes, and myriad other places. How convenient it would have been for a manager to point out a worker and say that he needed money and been seen messing around with the poison in a restricted area...but that was the stuff of Agatha Christie, not real life.

Is one little shred of evidence too much to ask, Dufort thought, feeling sorry for himself as he drove a little too fast down the hill leading south from Périgueux. Perrault looked out the window, hiding her morose expression. She had so wanted to make a splash as a gendarme while she was home, before her first deployment to another *département*. Be the one to figure out the puzzle before anyone else, spot the thing out of place, the crucial bit of evidence that had been overlooked. Make her family proud, after all the trouble she'd given them when she was younger and a faltering student.

She, and Dufort, were running out of time. In a matter of months, they would be gone from Castillac, and neither wanted to be leaving a possible serial killer behind, their duty undone.

Dufort dropped her off at her apartment, and Perrault mumbled, "Thanks," and went inside. Dufort felt a painful pounding on the side of his head. He didn't feel like going home but couldn't think of anywhere else he wanted to go either. He pulled away from the curb and drove through the village, north on rue des Chênes. He passed Molly's house and saw that the pallet of stones in her front yard had been moved, and wondered how her project with the pigeonnier was going. He kept driving, taking smaller and smaller roads until he was on a gravel track just wide enough for his car, deep in the forest. He stopped the car and got out.

The drumbeat in his head wasn't about Desrosiers, although she was in the front of his conscious mind. No, it was those two older cases—Valerie Boutillier and Elizabeth Martin, who had disappeared from Castillac and never been found—whose presences thudded into his brain so relentlessly.

The weather was mild and the moon was out. Dufort started to walk through the forest, bushwhacking, letting branches whip behind him, his eyes barely taking in where he was going.

Imagine how it would feel to be lost, and to know that everyone had given up looking for you.

That was the thought he couldn't shake out of his mind, no matter how many other cases had come along. No matter how many reports he had written up or matters resolved. He knew that a man in his position should be tougher, not let unsolved cases eat at him like that.

But they did. And Dufort sensed that all the herbal tincture, breathing exercises, and five-mile runs in the world were not going to change that.

He was either in the wrong job, or he needed to succeed 100% of the time. And he knew perfectly well that was impossible.

Circling back to his car, Dufort felt somewhat better thanks to the exercise, and perhaps also because he had faced the truth head on. The road was narrow with high banks on either side, and he was forced to back up all the way to an intersection before he could turn the car around and head for home. He planned to make himself a simple dinner, drink a bottle of beer, and see if he could think over the details of the Desrosiers case and have a flash of insight.

ॐ

BUT WHEN HE drove near La Baraque, Dufort slowed down, and then impulsively turned into Molly's driveway.

"Well, hello Ben!" said Molly, opening the door wide. She was covered in mango-orange paint. "Come on in! Sorry that every-thing's a mess. I started painting the hallway, as you can see—it looks pretty good, too, if I say so myself, such a nice cheerful color! It was gray before, which I didn't mind so much, and it went well with the white molding, but the former owners must have hired a painter with palsy or something because the gray was all over the white molding and the white came up on the wall—anyway, it looked sloppy and awful and every time I walked down the hallway, which is about thirty million times a day, I would notice it and grimace."

Dufort looked slightly stunned.

"I know, I'm babbling. Please, come sit. Can I get you a drink?"

Dufort surprised himself by asking if she had any cider.

"Sure, I adore it so I always have some, I'll get you a glass. Sit by the stove! It's warmed up a lot—which obviously you know, since you came in from outside..." Molly shook her head, wondering why she was gibbering like such a fool. She uncorked the cider and poured herself and Dufort bubbly glasses.

"I'm sorry to drop in unannounced," said Dufort. "I was out driving, trying to sort out my thoughts, and just ended up here."

A pause, during which they looked at each other frankly, and with affection. He said, "Have you ever wondered whether the path you've chosen for yourself has turned out to be a huge mistake?"

Molly let out an undignified hoot as she handed him a glass and sat down on the sofa beside him. "Have I made huge mistakes? Are you kidding me? Didn't I tell you about my marriage, my job, my whole life in the U.S. that I gave up to come here? One long string of unfortunate choices." She slapped her palms on her thighs and grinned.

Dufort nodded. Molly waited for him to elaborate, but he did not.

"Would it be indelicate of me to ask how the Desrosiers case is going?" she said softly.

"No. Horribly," said Dufort, and for some reason he started laughing. It felt as though being able to admit his failure to Molly lifted some of the weight off his back, and he laughed harder at the relief of it. "We've got nothing!" he said, and cracked up again, though by the time the laughter died out, most of the pressure was back.

"The case has some features I can't make any sense of. For

instance—the Arbogast poisoning. The poison was in a face cream jar, just as we suppose Desrosiers's was. But Arbogast was given several other jars of very expensive cream, and the cream was switched—Guerlain in the Chanel jar, for example. These other jars also had poison in them, but nothing lethal.

"I absolutely don't get it. What would be the point of going to all that trouble?"

Molly was looking off into space, not moving. "Wait," she said. "That reminds me of something..." She snapped her fingers. "Got it! Adèle told me that Josephine was really awful to anyone who worked for her. And that once she took all the gardening chemicals and switched them all up so they were in the wrong containers, and the gardener got seriously hurt. Acid burns, I think."

Dufort and Molly looked at each other. "So we have the modus operandi of a dead person."

"Less than helpful. Sorry." Molly topped off their glasses and then leaned back into the sofa cushion and sighed. "Okay, listen," said Molly, combing her paint-spattered hair back from her face. "I know I've no right to say this, but I'm just going to say it anyway. I don't think it's Michel. I think it will be a terrible miscarriage of justice if you arrest him. And I know it's none of my business and I have not one single bit of proof to give you."

"You like him?"

"Well, I...yes, of course. I mean, I don't *like*-like him, if that's what you mean."

"I am not sure what *like*-like means," said Dufort, amused.

"I mean he's a friend. Only a friend. Not a...a romantic interest."

"Ah."

Molly smiled to herself, because when she said it she knew it was true, which was something of a relief. It was easier to trust her thoughts about the case if her interest in Michel was only a friendly one.

"Have you checked out Jean-François, Sabrina's boyfriend?"

NELL GODDIN

"He's an activist, Molly. That arrest record has nothing to do with violent crime."

"I'm not talking about that. I saw him going into the Desrosiers mansion long after Josephine's death. I mean, I don't know the protocol about these situations, but I expect once the owner of a house dies, she isn't going to continue to pay for a housekeeper to come clean up when no one is living there? So why would the housekeeper's boyfriend be letting himself in the front door, carrying a bag?"

"I will talk to him," promised Dufort. "But don't get your hopes up."

They drank their cider and talked of other things, until Dufort glanced at his watch and saw that it was nearly midnight. He apologized for staying so late, they kissed cheeks, and he drove home on the empty streets of Castillac, feeling more confused than ever.

Chapter Thirty-Four

Molly was up early the next morning. She wanted to talk to her friend Lawrence and tried texting him in Morocco, but heard nothing back.

At least maybe that means there hasn't been another poisoning.

She drank two cups of coffee while staring into space, trying and failing to come up with a way to find out any information at all about Josephine Desrosiers's baby. Most of her mind knew that it was a total long shot, thinking that the baby had actually lived —a long shot that belonged in a melodrama, to boot. But families were weird, and people were secretive, and that was true enough for her to proceed.

She showered, mostly succeeding in getting the orange out of her hair, got dressed, and started the walk to the village. Because how many thorny problems did not seem easier while eating a pastry? Zero, was Molly's firm opinion. She was going to try a beignet for the first time, along with a third cup of coffee, thinking that was going to be a magic combination.

It had gotten colder again and the sky had that dirty gray, heavy look of snow. Christmas was the following week, and she realized she had made no plan except for ordering the bûche de noël—had bought no presents, had no tree. She felt as though she were disconnected from the calendar somehow, as though she had too many other things to think about.

Ben Dufort, for one...

As Molly reached the cemetery, she slowed down. Then stopped. Wait. Maybe there was a grave for the Desrosiers baby! Walking quickly, she went through the gate and under the 'Priez pour vos morts' inscription, looking for Josephine's grave. The cemetery was neat and orderly, with no sign of any disturbance. An old man was kneeling in front of a grave that was decorated with vases of artificial flowers. Molly could hear him talking.

She found Desrosiers's grave easily enough. The headstone was simple and the inscription said Josephine Faure Desrosiers. 1933-2005. On one side of her was the grave of Albert Desrosiers; his marble headstone was larger than hers and had a high polish. On her other side was a Franck Desrosiers who had died in 1958. Molly looked all down the row, and while she found several graves of children, she found none with the name of Desrosiers.

The small graves of the other children stabbed her in the heart, and she tried as she had many times before to tell herself that not having children had saved her the possibility of terrific, undying pain. It was a convincing argument, and yet she was not convinced.

She checked other rows, eventually covering the entire small cemetery, but there were no other Desrosiers graves, and the children she found all seemed clearly to belong to other families. Dead end.

But Molly did not give up so easily. Perhaps the baby had been cremated, or for some other reason hadn't been buried with his or her parents. Maybe she could track down the doctor who attended the birth? How about looking for a death certificate at the town hall or some other official building?

First to Pâtisserie Bujold, and then to the town hall, called the *mairie*. No doubt someone there could at least tell her where to search next.

❧

ADÈLE FAURE WOKE on that Tuesday morning, a week before Christmas, in a cold sweat. The days were ticking by, short and dark, and if village gossip was anything to go by—and Adèle rather thought it was—Michel was in serious trouble. That stupid Dufort had got it in his head that Aunt Josephine's will pointed inevitably to her brother's guilt, as though he couldn't imagine anyone having a motive for murder but not acting on it. As though all of us were not in that exact position a million times over the course of our lives, even if the motive was simply to remove the annoying person working in the next cubicle.

She swung her legs over the side of the bed and sat up, massaging her bad foot, which ached in the cold. It was time for someone to act, she thought, before this nonsense goes any further. She brushed her hair and teeth, got dressed with less care than usual, and prepared to set off for the bank. It was dark on that morning, one of the shortest days of the year, and the village itself felt dark in its heart to Adèle, as though all of its inhabitants had betrayed her and her beloved brother.

Back in *collège*, when they had been thirteen or fourteen, their schoolmates had teased them, saying the brother and sister loved each other too much and wanted to kiss each other. And the truth was that Adèle *had* wanted to kiss Michel. She had wanted to give herself to him in any way he would take her, and a few times, was on the point of telling him so...but she had held back in the end, fearing rejection. She had been tough as a child because she'd had to be, and she could stand teasing and her disability and any manner of difficult and painful problems—but not Michel's rejection. Not that.

Of course, it would have been quite a scandal if she and

Michel had had a romantic attachment, in public; but Adèle could brush that off, since Michel was adopted and they were not blood relatives—and who cared what other people thought anyway? It was true that they had grown up together, but that had only meant that they knew each other intimately and cared for each other profoundly, and in Adèle's opinion, that was the best basis for romance anyone could hope for.

All such thoughts and hopes were long buried in the past for the most part, and Adèle had been resigned to her single life and a close friendship with Michel. For his part, there had not been many girlfriends, and Adèle had never asked why, preferring to hold on to the belief that his deep love for her prevented anyone else from getting very close.

And now the love of her life was in trouble. She was sophisticated enough to know that his innocence wouldn't necessarily protect him—innocent people get sent to prison all the time, as Adèle and anyone who read the papers well knew. The question was...what was she going to do to stop it?

It is time to act.

Adèle wrapped a wool scarf over her head and around her neck so that everything but her face was covered up, and left the chill of her apartment for the cold of the street. Rue Tartine was empty that early in the morning, and the uneven clopping of her heels reverberated off the walls of the houses. Six blocks to get to the bank, two long and four medium. She had chosen her apartment because six blocks was comfortable for her to walk, but that morning, her whole body was tense and her bad foot throbbed worse than usual, slowing her down.

This whole plan is probably idiotic, she thought, and stopped in the street. *If I had done this before the murder, then maybe it would've worked.*

She was too late and she knew it, but pressed on because no other ideas had come to her. Suddenly starving, Adèle wished she had made herself an omelette and coffee before leaving home. She wondered if hunger went hand in hand with breaking the law and smiled ironically, thinking that once she was in prison herself for obstructing justice or whatever they called what she was about to do, she would be able to ask the other inmates in person. She imagined them standing out in the prison yard, blowing long plumes of breath in the freezing air, telling each other about all the dishes they had craved just before the commission of their crimes.

She could picture that omelette so vividly, how it glistened with butter, with a handful of bright green chives tumbling off it.

Thinking of food, Adèle picked up her pace no matter how it made her foot hurt, reached the bank before anyone else, and let herself in. She flicked on the lights. It was not strange to be the first one to arrive; she was generally an early riser and a dedicated employee, and before she was made an officer of the bank, she had come in early many times to make sure she could accomplish her work as perfectly as possible.

Her office was small but it had a window. Adèle sat at her desk and thought about how to accomplish what she wanted to do without leaving any sort of trail. She hoped, naïvely, that it wouldn't matter if someone eventually found out that she had transferred so much money into Michel's account—almost all of her money, everything but what she needed to live on this month and buy presents for Michel and her mother for Christmas. Adèle was not especially frugal, and spent far more on clothes and handbags than she should, so the sum was hardly exorbitant.

But she prayed that it would be enough to dissuade Dufort. That he would see, once he started poking around in Michel's affairs, that Michel was taken care of, that he was not remotely desperate for money, and in no hurry at all to get what Aunt Josephine ultimately intended for him to have anyway.

Chapter Thirty-Five

Over-caffeinated and with a mustache of powdered sugar on her upper lip, Molly left Pâtisserie Bujold with a white waxed bag filled with four beignets: two custard-filled and two plain. If she arrived back at La Baraque empty-handed, she feared what Frances might do, since she'd never forgiven Molly for showing up from a trip to the market with nothing but eggplants. As Molly headed toward the mairie, she realized that she had been so busy thinking about the Desrosiers baby that she hadn't even noticed Monsieur Nugent and his usual attentions.

The mairie was the center of all things administrative in Castillac. She got a little nervous going in because the stately building made her feel her ignorance acutely—so many rules and regulations, and she was probably not following half of them since she still, after not quite four months, had plenty left to learn.

She stuttered and garbled her French, feeling a blush creep up her neck. *Won't they wonder why in the world I am interested in death records, when I've barely just arrived?* Maybe she should have invented a cover story.

But the pleasant woman behind the counter was more than

happy to help, showing Molly to a room in the back that contained a series of tall wooden filing cabinets.

"Here is death," the woman said, pointing to three cabinets along one wall. "And here is birth," she said. "Alpha and omega, we have it all here at the mairie!"

Molly smiled, loving how the people of Castillac launched into philosophy at the drop of a hat. She went straight to the first cabinet along the wall and opened it up. Inside were folders by year, in chronological order, and documents of that year's deaths within each folder. The drawer she had opened contained 1899-1930. The drawer above it was 1931-1967. In a village of Castillac's size, there were deaths every year, but not so many that she wouldn't be able to find what she was looking for.

Hmm. Molly wasn't sure how old Josephine had been when she married so didn't know where to begin. At least she knew she had been seventy-two on the day she died, so that narrowed things down a bit. As intent as she was on finding evidence, the death records were so interesting she found herself getting distracted. The causes of death were particularly interesting. Such variety, and what stories they hinted at! Tuberculosis, cancer, and falling off a ladder. A drowning, more cancer, pneumonia. She couldn't help stopping at each document, reading the name and wondering what kind of life the person had, and whether she was missed.

She took so long that eventually she dipped into the waxed bag and ate one of the beignets. The custard burst into her mouth with such an amazing explosion of vanilla that she had to close her eyes and try not to moan out loud. And then back to work, plugging away through 1963, 1964, 1965...years before she was born, her main associations being Twiggy and the Beatles.

Up through 1967, and still no mention of any Desrosiers or any Faure. Maybe France does not keep records of stillbirths? But from what she could tell, France kept records about everything. She kept looking.

1968, 1969, 1970. She ate another beignet. By the end of the '70s, Molly was sure there was no death certificate for a Desrosiers baby in the filing cabinet, having gone through every single page in every folder for all the years when it would have been physically possible for Josephine to have been pregnant. She stood up, not sure what to do next.

Pulling her cell phone out of her bag, she gave Frances a call, but got sent to voice mail. She texted Lawrence asking him if he had any other tidbits to toss her way, though she figured if he did, she'd have heard from him already. Then she thought, well, hold on a minute. If the baby didn't die, there obviously wouldn't be a death certificate—I should switch over to looking at the birth records.

Stowing her bag away, she opened the first cabinet holding the birth records, leafing through the thick folders of *Extrait du Registre des Naissance*. Like the death forms, they were typed, which to Molly seemed wonderfully quaint. The letters did not align the way they automatically do on a computer, there were ink smudges and letters that made an impression on the paper but did not leave much of a mark otherwise. The occupations of the parents were listed: factory worker, farmer, shop owner, clerk.

With a sudden hoot, she saw ADÈLE with the last name of FAURE, and smiling, pulled it out of the folder to see it better. The paper was a little bent and not entirely clean. Adèle was thirty-nine, a year older than Molly. There was no father listed. Molly looked more closely. She almost didn't see it, but right over the space for the father's name was a stripe of discoloration. An edge was sticking up just barely, and had caught dust or dirt and so was lightly browned. A narrow strip of paper had been glued over the space where the father's name should have been typed.

With a glance behind her to make sure the woman in the other room was occupied, Molly picked at the edge with her fingernail.

It took a minute to come loose. The glue was old and brittle but hung on. Molly began to tremble, a sense of foreboding suffusing her body. Finally, she was able to pull the strip off completely, going very slowly, gently tugging it loose.

On the official birth form, Albert Desrosiers was listed as Adèle Faure's father.

Molly stared, unable to understand what that meant.

Her uncle was her father? Did that mean Murielle had had an affair with Josephine's husband? With her brother-in law? Molly sat down on the floor, unable to take her eyes off the piece of paper. Did Adèle know about this? And who had tampered with the form, trying to cover it up?

Without realizing she was doing it, Molly ate the last beignet. She looked at the paper once more, going over it from top to bottom and holding it up to the winter light coming in through a window above her. She saw that there was another narrow strip over the line for the mother—on which 'Murielle Faure' was typed—but it was glued more securely and harder to detect. It had no edge popping up either, but Molly had one decent finger-nail and she kept pushing it along the edge as she bent the paper, hoping it would snag along the strip and pull it up just enough to start separating it from the form.

A noise in the other room nearly gave her a heart attack, but it was only the door banging behind someone who was asking the woman at the desk about some parking tickets. Molly turned her back to the door so that if anyone came in, they wouldn't see that she was busy tampering with government records. She was nothing if not persistent, and eventually the top edge separated from the form just enough for her to get her little fingernail under it, and the strip popped right off.

Under the strip, listed as the mother of Adèle Faure...was Josephine Desrosiers.

"I'VE BEEN SAYING all along that families are nuts," said Frances, after Molly had told her what she found at the mairie. "And who eats four beignets, anyway?"

"Apparently I do," said Molly, unrepentant. "Now come on, Franny, help me puzzle this out. Is it possible that the form went from incorrect to correct—that those strips were put there by someone official, because a mistake had been made?"

"If it were something like the date, then maybe. But who puts the wrong mother on a form like that? I don't think so."

"So Adèle is really Josephine's daughter, not Murielle's? That is *huge*. Huge! For one thing, Michel can no longer be the prime suspect, because a child supersedes everyone else in French inheritance laws. Adèle will get most of that fortune, not Michel."

"That just means suspicion shifts over to her, right?"

Molly sat down on the sofa with a thud. "Oh jeez, I hadn't even thought of that. I was so busy celebrating about Michel that it didn't occur to me this might go badly for Adèle. But wait—she would have to know, right? If she doesn't know who her real mother is, she'd have no reason to kill her."

"But if no one knows, then Michel could have killed her out of ignorance, you see? And what about Michel's parentage? Did you see him in the files?"

"I was halfway down the block on my way home when I thought of that. I scrambled back to the mairie and went in to look for him—I'm sure the woman who works there thinks I'm a complete loon—anyway, yes, I found him. His form looked original and not tampered with, and his parents were...I don't remember their names but I made a note on my phone...anyway, nobody I'd ever heard of. He appears to be adopted, just as he says."

Molly got up to check if her paintbrushes and roller were dry. "I just don't get this at all. I know back when the world was more conservative, sometimes a married couple or a grandmother might have taken in a child born out of wedlock and pretended it was theirs—but this is sort of the opposite of that. A married couple giving up their child to a sister who's single. Explain please."

"Maybe if I had a beignet, my mind would be clearer," said Frances.

"You're like a dog with a bone."

"And that bone is not pillowy soft and filled with vanilla custard."

Molly laughed. "Okay, I'm going to go see how Pierre is doing with the pigeonnier, and then try to finish up this paint job. I need to decide what in hell to do with this information I've got, and so far, I have no idea."

"You mean whether to talk to Adèle about it? Or Ben?"

At Ben's name, Molly blushed furiously. "Both. So wait. I've been so gobsmacked about this news that I haven't asked about last night. How was it with Nico?"

Frances made a little peep and smiled, not making eye contact.

"That's it? Just mhmm? What did you guys do?"

"Okay Molly, I'm going to put in a few more hours of work and see if I can get this jingle in good enough shape to send to the client. And then maybe I'll wander into the village and see if I can find a morsel to eat before I starve to death."

Molly smirked, knowing a brick wall when she hit one. At least Frances's usual black cloud of drama seemed to have stayed on the other side of the ocean.

She went outside without putting on a coat. It was cold and the air felt moist—all her years in Boston had taught her to recognize when snow was coming, and she guessed it was coming soon. She walked quickly out to the pigeonnier and called to Pierre Gault, who was on top of a ladder leaning against the half-finished building.

"Salut! How is it going?"

"Better than expected," said Pierre, climbing down. "All those stones that were hidden in the tall grass turned out to be in good shape, and even the part of the wall that was falling down is shaping up to be more easily repaired than I first thought. I should be done with the exterior in a few days, before Christmas, at any rate."

"I'm glad that's going well at least," she said.

"Are other things not going so well?" asked Pierre.

"No. Well, maybe. I don't know."

"Ah. All cleared up, then."

Molly thanked him for his fast work and walked out into the meadow. The grass was crusty under her feet, frozen in spikes that crunched under her sneakers. For a brief moment, she forgot about the Faures and Desrosiers, and Ben, and Nico and Frances, and thought about the surprise she was going to get when spring finally came. La Baraque had old gardens, and the meadow was old too—she expected to see all kinds of things come up that past inhabitants had planted before they died or moved on. A few apples trees hung on, their bark scarred and showing signs of ill health. Then the forest, dark and impenetrable, at least from the edge of the meadow. Molly was in no rush to blunder around back there, out of the sunlight.

She was sure the secret of Adèle's parentage meant something. But what? And what in the world was the right thing for her to do? She felt as though she were walking around the meadow with a grenade in her pocket. With no idea how to set it off to cause the least amount of damage.

Chapter Thirty-Six

The third cyanide poisoning in Castillac occurred the next day, a Wednesday notable for an unusual amount of snowfall. Castillac generally got a dusting or two each winter, rarely more, but this was a real snow. Not to Molly, who was used to close to four feet a year in Boston, but to the residents of Castillac, the five inches was a dire emergency.

But no ambulance skidded through the storm on the way to Madame LaGreffe's house that night. Madame LaGreffe lived alone in a little house on rue Saterne, and there was no one to call for help.

That morning she had gotten up early, as she always did, never able to sleep through the night after she hit her mid-fifties. Now she was nearly eighty. At least, she told friends, for these last years of my life, I will be awake nearly all the time, so I shan't miss a thing.

Madame LaGreffe had done her marketing as soon as the épicerie and the butcher opened their doors. She had splurged on a case of Perrier and arranged for the delivery boy to bring it later in the day. Unlike a lot of old people, she adored snow and was excited to sit in her cozy house and watch the village turn white.

When she reached home again with her basket under one arm, she saw a small paper bag sitting on her front step, right up against the door as though to keep it from getting snowed on.

Inside was no note, just a jar of face cream—Chanel, of all things. Madame LaGreffe had never used anything so fancy and she let out a little cackle when she saw it. Never for a moment did she wonder where the face cream had come from, or whether there could be anything shady or unsafe about it. The rest of the day passed as most of her days did: she vacuumed the upstairs, ate lunch and washed the lunch dishes, thought about dinner, did a little knitting while listening to the radio. She was lonely, but so used to loneliness that it caused her no pain, but was rather like a joint with an ache that never really went away, so constant she barely noticed it.

In the back of her mind, all day long, she was looking forward to her bath, and then using that expensive face cream before going to bed. It made lunch more exciting. It had even made washing out her underthings after dinner more exciting. She thought that if she had suddenly inherited a million euros, she still would never have bought such an expensive jar of face cream for herself—it was just not in her nature to indulge herself that way. But how lovely to be able to do it without having to make the choice!

Madame LaGreffe lingered over her bath, washing herself thoroughly and for a moment splashing about like a little girl, slapping the water and letting it spray up against the tile. She dried herself and put on a flannel nightgown that a friend had brought her from England fifteen years earlier, and then, fatefully, she sat down on the edge of her bed and opened the jar. She leaned down and smelled the fragrance, and for an instant she closed her eyes and remembered being a teenager, when her mother had allowed her to use a quick spray of good perfume before going out on a date.

Then she dipped her finger in and smoothed the cream across

her cheeks, her forehead, her chin. Carefully she screwed the cap back on the jar, slid her feet under the covers, and went to sleep with a smile on her face.

She was awakened later, but at first it didn't register that anything was wrong because she was used to waking up in the middle of the night. She did not get up and walk to the window and watch the snow come down; instead she lay gasping for breath, feeling sick to her stomach, and wondering why in the world she suddenly felt so terrible.

She never suspected the face cream. She did suffer, but not for long, and there was no one to watch or to help, as the village slept through the storm, and all of Castillac got whiter and whiter.

Chapter Thirty-Seven

Dufort was furious. Another death just a few blocks from Desrosiers's house, and nothing he and the other gendarmes did seemed to get them any closer to apprehending the murderer.

"How did LaGreffe not know about the danger?" he demanded. Perrault leaned against the wall with her head bowed. Maron was expressionless.

"We put notices up all over the village," Perrault said. "And made plenty of noise online. Thing is, the people the murderer is targeting—women over seventy years old—a lot of them don't have computers. We need to think of a better way to reach them."

"Look, we can go door-to-door to every single house and warn people, but the murderer will just switch her delivery method," said Maron. "It's face cream today, but it could be, I don't know, a fruit drink tomorrow."

"'Her'?" said Perrault witheringly. "You're not going to let go of your whole 'poisoners are all women' idea are you?"

Maron stared straight ahead, not allowing himself to take the bait.

"It's eight o'clock," said Dufort. "I want the two of you out canvassing that neighborhood until lunchtime, and take more time if you need it. Number one, ask all the neighbors on that street if they saw anybody hanging around, anybody who doesn't live in that neighborhood. I want a list of names. And number two, as long as you're talking to people, warn them to make sure not to ingest anything they don't know the provenance of. Don't put anything on their skin, in their hair, in their mouths... anywhere on their bodies at all. And three—tell them to try to do their best to look after the older people in our community. It's obviously only been women targeted so far, but that doesn't mean our murderer won't branch out."

"Yes sir," said Perrault, heading for the door.

"Maron, hold up, I'd like a word with you." said Dufort. Maron stayed still and did not react. "I want to know if you have any further reason to think Claudette Mercier has been involved in this."

"Uh, I can't say I have anything new specifically, but I'd like to look into whether there is any connection between Mercier and LaGreffe. I know LaGreffe was older, not one of Mercier's school-mates, but that doesn't mean there's not something else. Maybe Mercier is unhappy about growing old, and she's displacing all that fear and unhappiness onto her victims, as though killing will somehow slow her aging, psychologically, I mean."

Dufort moved around the side of his desk and got up close to Maron. "That is probably the most idiotic, implausible theory I have ever heard spoken in this office. Drop it, Maron," he said, his tone like iron. "Now get out there and find out who was on rue Saterne yesterday. I want a report from you that's as thorough and precise as if we had CCTV all up and down the street. You under-stand me?"

"Yes sir," said Maron. His dark brows furrowed, making him look angry. He had more to say, but had the sense to know this was not the time. He put on his heavy coat and followed Perrault out onto the snowy street.

੬

THIS TIME Molly heard about the latest murder not by stumbling across the body or by a text from Lawrence. She found out at the épicerie where she was ordering the delivery of a case of Perrier just like Madame LaGreffe had the day before. A number of people were in the épicerie talking about what had happened, but Molly didn't stop to find out the details. She went straight to the bank where Adèle worked, and after a wait at the reception desk, asked her if she was free for lunch—there was something important she wanted to talk to her about.

Adèle looked at Molly carefully, her head to one side. She liked the American and enjoyed her company, but she wasn't sure that she trusted her. A new friend is untested, nothing like the sort of friends one grows up with, or family. She appeared amiable enough, but it was not absolutely clear where Molly's loyalties lay; she was friendly with Dufort, after all. Adèle told herself to be a little careful and not get swept up into Molly's energetic chatter and say something she would regret.

"I can meet you for lunch," Adèle said, smiling. "Did you know that a little boutique has opened only a few blocks from here? Perhaps we could swing by after we eat, if there's time. I hope your news...isn't bad? Nothing too serious?"

Molly looked at Adèle blankly. She had no idea what her news meant, so had no way to answer. "I'll see you at 12:30," she said awkwardly, and went back outside. She had an hour to kill and she spent it wandering the streets of Castillac, trying to enjoy how pretty the village looked in its fresh blanket of snow. But she couldn't block out her nervousness, and even fear. She told herself she wasn't in the killer's demographic and wasn't in any danger, but fear does not go by logic. There was a killer in Castillac, his motive was unknown, and Molly was starting to have serious misgivings about her new friends.

She wanted to believe in Adèle and Michel. But what was the

friendship based on, anyway? A few ephemeral meetings in which they had felt a spark of attraction and congeniality? That wasn't much. It wasn't really wasn't anything at all, at least not anything she could count on. She didn't really have any idea what kind of people they were, deep down. And she knew her history was full of examples of being smitten with people for one small bit of charm—a joke they made, or an apt line of poetry quoted—and ignoring evidence of serious character flaws.

The snow was wet and Molly could feel dampness getting inside her boots, but she ignored it. Without thinking about it, she found herself on rue Simenon headed for the Desrosiers mansion. She peered over the wall into the empty back garden. No footprints in the snow. The front of the house looked sort of sad to her, as though the building missed having inhabitants. A shutter on a downstairs window had come loose and sagged on one side. The steps were not shoveled. It's like a beautiful tomb, thought Molly, shivering.

Why in the world had Josephine given Adèle away? Molly went through all the reasons she could think of that a mother would choose to give her baby up, but as far as she could tell, Josephine matched up with none of them. She stood for a long moment feeling rage at the dead woman for giving away what Molly wanted so deeply.

So many unanswered questions.

The hour was nearly up, and Molly got back to the bank quickly, wishing she had thought of a clever way to find out whether Adèle knew who her real mother was.

"Nice bag," said Molly, unable to keep herself from grinning. The leather was a saturated shade of green and it looked soft as a baby's bottom.

Adèle shrugged. "No children, you know? I don't have many expenses."

Molly took a deep breath. They weren't starting on the right foot—Adèle was defensive and brittle, and Molly was already having to stop herself from blurting out a stream of questions. "I'm starved," she said. "How about we get something to eat before going to look at that boutique you mentioned?"

Adèle nodded. She had put on short waterproof boots, and the two women went outside. "There's a little place right around the corner where I've been many times," said Adèle. "Very good soup sound good?"

"Perfect for a snowy day," said Molly, inwardly cringing at how they were reduced to talking about the weather again.

They had barely been seated when Molly burst out. "Listen, I'm sorry it's awkward. I don't really—well, I do actually—listen, Adèle. I know I've probably butted in where I don't belong. But I do want you to know that my intentions were good. I mean, I was trying to do what I could to help Michel, you understand?"

"No," said Adèle, "I don't understand. What are you trying to say?"

The waiter approached and then backed away when he heard the intensity of the conversation.

"I'm trying to explain that I did some digging," said Molly, keeping her voice low. "I heard that your aunt had a stillborn child, and that got me wondering...if the worst thing against your brother is that he stands to inherit your aunt's money, then if someone else were to inherit, wouldn't he be free of suspicion? So anyway, again—I know it's none of my business, but I checked the records at the mairie." Molly was hoping that Adèle would jump in and tell her none of this was news to her, but Adèle said nothing. Her face was inscrutable.

"What I found, Adèle—it says on your birth certificate that Josephine Desrosiers is your mother."

Adèle's eyelid twitched but otherwise she did not move; she did not speak.

"I know it was a terrible breach of privacy," said Molly. "I just thought—if Michel didn't inherit, then really the only evidence Dufort has against him evaporates, you see? I...I never imagined...

I didn't intend to…I'm sorry if this causes you pain. I was shocked to see Josephine and Albert's names on your birth certificate. And I do see that it complicates matters rather than resolves them."

Adèle did not move or speak, her gaze directed out of the window.

"Adèle? Talk to me!"

Adèle whispered, "I don't think I can find words." Her eyes welled up. "What you're telling me is that my entire life has been based on…a lie…"

"Well, I don't know that your entire life is about who your parents are." Molly put her hand on her friend's shoulder and then took it back. "But yes, it certainly looks as though there has been some lying. I don't understand it, and I guess I was hoping you'd be able to explain why your family did what they did."

Adèle shook her head. She used a napkin to wipe tears from both eyes and took a deep breath. "My mother has been a wonderful mother to me," she said. "And I suppose I should thank God that I did not have to grow up living with horrible Aunt Josephine." She took a deep, jagged breath. "And now that I stand to inherit, I suppose I will be the next target of the investigation."

Molly signaled to the waiter, unable to wait for lunch any longer. "If you had no idea about this, I don't see how Dufort could start looking at you for her murder. I don't think you have to worry about that," although Molly was worrying, herself. Worrying that her meddling had only made things worse for the people she was trying to help. "You should be coming into enough money to buy any handbag in the world," said Molly, trying to look on the bright side.

"I don't want that witch's money," murmured Adèle, pushing back from the table. "And if you'll excuse me, I can't eat anything. I need to find Michel."

"Adèle, I'm so sorry—" said Molly, but Adèle had gotten up quickly, her napkin dropping to the floor, and was halfway out the door.

Chapter Thirty-Eight

Perrault flew down the street, slipping in the snow. For once, she had accomplished something tangible! Who would ever have guessed that old Madame Tessier would turn out to be a gendarme's best friend?

"Chief!" she shouted, a little too loudly, as she burst into Dufort's office. "I just talked to Madame Tessier, and I think we've got Michel Faure!"

"Slow down, Thérèse," Dufort said. His voice was gentle, but his gaze was intense. "Now tell me what Madame Tessier said."

"Well, you know she's the biggest gossip in all of Castillac. Sits on her stoop when it's warm, peeps out of her window when it's cold."

"Yes, I know all that, I've seen and spoken to her quite often."

"She saw Michel on Wednesday, walking down rue Saterne. Carrying a paper bag. Which he put on Madame LaGreffe's front step!" Perrault had leaned farther and farther forward, but when she delivered the last line, she leaned back in triumph and slapped her palms on Dufort's desk.

Dufort rubbed his hand over his brush cut and thought about this. "She was sure it was Michel?"

"No doubt whatsoever."

"What sort of bag?"

"Brown paper. Not as large as a grocery bag."

"And she saw him walk up LaGreffe's front steps, and put the bag there? Did he ring the bell?"

"No, she didn't think so."

Dufort scratched his ear. It seemed damning. So why didn't he feel satisfied?

"All right, nice job Perrault. Let's bring him in for a chat."

"IT DOES SEEM like a thirty-four-year-old man should have someone to call besides his mother," said Michel, having been brought to the station by Perrault. "But that's how things are," he murmured to himself, and dropped down into a chair. "I'll tell you right from the beginning that you're going to think my version of events sounds ridiculous. And honestly, my life at the moment—it *is* rather ridiculous. I've been out of work for nearly a year, I don't have two *centimes* to rub together, and for some reason unknown to me, I can't seem to keep the shadow of suspicion off my back. You know, I had a decent job, in Paris, for a short while, working in advertising. But things...sometimes things don't work out the way we'd like, I think we can all agree on that?"

Perrault and Dufort let him talk, since he was feeling so voluble. It was unusual for suspects, but always welcome, since almost invariably they said things that they later wished they had not.

"I seem to have the worst luck," he said, shrugging. "On Wednesday, just before the snow, I was on rue Saterne. And I did carry a bag and leave it on Madame LaGreffe's front step—that's all true. But the rest of the story is that I'm out of work, as I've said. I have an abundance of free time, you understand, and so I do a lot of walking around the village and sometimes farther afield. Since my aunt lived on rue Saterne, I've walked down that street hundreds of times, and I noticed that Madame LaGreffe gets milk delivered every Wednesday.

"Maybe if my unemployment allotment were more generous, I wouldn't have given it a thought. But the amount of support is based, as you both no doubt know, on how much one contributes to the system over the course of one's working life. But my work has been, well...do you think I could have a glass of water?"

Perrault jumped up to get him one. Dufort stayed casual, leaning back in his chair with an expression of affability, as though he and Michel were just relaxing in his living room before watching a soccer game on television together. When Perrault returned with the water, he kept silent.

"So what was I saying? All right. This is embarrassing for me so I'll just come out with it. The fact of the matter is that I was hungry. I knew about Madame LaGreffe's milk on Wednesdays. And every so often I made sure to be walking along rue Saterne just after the delivery so I could steal it. I didn't know anyone even got milk delivered anymore, but this milk is so fresh and delicious—it's indescribably good. I've never drunk glasses of milk in my life until I started taking Madame LaGreffe's, but you understand, when you're hungry, you tend to try new things. The milk was especially good when it was very cold, as it was on Wednesday.

"So yes, I fully and shamefully admit—I took the milk. Here I am, thirty-four years old, stealing an old lady's milk! I'm well aware, Chief Dufort, that this is reprehensible behavior. I didn't steal it every week, not by a longshot. And I tried, whenever I did steal it, to leave her something as recompense. This last time, I brought her a bag of pine cones I'd collected. I know, it's hardly anything valuable, but you can use them to start fires or they make a nice rustic decoration for the table." Michel shrugged again. "How I managed to choose the same day poor Madame LaGreffe was poisoned—" He shook his head with a wry half-smile.

All three looked around to see Murielle Faure walk into the room. "What sort of ridiculous goings-on is this?" she demanded of Dufort. Her graying hair was pulled back into a tight ponytail and she was wearing a corduroy skirt that went to her shins. Perrault, who was not exactly fashion-minded, winced at that skirt, wondering how in the world Adèle and Murielle came from the same family, considering how opposite their approach to clothing was.

"Bonjour, Madame Faure," said Dufort. "We are having a talk with Michel because he was seen leaving a bag on Madame LaGreffe's doorstop the day she was poisoned with cyanide. The same poison that killed your sister." Dufort kept his voice even, almost nonchalant.

"Well, I don't know anything about poison or any Madame LaGreffe, but I can tell you that of all people, Michel had absolutely nothing to do with anything illegal!"

"Can you say how you are so sure of that?" asked Perrault.

"Michel is my son. I know him deep down, like mothers know their children. Michel is a kind-hearted boy, always has been. He is the last person on earth who would hurt anyone."

Dufort leaned his head to the side, and waited to see if Murielle would keep talking.

"Maman, I might as well tell you, since I've just told the chief —I'd been stealing Madame LaGreffe's milk sometimes. I know, it's very embarrassing. Mortifying, really. It would have been much better if I'd come up with a more glamorous way to break the law, something that would at least make a better story."

"Oh, Michel," said Murielle, going to him and kissing him on the head. "Don't you know that you can always come home for a meal if things get tight? Always." Murielle looked to Dufort. "So you see? Of course if he must pay a fine or something, I am more than happy to take care of that. But his crime is petty theft, not murder."

Dufort nodded. "And Madame Faure, since you're here,

perhaps I can ask you—who do you think murdered your sister, if it was not Michel, who is the main beneficiary in her will?"

Murielle gasped. "I was unaware that Josephine had made a provision for him." She kissed Michel on the head again. "It's lovely for her to have done that, especially since she and I weren't very close. But I know she was very fond of Michel and I'm so pleased that she showed her affection in that way."

"But you see the trouble, Madame Faure? That the inheritance endows your son with the only motive for killing her that we've been able to find?"

"Chief Dufort! Michel—he is not capable of doing anything!"

"Maybe I did do something. For once," Michel muttered, almost inaudibly, but Perrault caught it.

"Are you arresting him? Because if not, I would like to take my boy home and cook him a good dinner. As far as I can see, that is the solution to any crime committed by Michel. It's nothing a square meal won't fix."

"No, we're not holding him," said Dufort reluctantly. "He's free to go. But Michel, I would listen to your mother. If you don't have enough to eat, take her up on her offer and leave the residents of Castillac alone, *comprends*?"

The Faures left, arm in arm, though Michel did not look vindicated. He gave a backward glance to Perrault and she smiled at him.

"So what do you think?" Dufort asked her.

"She treats him like a child."

"Yes. A mixture of adoration and contempt, isn't it?"

Perrault nodded. Then she told Dufort about hearing Michel mumble something about having "done something, for once". The two gendarmes puzzled over it, but the meaning remained obscure.

Chapter Thirty-Nine

O n Friday morning, Molly and Frances took their coffee cups to warm their hands, and walked around the frosty garden. The snow had half-melted, but it still lingered where the sun hadn't struck it, and Molly could easily see how much shade everything got—good to know when planning what to plant, though that morning she was too distracted to pay much attention.

"I've decided to tell Ben," she said, stopping by an oak tree that hadn't yet let go of its brown leaves.

"I don't know," said Frances. "Shouldn't he have to find out stuff like that on his own? Why do you have to do all the legwork?"

"You say that like it's drudgery. I *like* finding stuff out. And besides, I want whoever killed those two women brought to justice as much as anyone! Don't you?"

"Well, you're not going to get me to argue the side of the murderer," Frances laughed. "I guess I'm just not clear on why who Adèle's mother is or isn't would make any difference to the case."

"I don't know either," said Molly. "Not if it was this big secret that neither Adèle nor Michel even know about."

"Maybe you just want an excuse to consult with the foxy policeman," said Frances.

Molly leaned down and put her coffee cup on the ground, then picked up a handful of wet snow and hurled it at her, hitting her right on the back of the neck so that the snow dripped down her shirt.

"You're going to pay for that, Molly Sutton!" yelled Frances, running for a good patch of snow.

Molly shrieked and ran inside. She and Frances loved occasionally acting like eight-year-olds. She refilled her coffee and went to get dressed. It was a little bit true; she liked seeing Ben and working with him on a case. But it was also true that the business of lying about whose baby was whose—it begged for more investigation, and the more she thought about it, the less doubt she had that Ben ought to know about it.

It was perhaps a betrayal of her friend. But the truth was the truth, and Adèle was going to have to come to terms with it one way or another. Molly's continuing to keep the secret wasn't going to protect her from that.

"MOLLY! BONJOUR," said Dufort, standing up from his desk.

"Bonjour, Ben. I was wondering if you had a moment?"

"Of course." Dufort ushered her into his office and went around to close the door. "What's on your mind?"

"Probably nothing. But I found something out that I thought you should know." She sat down.

Dufort moved next to Molly and half-sat on the front of the desk. He admired how her red hair was flying out from under her hat in a wind-blown tangle. "Yes?"

"Well, I heard that Josephine Desrosiers had a baby—a still-born baby. Did you know about that?"

Dufort shook his head. "This would have been…in the sixties or seventies?"

Molly nodded. "It was in 1966, to be exact. So I thought, well, I've heard about how different the inheritance laws in France are from in the States. See, Americans can leave anything to anybody —or not. They can will a fortune to their unpleasant cat and leave the children out in the cold, if they want to."

"Not so in France. The children are protected under the law."

"That's what I understood. So I thought: what if Josephine's baby *wasn't* stillborn? If he or she was alive, then the biggest share of the Desrosiers money would go to that child, no matter what Josephine might have wanted, right?"

"I believe so, yes," said Dufort, looking at Molly carefully. "Is this about trying to take suspicion off Michel Faure?"

"No. I mean, yes, sort of. I did start down this path thinking that if he didn't inherit, his motive disappears. But then I realized that as long as Michel believed he was the beneficiary, the truth about Desrosiers's child didn't really matter. As far as motive, I mean. I followed the lead anyway, because I was curious."

"And what did you find, Molly?"

She told him.

Yet again, Benjamin Dufort found himself utterly baffled by the things people did. He and Molly spent several minutes agreeing that it made no sense at all. They wondered whether the strips of paper over the names were actually correcting a mistake. And in the end, they decided that there was a reason the Desrosierses had given their baby to Josephine's sister and then covered it up—they just had no idea what it was.

"I will tell you, I'm no less inclined to think Michel is involved in the murder. Maybe he and his sister planned it together? We brought him in for a chat this morning, and he admitted that he left a bag on LaGreffe's doorstep on the day she died. He was seen doing so by Madame Tessier who lives two doors down on rue Saterne, so there was little point in denying it. Had a preposterous story about leaving her some pine cones." Dufort shook his head. "I know Josephine Desrosiers was not a well-liked woman. But in a case like this, family is where to look for the murderer, Molly. Family is where the emotions are deepest, and the pain sometimes intolerable."

"I didn't know you had such a rosy view of home life," said Molly.

"Heh. Well, let me misquote Tolstoy—happy families are all well and good, but when families get unhappy, that's when the gendarmes might get involved."

Molly hooted, and then she got serious. "But Ben, there are other possibilities. Have you really been able to make absolutely sure it was not Sabrina, for instance? I heard Desrosiers treated her horribly. And how about Sabrina's boyfriend, that hotheaded political dude? He could have killed her for ideological reasons alone, not to mention how she treated his girlfriend."

Dufort shrugged. "Are *you* convinced either one of them did it?" he asked gently.

She paused before continuing. "But Michel and Adèle—I just...I just don't *want* them to have done this! And you're saying they also killed Madame LaGreffe, to cover up the first murder? That's so much worse, isn't it? When is it going to end?"

"When I have the evidence to stop them," said Dufort.

They both looked down at the floor, wondering how—and when—and if—that was going to happen.

Chapter Forty

Adèle was so undone by Molly's revelation that she did not return to the bank. After standing outside in the cold trying to calm down and figure out what to do next, she walked all the way to her mother's house. Probably the best thing would be to wait, think things over, maybe go to the mairie herself to look at the records. But sometimes the best thing is not the most pressing thing, and what Adèle needed to do as soon as possible was look her mother in the face and ask her if it was true.

Had her real mother been Josephine? And if yes, why had Josephine given her up? And why in the world was her sister the one to take her?

It made no sense. No matter from which direction Adèle tried to approach it—it made no sense. She wanted to run to Michel, but what could he do? The only thing was to confront her mother and see her reaction, and then hope she was willing to explain everything.

In the meantime, Adèle felt as though her world had tilted dangerously, like her balance was lost and she was sliding one way, barely hanging on, only to pitch the other way; her thoughts tumbled around in her head, incoherent, and her heart raced.

She wanted to go home to talk to her mother, and also to be back in the familiar surroundings of her childhood. Home was still home, almost unchanged; the smells and sounds the same, the pattern on the wallpaper and the appliances and the creaky spot on the stair...all the same. She had uncountable happy memories of the three of them—her mother, Michel, and herself—laughing at her mother's latest culinary disaster, or making ant farms, or, less happily, working in the garden under her mother's strict guidance.

Adèle loved Castillac and had never had any desire to live anywhere else, but at the same time, she had felt separate from the village as long as she could remember. In school, she was the girl who limped. But at home, with Maman and Michel, she was just Adèle, and their closeness made any of her difficulties always easier to bear.

When she reached the house, she looked at it with different eyes. It looked run down and dingy. The windows were dirty, and a pile of boxes crowded the small entry-porch. Adèle went around to the back where she fished a key from under a rock, and let herself into the back door, into the kitchen.

"Maman!" she called, though she knew it was too early for her mother to be home from the lycée. Nevertheless, the silence felt sad, not peaceful. "Michel!" she called, knowing he was not there; he never came to Maman's unless Adèle was going to be there too.

As she had done so many times before, Adèle wandered through the house, trailing her fingertips over familiar things: stacks of books, an old vase, a lopsided pottery bowl she had made for her mother back in *primaire*, a stack of dishtowels printed with pears. The only sound was her footsteps on the wooden floor. It was so quiet she became conscious of her own breathing, a little noisy thanks to a minor cold, and never had she wished more for a dog in that house—something she had begged for, but never succeeded in convincing her mother to get.

She drifted into her mother's bedroom. It was sparse-looking:

a plain single bed with an iron frame, a cheap armoire with a smudged mirror on one of its doors. Adèle looked at herself. She brought a hand up to her face and touched the lines that were just starting to appear at the corners of her eyes and mouth. She saw that she looked tired and older than she expected herself to look, and that her makeup had not lasted through the afternoon.

Who am I now?

She couldn't stop herself from wondering about Josephine's bedroom, and had a sharp and sudden desire to go to the mansion on rue Simenon and see for herself.

Adèle sat down on her mother's bed—or her aunt's bed, she wasn't completely sure—and wept. She put her face in her hands and let herself be taken over by her sorrow and confusion, her body shaking, her breath heaving. And then the gust was over, and she stood up and went looking for a handkerchief or a tissue to wipe off her face.

She couldn't have said why she went to her mother's desk to look, because if she had thought about it, it wasn't the place to find tissues. But sniffling, she sat at her mother's desk, where Murielle had made her lesson plans through the years of Adèle's childhood. It felt a little strange to sit in Maman's place, and she half expected her to walk in and demand what she was doing. Adèle realized that the desk had had a sort of spell cast over it, an unspoken boundary which she and Michel were not to cross.

Adèle opened the top drawer and found a couple of test tubes and some felt tipped markers. There was only one other drawer. It was stuffed with papers of various kinds; Adèle riffled through them and saw bank records, utilities bills, and so forth, all ordered by date. Under the household papers sat a stack of letters, and Adèle paused only a moment before taking the first one out of its envelope and reading.

Ma belle, it began. Adèle's eyes widened. Had her mother had a lover, a boyfriend? If so, she had never heard a word of it.

. . .

Ma belle,

I know that there are no words powerful enough to express my regret, and no words magical enough to wipe away the pain I have caused. Or maybe there are and I am too inept to find them. Please know that you are dearest to me and will remain so forever.

THE LETTER WAS UNSIGNED. Adèle read the others, and they all said more or less the same thing, pleading forgiveness for some unmentioned act. The last letter was in a blank envelope, and as she unfolded it, she recognized her mother's handwriting.

Albert,

You call me pretty things, you say 'ma belle', but your actions are not pretty at all. I would have said that my sister did not deserve you, but now that I see your character more clearly I think perhaps I was wrong.

I do not wish to seem obdurate but all I can say is that you made the choice you made, and now it is your challenge to live with it. I would be sad but I fear your conduct has turned my heart to stone.

M.

ADÈLE SAT with the letter in her lap for a long time. The house was cold and she was shivering. It felt to her as though she had lifted a lid and all kinds of horrors had flown out, truly a Pandora's Box—she still couldn't see them clearly, still didn't really understand—but she knew for certain that everything was changed now, and it was not a change for the good.

❧

IT WAS dark and Maman had not come home. Sometimes an event or a meeting at school tied her down. Sometimes she was out in the ditches and woods collecting things for her science classes. The desire to confront her had dwindled like a sputtering fire, and Adèle stood at the window watching for her, frozen, with no idea what to do next.

So she couldn't have Albert, thought Adèle. So what, people get their hearts broken all the time.

Maybe not by their sisters.

Adèle sighed deeply, trying to calm her frazzled brain. And Michel? Has she spoiled him so much that now he does her bidding? Even all the way to murder?

No. No, Maman spoiled me too, Adèle reminded herself. She generously made me the best-dressed girl in the whole village. And all those evenings helping me with chemistry, the picnics in the woods she took us on, the games of chess...

But still. She had this awful nagging worry that Michel...that Maman and Michel...could they possibly have...

Adèle went to the foyer where she had left her bag, and took out her cell phone. She hesitated, uncertain of whom to call.

She chose Molly.

"Salut. I'm sorry to disturb you," she said, when Molly answered. "Something's...I'm at home, at Maman's house. I found some letters. It looks like there was something between Uncle Albert and my mother, I don't entirely understand what went on. But Molly..."

Molly waited, all her senses sharpened. Gently she suggested, "Want to read me a bit of it?"

Adèle nodded and walked back to her mother's desk, but avoided sitting in her chair. She took the packet out and read Molly the one in her mother's handwriting.

"When I got to the line, 'my heart has turned to stone'—I... I...an icy feeling went through my chest. I'm frightened, Molly. It's like this abyss has opened up right in front of me and—"

"I understand. Do you have a car?"

"No, no, I walk everywhere. Not even Maman—"

"All right, listen to me," said Molly. "I want you to follow my instructions, all right? I want you to leave the house, right now, while I'm talking to you."

"But Molly—"

"Adèle, it's not safe there. Not right now. I want you to grab those letters and then leave the house, and walk north on that same street. Isn't there a café a few blocks down?"

"Yes but—"

"Meet me there. I'm leaving now. *Please*, Adèle."

FRANCES WAS in the cottage and Molly decided to leave her a note rather than take the time to explain. She hurried into a coat and hat and took off for the village. It was a longish walk to Murielle's house, and Molly wished she hadn't put off getting a car.

She was afraid for her friend. She didn't understand what had happened between the Faures and Albert Desrosiers any better than Adèle did, but she was certain that whatever it was had everything to do with the murder of Josephine. From what Molly had seen, Murielle appeared to be a devoted mother and a dedicated teacher, and confusingly, she *was* those things.

But when Adèle had read the letter, Molly got the icy stab in her chest as well. And she thought, given the limited number of possible suspects in the case, that all signs right now were pointing straight at Murielle Faure.

The night was especially cold, in a month that had been far colder than any December in anyone's memory. Molly pulled her scarf up to her nose and jammed her hands in her pockets, walking as quickly as she could. A few people were out on the streets but most of Castillac was inside, getting ready to have dinner. Molly caught a few delicious smells as she passed some houses, roasting meat mixed with pine logs burning.

Should she call Dufort? She brought out her phone but then decided against it. She had no proof yet, no evidence that Murielle had done anything at all besides possibly gotten her heart broken. But at the same time, when Adèle had read her what Murielle had written, Molly had thought: *she killed her sister.* Just like that. The cold rage in the letter had come across with utter clarity, and Molly did not think for one second that somehow Murielle had gotten over whatever injustice she wrote to Albert about.

Molly was glad the streets weren't empty. At a moment of such high stress, she wanted to be surrounded by other people, by laughing, normal people, out doing ordinary things. Their presence was a kind of balm to her nerves. Because if Murielle had killed Madame LaGreffe to cover up the first murder, what would stop her from more killing, for the same reason? Anyone connected to the Faures was potentially in danger.

And that was her main thought as she walked as quickly as she could toward Murielle Faure's house.

Chapter Forty-One

The café a few blocks down the street from Murielle's was open, but there was no sign of Adèle. Molly felt a punch to the pit of her stomach even though she hadn't really expected Adèle to follow her instructions. She went on to the Faure house, seeing a light on from a block away. The sidewalk was icy and she didn't dare run.

Finally, Molly reached the house and trotted up the front steps. Her hand was up, reaching for the knocker, when she thought better of it and let it drop. She stepped back down to the sidewalk and tried to look in the living room window instead, wanting to know if Murielle was inside before she went barging in.

She didn't see anyone. But she heard raised voices—she heard crying—she heard Adèle—couldn't make out her words but the tone of her voice was like a steel string pulled so taut it was about to snap.

Molly sneaked around the side of the house, praying no neighbors were watching. A light was on in the kitchen, and the window was high up, which made it easy for Molly to crouch down so as not to be seen, and get as close as possible. The walls of the little house were not thick and after catching her breath, she started to be able to understand some of what the mother and daughter were saying.

"You must understand. I had no choice. I couldn't let her take him away too."

"No choice? Are you joking? No one forced you to kill anyone, Maman!"

Molly got out her phone and called Ben.

🐌

DUFORT ARRIVED BY CAR, no siren, just as Maron pulled up on the scooter. Molly saw them coming and ran over.

"It's Murielle—she's the killer," she said breathlessly, in a whisper. "I heard her more or less admit it to Adèle. Kitchen," she said, pointing toward the back of the house.

"Cover the back," Dufort said to Maron. Then he smiled grimly at Molly. "How about you wait in the café?"

Molly looked incredulous. Unless gunfire broke out there was no way she was leaving, not unless he physically forced her.

"I may be able to help," she said. "You know Adèle and I are friends. Her whole world has just been shattered. At least let her have an ally."

Dufort thought for a fraction of a second, then nodded and went up the front steps of the little house. "Keep quiet," he said to her before raising the knocker and banging it down hard.

No answer. Molly thought she could hear talking but she wasn't sure. Dufort tried the latch and the door was unlocked. "Not a word," he cautioned Molly again as he went inside.

The light was dim and everything looked even shabbier because of it. Dufort moved quietly down the hallway toward the sound of voices, Molly following. He paused to listen.

"Eh, she was old! Perhaps regrettable but as I have said, I had no choice," Murielle was saying to Adèle.

"No, Maman," said Adèle, her voice sounding thin. "No."

Dufort entered the kitchen with Molly close behind. Murielle was hugging Adèle, but Adèle's arms were at her sides.

"Bonsoir, Madame Faure," Dufort said, his voice calm and friendly. "Adèle," he added, nodding at her. "If it wouldn't trouble you too much, I would like to have a word. With both of you actually."

Molly marveled at Ben's voice, how the tone was so gentle it was practically lulling her to sleep. He sounded so unthreatening, so kind and helpful, as though he were talking to a skittish animal.

"I said all I had to say earlier today," said Murielle, letting go of Adèle and standing up tall. Her face looked gray and drawn, perhaps betraying less ease of spirit than she was trying to project. "Michel may have made some mistakes, but he most certainly did not do those things you accuse him of. Now then, I am about to make a late supper for my daughter and me. If there's anything else, I'm certain it can wait until morning."

"I'm afraid it cannot," said Ben, his voice still soothing. "I'm not here about Michel. What I'm interested in is your side of the story, Murielle. In the village, everyone knows the story of Albert Desrosiers and his invention. Everybody knows how your sister married him before he was wealthy, and ended up living in the grandest house in Castillac. A mansion, really, isn't it? But maybe the house is of no consequence to the story. What matters is *you*, Murielle Faure, whose story has not been told."

Molly held her breath.

Adèle looked at her mother, expecting her to cut Dufort off at the knees.

But Murielle did not. Tears glittered in the corners of her eyes. "I couldn't tell it, during all these years," she said in a low, breaking voice. "I was trying to protect Adèle."

Adèle looked at her sharply. "Me? How was keeping all these secrets supposed to be good for me?"

"All I wanted was for you to have a good life, a decent life," murmured Murielle.

The others waited for her to continue but she bowed her head and did not speak.

"My mother killed Josephine," said Adèle to Dufort, her voice strong. "As far as I can tell, she has a pack of reasons and excuses for what she did, but she has admitted to me that she did it. Oh and wait, in case you haven't heard? Murielle is not my mother. So to put the situation correctly, the woman who has pretended to be my mother killed my actual mother. I know, you might need to take notes, it gets very complicated!" Adèle laughed harshly, a sound Molly had never heard her make.

Dufort reached out and touched Murielle on the arm. "I meant what I said. I want to hear your side of the story, Murielle. Could you tell a bit more of it?"

She looked up gratefully at Dufort, as though he was offering her water after she had crawled across a desert.

Adèle sat down in a chair and crossed her arms. "Yes, let's hear it, Maman. Let's hear all about poor, poor you and how you had no choice but to go on a murdering spree! Because let's not forget, it's not only your sister you decided to kill, there's Madame LaGreffe whom you didn't even know. And Madame Arbogast—not so smart picking the mother of a nurse, was it?"

"Molly, would you take Adèle into the living room for a moment?" Dufort asked.

Molly nodded, afraid to say a single word. She put her fingers on Adèle's elbow and gave it a tug, and gave her an encouraging look. Adèle said "Fine," meaning it was not fine at all, and went down the hallway with Molly.

Dufort looked into Murielle's eyes, seeing her pain.

"The thing you must understand," she said softly, "is that I loved him. I never stopped loving him, even after—"

Dufort nodded, guessing she meant Albert, but not at all sure.

"We had just started a relationship," Murielle continued. "This was in the 60s, you understand, another lifetime ago. A time of upheaval, as you are too young to remember. No one knew about Albert and me. We were shy. It was our own private delight, falling in love, and keeping it a secret so no one would tease us. We were not children, you know. I was already teaching at the lycée, and Albert worked as an electrician. He was thirty-three years old and never married. Never had a girlfriend, I don't believe, not until me.

"It was science that brought us together, you see. He was always making inventions, teaching himself electrical engineering—so ambitious, Albert was! And I was doing the same in my backyard garden, breeding roses and doing other botanical experiments...we had a lot in common, so it's no surprise that we got along as well as we did. But," and Murielle looked intensely at Dufort and her face hardened, "there was a great deal of passion as well as shared interests. I loved him unreservedly."

Dufort gave her his full attention. "Yes," he said, very softly.

"But then Josephine...Josephine found out about it. If she had simply made fun, that would have been one thing. But no. Josephine could not stand the idea of my finding happiness. She... she *seduced* him," spat Murielle. "And much worse, she became pregnant with his child. Think for a minute, Chief Dufort! I know you have no wife, no children, perhaps you do not want them, perhaps this sort of thing only seems tawdry to you and pointless. But can you try to imagine how it felt to have my sister, my hated sister of all people, impregnated by the man I loved? The man who had sworn his love to me?"

Murielle paused. "*Sworn*," she said sarcastically. "As though his words meant anything at all."

And then, so quick she was almost a blur, Murielle leapt to the back door and slipped outside. Dufort had not seen it coming and his reaction was too slow. "Maron!" he shouted.

Molly and Adèle came running from the front of the house;

well, actually from the hallway where they had been doing their best to eavesdrop.

They found the backdoor open and the kitchen empty, and the two gendarmes shouting at each other in the cold dark of the snowy garden.

Chapter Forty-Two

Dufort and Maron split up to search the neighborhood on foot. Dufort told Molly to take Adèle and go home, and he spoke with such authority that Molly did not argue.

They barely spoke as they walked toward La Baraque. It was cold, but they hardly noticed. After about fifteen minutes, Adèle's limp was noticeably worse; Molly had an urge to scoop her up and carry her the rest of the way, but knew she wasn't strong enough to do so even if Adèle would let her, which she highly doubted.

At the halfway point, Molly texted Frances to let her know they were coming, but left out any mention of Murielle. She was hyper-alert, flinching at any sudden noise, scared that Murielle might step out from the shadows at any minute even though she knew that was unlikely. But her body didn't seem interested in probabilities—her heart was pounding and her hands were clammy. As best as she could tell from listening in the hallway, Murielle had completely flipped, and who knows what she might be capable of? If she could murder the innocent Madame LaGreffe, why not kill off Molly and Adèle, who had witnessed her confession?

Molly had a million questions for Adèle, but since Adèle

wasn't talking, she kept quiet. By the time they reached the ceme-tery on rue des Chênes, both women were exhausted.

"Molly," said Adèle finally. "Is it much farther to your house? And listen, I'm sorry you got all mixed up in this."

"No, not far. Just around this bend there's a straightaway, and then we're home. And please, don't apologize. We're friends, right?"

Adèle nodded but did not smile.

When they turned into the driveway of La Baraque, they heard barking.

"What in the world," said Molly under her breath, as a big speckled dog came streaking around the side of the house and slammed into her leg with the force of a freight train. "Hey!" she said, stumbling.

Frances came out of the cottage, pulling a sweater tight around her. "Come to the cottage!" she shouted. "It's toasty inside. And you can meet Dingleberry!"

"We've already met," said Molly. "And her name is not Dingleberry."

"Just come in where's in warm. I made some mulled wine, you want some?"

Molly and Adèle gratefully came inside and dropped onto the small sofa. Molly started to speak, but didn't know where to begin.

"My mother is a murderer," said Adèle, and Molly figured that was as good a beginning as any.

MOLLY WAS AWAKENED EARLY the next morning by a strange noise that she finally woke up enough to understand was her cell phone.

"Bonjour, Molly, it's Ben. Are you up?"

"Yes," she lied.

"Adèle is there with you, yes? Would you bring her in, as soon as possible? I'd like to see the letters. And I'm hoping she may be able to help us find Murielle."

"She's still at large?" Molly snapped awake.

"I'm afraid so. Hard to believe, but it was very dark last night. And of course she would know the neighborhood like the back of her hand; she's lived in that house for over thirty years. We'll find her, Molly. And in the meantime, we want to nail down some of the details of the case, and Adèle will be helpful with that."

"Give us half an hour? Make that forty-five minutes," she added, running her hands through her hair and wanting time for a quick shower.

They said goodbye, and Molly texted Frances and Adèle, who had stayed in the cottage last night, not wanting to walk even the few steps to Molly's house after drinking a few glasses of Frances's special recipe mulled wine.

Molly lay in bed thinking about the day before. The speckled dog flopped her big paws up on her bed and nosed at her. "Well, good morning to you," said Molly. "I'm warning you though, I have no dog food. Where did you come from, anyway?"

She found some scraps to give the dog, and within twenty minutes, Adèle and Molly were on their way to the station. To Molly, it felt awkward not to chat, but even more awkward to talk about what was on their minds if Adèle didn't bring it up first. So again, they walked in silence.

"At least it didn't turn out to be Michel," Molly blurted out once they got to the village.

"Yes, at least that," answered Adèle, and made that harsh laugh Molly had first heard the night before in Murielle's kitchen.

Perrault jumped up when they entered the station, and led them into Dufort's office. "Can I get you anything, a coffee maybe?" she asked.

"Yes," said Molly gratefully.

"Bonjour, Molly. Bonjour, Adèle," said Dufort. He kissed

Molly and called to the other room, "Maron! In here and bring the letter!"

"Another letter?" said Adèle, looking as though she wasn't sure she could take any more surprises.

"Would you give me the ones you found last night?" Dufort asked her. "I think the heart of this case is turning out to be what the principals have written. Let's have a look."

"What about Murielle?" asked Adèle.

"Maron is about to go continue the search," said Dufort. "Though I believe she is no danger to anyone at this point. Now that she's already confessed, there's no point to making any more attempts to cover up the original crime."

"Maybe she won't act out of logic, though," said Molly quietly.

"Oh, sure she will," said Dufort. "It's an emotional logic, granted, but all of her actions thus far have made a kind of sense, and I'm confident they will continue to do so. Madame Faure is at the moment trying to escape the consequences of her killings by hiding out, but I don't think she has the resources to get far.

"Would you agree, Adèle?"

Adèle didn't answer. She was appearing to be further and further disconnected from the present moment, and looked physically deflated, as though shrinking inside herself.

Dufort read over the letters Adèle had brought, had a private word with Maron before he left, and then removed all four letters from their envelopes and spread them on his desk, taking his time, smoothing out the creased pages.

"Here is the story, written out for us," he said. "First we have a letter found in Josephine Desrosiers's desk. A love letter. We thought the letter was written by Albert to Josephine, since it was in her desk and carefully tied with a satin ribbon as though it was something treasured. But notice it begins with 'Ma belle', not Josephine's name. And then here—" Dufort pointed to the letter Adèle had brought. "You're absolutely sure this is your mother's handwriting?"

"Yes," said Adèle, not looking at the letters.

"See, she is accusing Albert of calling her 'ma belle'—and saying, essentially, that his words don't match his deeds. The first letter was not a love letter written to Josephine, but to Murielle. Possibly from before Josephine seduced Albert, judging from the tone."

"Maybe Josephine found that letter, and that's how she knew Albert and Murielle were in love?" said Perrault, coming back with two coffees.

"And she had to get in there and wreck it," said Molly. "I guess that could explain why Murielle poisoned her, even after all this time. But what about Adèle? It still makes no sense that Murielle raised their baby as her own, or am I missing something?"

Molly and the two gendarmes looked at Adèle, but she only shrugged.

Dufort continued, "Then we have the second letter, which was found at Claudette Mercier's house. It is unsigned, but as Maron pointed out, anyone with the slightest knowledge of handwriting analysis can see it was written by Josephine, as we have her signed will and other papers for comparison. We would call it 'hate mail,' the old term was 'poison pen letter.' I believe it has bearing on the case because it demonstrates Josephine's viciousness. It couldn't have been easy being her sister."

Molly shot a glance at Adèle but she did not seem to have heard.

"The third letter—thank you for bringing it in, Adèle—was written by Murielle to Albert. It looks as though it was never sent. She is cold and furious, understandable emotions given the depth of the betrayal."

"It's bizarre that these letters, except for the Mercier one, are all over forty years old. Get over it, people!" said Perrault. Dufort and Molly shared a quick look of amusement.

"It's sort of sad that Josephine kept love letters her husband wrote to another woman," said Molly.

"All three of the recipients kept letters that must have been extremely painful," said Dufort. "You do wonder why they didn't just toss them in the trash."

"But if they had," said Adèle, standing up from her chair, "we might never have found out who did this. And Murielle might have kept on killing, who knows? Maybe she started to enjoy it. I don't pretend to know. Everything I thought I knew has turned out to be a lie."

"Adèle, do you have any thoughts on where we should look for Murielle? Any places she especially liked, anything like that? We have her bank account shut down and her house being watched, so unless she somehow happened to be carrying a lot of cash, she won't get far. Unless you might know of other resources we're not aware of?"

"Murielle is obsessed with plants," said Adèle, walking toward the door. "I'm going to find Michel, if you don't need me further. I would keep plants in mind, if I were you."

"She must have made the cyanide herself," mused Dufort. "Does she have fruit trees in her backyard?"

"Apricot, apple, and peach."

"Oh yes," said Dufort. "Of course. That would do nicely."

Chapter Forty-Three

W hen Murielle knocked on Michel's door in the morning, he scrambled out of bed and put on a robe. He was not used to visitors, preferring to meet friends somewhere more aesthetically pleasing, where they also might buy him lunch.

"Maman! To what do I owe this pleasure? I'm not sure you've ever come to my apartment!"

Murielle pushed past her son and looked around. "I see you keep it nice, just as I taught you."

"Of course," he laughed. "Your tutelage in dusting and vacuuming was quite exhaustive. Can I get you something to drink?"

"Yes, actually, something to drink would be exactly what I need." She reached into her pocket to make sure the small packet was safe, and then perched on the edge of the cheap sofa. "There are a couple of things I need to talk to you about," she said, and felt her eyes welling up, just as they had the night before with that damned Dufort. It was both difficult and strangely wonderful to finally begin to talk about the things she had held back for so many years. Exhilarating, yet disquieting.

"Sit," she directed him, and Michel handed her a glass of water and flopped down in a tattered armchair and guzzled part of a

Coca-Cola. Then he looked more carefully at his mother. "Maman? You look...you've got leaves in your hair," he said in a wondering tone.

"Not surprising," she said, taking a sip of water. "I slept under my trees last night."

"You what?"

"Under the apple in the back garden. But never mind that, it is not something you would understand. Michel, I want you to know everything, finally," she told him, and was gratified when he looked startled and interested. "I know you think you are adopted and your sister is my birth daughter, yes?"

Michel nodded.

"That is incorrect. Well, you were adopted, that much is true. But didn't you wonder where Adèle's father had disappeared to? I always thought it odd that you and Adèle were so incurious. I don't believe you ever once asked where her father was, or who he was, so I had no occasion to lie."

"Maman, what are you talking about? We did ask you, numerous times! But you would get this stony look on your face and refuse to answer. We decided it was all highly romantic and your heart had been broken so you could not speak of it."

"I have no memory whatsoever of any questions. But in the event, you were correct. My heart *was* broken. I loved your uncle, Albert Desrosiers. I loved him desperately. And he loved me back, until my sister ruined it.

"Josephine enticed him. Just the one time—she got him alone and tempted him, *beguiled* him, Michel—and that one time was enough to make her pregnant. Albert was a decent man, and his family was religious. He felt he had to marry her even though he did not love her or want to be her husband. Because of the child. He married a woman he did not love, for Adèle.

"Of course, no one was doing anything for *me*," she said, her voice low and gravelly.

"You're saying Adèle—"

"Just hush a moment, Michel. Let me tell my story. Please. The minute I heard about Josephine and Albert, I went to stay with some cousins, up in Franche-Comté. I never should have come back, especially once I heard she was pregnant. I knew Josephine would be parading around the village like she was about to give birth to royalty—you know very well what she was like. I should have stayed away for good. But I couldn't help myself.

"I missed Albert. Even though by then I was his sister-in-law, and there was of course no thought to an affair or anything like that—I wasn't that kind of person, as I think you know. But still, I wanted to live where I might run into him from time to time. Even if I would not allow myself to speak to him.

"And then the truly appalling thing happened. Josephine gave birth to Adèle, at home. They lived in a small house then, on the edge of the village, I forget the name of the street. Adèle was born with a clubfoot. And when Josephine saw that foot, she pushed the baby away and said she refused to raise her. That she would not have a deformed daughter. And that was the end of it. I don't even believe Albert argued with her much, because he had already learned that arguing with Josephine was fruitless. She always got her way. The luckiest woman on earth, that's what she used to say about herself, but it wasn't luck. It was domination.

"Anyway, the midwife got hold of me, told me Josephine had rejected her own baby. Said she had never seen anything like it. Well, what was I going to do—let my niece be given up for adoption and never see her again? The daughter of the man I loved more than anything in this world?

"You took her." Michel was sitting up, listening intently to his mother.

"I took her. Of course I did. Josephine didn't like it. But at least that one time, Albert insisted and got his way. They had to bribe the midwife somehow, and they all told a story about the baby being stillborn."

Michel sat with his eyes wide. He drank some of his Coke. "Aunt Josephine is Adèle's mother?"

"Yes, Michel—that is precisely what I've been saying."

"But that means...not to jump immediately to the mercenary... that means Adèle inherits the bulk of Aunt Josephine's fortune."

"Indeed it does. As it should be, and not a minute too soon."

"What do you mean, not a minute too soon?"

"After what her parents did—disowning her like that because of a small imperfection—Adèle deserves that money. She should have had it all along."

Michel had a moment's regret for all the evenings wasted in the company of his vile aunt, but he was not one to dwell on his mistakes. "So you just got impatient, is that it?" he asked.

"And you wouldn't stay away from her," said Murielle, shaking her head slowly. "I tried to suggest a different path for you, I gave you that money to settle in Paris, out of her clutches. Why would you not listen to me, Michel, dearest boy?"

"Oh, Maman." He couldn't help feeling a pang of sympathy for her. "I detested Josephine, you know that."

Murielle gave Michel a quick hard look, then reached into her pocket and drew out the packet. "I've heard that before," she said. "You say you detested her, but you couldn't stay away. She was like a spider wrapping you up in silk, feasting on you until you'd have ended up a dry husk, no longer a man but an empty husk."

Michel's eyes widened even more and he noticed a jittery feeling in his legs that he recognized as fear.

"Give me your soda," she said. "How you can drink this disgusting fluid I will never comprehend."

Michel held out the can. "Yes, I know, no nutritional value whatsoever. Don't dump it out, Maman."

She tipped the packet to the hole in the can and tapped it to make some powder drift down inside. Then she did the same to her glass of water.

"What is that, some new vitamin?" laughed Michel, trying to

believe she was joking around. "And go on with your story. I can't decide whether you're pulling my leg or not."

"It's not a vitamin, no," said Murielle. "But it will make us both feel better, I believe. It will take the pain away at long last."

Michel had a sudden feeling of cold sweep through his body and he put his hand over his heart as though to make sure it was still beating. In that moment he understood very little of the convoluted tale his mother had been telling, but he grasped very well that she was deeply, deeply disturbed.

And that whatever she was putting into his drink, he had better avoid at all costs.

Chapter Forty-Four

"So how did you get away?" Adèle was asking Michel, as they sat with Molly and Frances at Chez Papa the next afternoon.

"You won't believe it," Michel said, laughing and taking a sip of his beer. "I told her I'd be right back, I had to go out and get a pack of cigarettes, I was dying for a smoke. And she started in on how terrible smoking is and how stupid must I be to take up such a filthy habit at my age. There she was, trying to kill me—and nagging me about the danger of cigarettes."

Molly and Frances were speechless.

"I guess that sort of sums up how lost she was," said Adèle sadly.

"I'm laughing but there is nothing funny about it," said Michel.

"And so she let you leave?" asked Molly.

"Oh, she protested. My place only has one room, and I had to get dressed in front of her which was awkward. I was shaking like a leaf. You can't imagine...one minute, she was telling me this crazy mixed-up story, and the next minute, I felt this cold, stabbing feeling in my chest. This *fear*. She had this expression on her face—I've never seen anything like it. It was an expression of

NELL GODDIN

overwhelming assurance that she was doing the right thing, even though quite clearly it was insane. Literally…insane."

"She told you about killing Aunt Josephine?"

"Not directly. Heavy hinting. I had been suspicious of her anyway, you know. Suspicious of you, too, Adèle, if I'm honest. At first I thought maybe it was Sabrina, because doubtless Aunt Josephine had been making her life a living hell. But it just made sense that it was somebody in our family, and obviously I knew it wasn't me."

He shrugged. "So when I got out on the street, I called the gendarmes and they got there right away. But it was too late for Maman." Michel squinted, looking out of the plate glass window onto the street. "It'll sound a little weird, but you know? I felt bad that she died by herself like that. I hung around outside, freezing my ass off with no coat on, no way was I going back in there with her and her little packet of cyanide. But even so…I'm sorry she was alone."

"Michel, she tried to *kill* you," said Molly.

"I know," said Michel. "But the thing is, and Adèle will back me up on this, she did do her best for us. Our childhood was a whole lot better than it would've been without her."

"I'll say," agreed Adèle.

"So that's it? Two murders and a suicide, and in three days it's Christmas, and everything will be back to normal?" asked Frances.

"No more 'normal' for Adèle—she's going to be rich!" said Michel, lifting his glass to toast her.

Adèle smiled a smile of wonder. "It's not real to me yet," she said. "Eight million euros, Perrault told me yesterday when we were at the station."

"That's a lot of handbags," said Molly, grinning. "Are you going to move into the mansion? I bet Lapin is itchy to get his hands on that place!"

"No plans yet, Molly. It's going to take some time before I can get used to so much change."

262

Molly nodded and put her arm around her and gave her a squeeze.

The four of them finished their drinks and then walked to La Baraque, Molly having invited the Faures over for a makeshift dinner. Molly and Michel got ahead of the other two—Adèle's foot was still suffering the effects of the long walk the other night and she made slow progress—and Molly asked in a low voice, "So Michel, did your mother say anything about why Josephine gave up Adèle? That's the part about this whole thing that I haven't been able to wrap my head around. I keep thinking about it and trying to work it out, but I get nowhere. Did she give you any explanation about that?"

Michel shook his head. "Not a word," he said, hunching his shoulders to keep the cold off his neck. "Now tell me what amazing things you're going to make for dinner. Frances says you're an absolute magician in the kitchen—and I'm a French-man, in case you haven't noticed!"

"I wasn't wrong about the poisoner being a woman," said Maron to Perrault, who rolled her eyes.

"I never said you couldn't make assumptions about what kind of person a poisoner is," said Perrault. "Obviously, it's someone who likes to plan. Someone who doesn't want to get her—or his—hands dirty. Who doesn't mind causing pain. But you can't assume gender, Gilles, that's all I'm saying. And I'm sticking to it like glue. Hey, Chief—I went by Madame LaGreffe's this morning, and caught her daughter at the house. Guess what I found sitting on the kitchen table?"

Dufort shook his head.

"A bag of pine cones!"

"Huh," said Dufort. "I wouldn't have expected that."

"That loose thread was nagging at me," said Perrault.

NELL GODDIN

"Suck up," said Maron under his breath, but he flashed Perrault a rare—and small—smile.

"All right, the two of you. You did some good work. I want you both to go out on the street for the rest of the day, enjoy yourselves, talk to people, see if there's anything that needs our attention. Pay close attention to the elderly who might need an extra bit of help during this bad winter."

Perrault and Maron jostled each other jokingly as they went out, and Dufort sank down in his chair, at his desk, and rubbed his face with both palms.

I've been wrong, he was thinking. Wrong about what I should be doing with my life. There've been too many mistakes, too many deaths, and it's time I heard what those mistakes are saying.

He jiggled his mouse to wake up his computer and opened a new document, and started to type a letter of resignation. Dufort had no idea at all what he was going to do next, but whatever it was, he would not be accepting the new posting from the gendarmerie that he expected to come in January.

He would stay right here in Castillac.

The letter was brief and to the point. He saved it, printed it out, and then without wasting any time, pulled out his cell and called Molly Sutton.

Chapter Forty-Five

T he next day was Christmas Eve-Eve, as Molly had called it as a child, and she let Frances sleep and walked into the village to finish up her shopping. There was the goose to pick up at the butcher's, and the bûche de noël from Pâtisserie Bujold, and she was talking herself into splurging on some organic foie gras. Constance had promised to come over that afternoon for a whirlwind cleaning followed by a holiday cocktail. And she had to remember to pick up some dog food. But all of these things, which normally would be giving her pleasure, felt a little flat.

Whenever a period of excitement was over, there is always a letdown, she thought as she walked along rue des Chênes. Molly felt she should be happy that Murielle could no longer hurt anyone else, and that her friend had come into a huge sum of money. But somehow, they weren't enough to keep the letdown feeling away. Part of it was still the incomprehension over a mother rejecting her baby for a correctable flaw. And part of it, if she was honest, was that she relished the stimulation of having a problem to solve—a good, meaty mystery—and when it was over, and she had nothing on the docket besides making dinner, she ended up needing some time to readjust to everyday, ordinary life.

Molly visited the butcher, got the foie gras, and was just coming out of Pâtisserie Bujold with a large bag, when her cell phone buzzed in her pocket.

"Âllo?" she said, stepping into the middle of the street where the reception was better.

"Salut, Molly, it's Ben."

Molly smiled. She and Ben talked about the case, trying to tie up a few little loose ends, and then they talked about things unrelated to murder or poison or betrayal. He made her laugh, and then finally, after she had been standing in the middle of the street for fifteen minutes, he asked her out to dinner.

"Probably not at La Métairie," he said.

Which was completely fine by Molly.

THE END

Glossary

1:

comment vas-tu?...How are you?
La Baraque...the house or shed
pâtisserie...pastry shop
Café de la Place...café on the square
café crème...espresso with milk

2:

pigeonnier...dovecote
gîte...holiday cottage
ma belle...my beauty

3:

châtelaine...mistress of a castle
merde...excrement
la métairie...farm

4:

salut...hi

bon anniversaire...happy birthday

amuse-bouche...literally, mouth-amuser. An appetizer not ordered but sent out free by the chef

6:

crétin...cretin

crème brûlée...burnt cream. A custard with a hard caramelized top. (Swoon.)

à bientôt...see you later

7:

petit, s'il te plâit...espresso please

8:

rue des Chênes...Oak Street

priez pour vos morts...pray for your dead

la bombe...hot woman, bombshell

café grand...large coffee

9:

grand-mère...grandmother

lycée...high school

merci et à bientôt...thanks and see you later

11:

la grisaille...grayness; dreary weather

frites...French fries

14:

épicerie...small grocery store

16:

félicitations...congratulations

bon...literally, good. Used as a conversational filler: well, all right, fine

17:

toilette...toilet
cèpes...the mushroom boletus edulis
girolles...chantarelle mushrooms

18:

oui...yes

20:

boulangerie...bakery

21:

bûche de Noël...Christmas cake, often sponge cake and buttercream rolled up. Made to look like a Yule log.

26:
à table!...to the table! Come to dinner!

28:

liberté...liberty
fraternité...fraternity

30:

département...regional area in France similar to a state or county

31:

mairie...town hall
collège...middle school, junior high

32:

Extrait du Registre des Naissance...birth records

35:

centimes...pennies
comprends...understand

37:

primaire...elementary school

Also by Nell Goddin

The Third Girl (Molly Sutton Mystery 1)

The Luckiest Woman Ever (Molly Sutton Mystery 2)

The Prisoner of Castillac (Molly Sutton Mystery 3)

Murder for Love (Molly Sutton Mystery 4)

The Château Murder (Molly Sutton Mystery 5)

Murder on Vacation (Molly Sutton Mystery 6)

An Official Killing (Molly Sutton Mysteries 7)

Death in Darkness (Molly Sutton Mystery 8)

No Honor Among Thieves (Molly Sutton Mystery 9)

Acknowledgments

Editing by the incomparable Tommy Glass. Proofing by 4eyesediting.com. Beta reading by Nancy Kelley. Big thanks to you all and I toast you with a big glass of Médoc!

About the Author

Nell Goddin has worked as a radio reporter, SAT tutor, short-order omelet chef, and baker. She tried waitressing but was fired twice.

Nell grew up in Richmond, Virginia and has lived in New England, New York City, and France. Currently she's back in Virginia with teenagers and far too many pets. She has degrees from Dartmouth College and Columbia University.

www.nellgoddin.com
nell@nellgoddin.com

Made in United States
North Haven, CT
21 August 2024

56321764R00171

Another pastry, another dead body....

Things have started to look up for Molly Sutton. Her new life in the French village of Castillac isn't as peaceful as she expected it to be, but maybe that could be a good thing. Turns out a little mystery, a little excitement—it gives a girl with imagination something to do besides obsess about croissants.

After Molly stumbles on another dead body, our amateur detective wastes no time before eavesdropping and butting into conversations all over town, gathering as much information as she can on everyone.

But when Dufort is about to clap handcuffs on the wrong man, she's got to do more than eavesdrop to save him. Will she have the chops—and the cleverness—to pull it off?

Nell Goddin has published a grammar book, a math book, stories in literary journals, and a vampire romance or two. This is her first mystery.

She lives in Charlottesville, Virginia.

ISBN 9781949841022

90000

9 781949 841022